Jane's Baby
by
Chris Bauer

Copyright by Chris Bauer June 2018

All rights reserved. No part of this book shall be reproduced or transmitted in any form or by any means, electronic, mechanical, magnetic, and photographic including photocopying, recording or by any information storage and retrieval system, without prior written permission of the publisher. No patent liability is assumed with respect to the use of the information contained herein. Although every precaution has been taken in the preparation of this book, the publisher and author assume no responsibility for errors or omissions. Neither is any liability assumed for damages resulting from the use of the information contained herein.

This is a work of fiction. Names, characters, places, and incidents either are the product of the author's imagination or are used fictitiously. Any resemblance to actual events or locales or persons, living or dead, is entirely coincidental.

ISBN-13: 978-1-940758-77-0 Paperback
ISBN-13: 978-1-940758-78-7 E-Pub
ISBN-13: 978-1-940758-79-4 Mobi

Cover design by: Rae Monet

Published by:
Intrigue Publishing
11505 Cherry Tree Crossing RD #148
Cheltenham, MD 20623-9998

ACKNOWLEDGEMENTS

These are the folks who provided input, feedback, suggestions, chastisement, ass-whoopings, encouragement, and shoulders to cry on while I readied the manuscript for public consumption. Thanks to you all. My family (wife Terry Bauer, daughters Jenn Helenbauer Soliah and Jill Bauer-Reese). My literary agent Jessica Faust, President, Bookends LLC. It took a few rewrites for us to determine what *wasn't* working, Jessica; by process of elimination and sheer doggedness, I'm hopeful I/we finally got it right. The iconic, wonderful Ms. Buffy Sainte-Marie, singer-songwriter, musician, composer, artist, pacifist, social activist, whose feedback helped me resurrect a fond, tender memory and elevate it "up where (it) belong(s)." Jeffrey Toobin, whose *The Nine* kept me riveted on the real-life workings of the U.S. Supreme Court. Melanie Rigney, editor. Anything that doesn't work here is not Melanie's fault. Lyle Sankey, Sankey Rodeo Schools. "Quinn" at Throwflame.com. The stable of rich writing and critiquing talent that wanders into and out my writing life in Bucks County, PA, and other Philly environs: Don Swaim, Daniel Dorian, Jim Brennan, Jackie Nash, Alan Shils, Bill Donahue, Natalie Dyen, Beverly Black, Kevin Knabe, Bob Cohen, Bill O'Toole, Candace Barrett, Martha Holland, Jim Kempner, Wil Kirk, Stephen Buerkle, John Schoffstall, Fran Nadel, Lindsey Allingham, Cathy Hilliard. Also, from the much hallowed Rebel Writers of Bucks County: author/agent Marie Lamba, author/agent Damian McNicholl, Jeanne Denault, Russ Allen, Dave Jarret, John Wirebach. Alan Grayce (the talented writing team of Al Sirois and Grace Paredes Marcus Sirois). Author Kelly Jameson, who somewhere, somehow, influenced something about my protagonist. Kelly Linko, who suffers through reading all my stuff in its early stages. The Facebook Military Working Dogs community. Travis Pennington, among the first in the publishing industry who saw the merits of this manuscript. Multi-talented musician, songwriter, folksinger, author and all around gentleperson Tracy Grammer. Austin Camacho and Denise Camacho of Intrigue Publishing, who took a chance at publishing this beast.

Rave Reviews for Jane's Baby

Jane's Baby is a stunning thriller, pitch-dark and filled with twists you never see coming. Chris Bauer's complex cast of characters headed by bounty hunter Judge Drury and his K9 partners pulled me in from the beginning and never let go. Bauer is a novelist to watch.

–Margaret Coel, New York Times bestselling author of the *Wind River* Mystery Series

Jane's Baby is both topical and enduring. Chris Bauer's knack for creating unconventional characters is exceeded only by his intense and vivid prose.

–Don Swaim, author of *The Assassination Of Ambrose Bierce: A Love Story* and host of CBS Radio's *Book Beat*

Chris Bauer came up with a doozy of a 'what if' question in *Jane's Baby*. I just wish I had thought of it myself.

–Alan Russell, bestselling author of *Burning Man*

In *Jane's Baby,* Chris Bauer weaves unique characters into a compelling story. Readers will love bounty hunter Judge Drury's two deputies, who happen to be retired military dogs.

–Margaret Mizushima, author of *Hunting Hour: A Timber Creek K-9 Mystery*

Jane's Baby has it all--fresh and quirky characters--an ex-Marine bounty hunter with Tourette's Syndrome and bomb-sniffing dogs, an alcoholic little person blogger sidekick, an angry bull, a female Native American Supreme Court Justice, an obsessive assassin-- and a plot loaded with tricky twists and troubling timely issues. Chris Bauer pulls them all together with wrenching seat of your pants suspense. He's clearly a writer to watch.

–Merry Jones, award-winning author of *Child's Play* and *The Nanny Murders*

*To the women who struggle
with making these decisions*

PROLOGUE

I want the boy institutionalized, Judge's father told his mother. Try it, his mother said, and I will leave you.

His father, a U.S. senator, decided on a different approach: The Marine Corps.

When Judge left for boot camp, they didn't hug, didn't shake hands. There was no imparting of keen insights or wisdom, no fatherly advice. His father made one final, rid-of-your-fucking-afflicted-existence comment that came directly from his black heart: *They'll either kill you or cure you.*

His father would have been satisfied either way.

Judge's affliction had embarrassed them on the grandest of stages: Nixon's second inauguration, when Judge was fourteen. When he turned nineteen, his senator father wrote the letter. The president said yes, he'd make his enlistment happen. A senator had this access, the Commander-In-Chief this power.

That was thirty-eight years ago.

Kill you or cure you.

Judge waited for his bounty, a bail-jumping pedophile, outside a Shreveport, Louisiana Starbucks, a long way from home for the both of them. Judge sat in the van, smooth talking his K9 deputies, waiting for the guy to exit, wanting, praying the guy would run…

Judge had proved his father wrong. The Marines proved his father wrong. Win-win.

His father died knowing this. His father died horribly. Win-win.

Judge had Tourette's. There was no cure, but they had an arrangement, this affliction and him. Win.

His full name, Judge Terrence Drury. USMC rank at retirement, Gunnery Sergeant. His current profession, bounty hunter.

Semper Fi.

ONE

June 1985
Hotel Indigo Ballroom
South Dallas, Texas

Difficult beginnings, U.S. Senator Mildred Folsom knew from her experience, often shaped a child's worldview in ways that remained unrecognized far into adulthood. Ways that were permanently unhealthy, that could stunt a child's emotional maturity and hinder her from becoming a responsible, God-fearing, conservative adult. It wasn't much different today, the senator told her audience, than it was twenty-five years ago, when she herself was still in the system. A small lamp on the podium illuminated the senator's speech, the light reflecting onto her face, her platinum hair.

"Many displaced children, if they age out un-adopted, will forever feel hungry and alone," the Texas senator said. She was the last speaker for the evening, her speech a voice-over for a slideshow that to this point had only shown images of proud parents with their smiling adopted children.

The tone of the slides changed. The images shifted, became interspersed with pictures of twentieth-century group home despair. Children in dignified poses but with no individuality, at attention at the foot of their beds, lost and frightened, or in foster home kitchens seated stiffly upright, their adult caregivers smiling but the children rigid, with severe faces.

"Many, regardless of their achievements as adults, will feel colder than you in winter, or uncomfortably warmer than you in summer. Many will feel sick their entire lives. And many children…"

Three hundred moneyed Texan benefactors were in attendance at the senator's fundraiser for the agency. By the end of the

Jane's Baby

slideshow she expected their eyes to be moist, and their noses to be sniffling. Her voice caught in her throat. She tapped the podium lightly and pursed her lips, both meant to pull her out of some maudlin personal memory the audience was expected to conjure up for themselves.

She was good at this. She had them.

"…so many children will feel perpetually unloved, perpetually unlovable. I'm sure our guests of honor have all had similar feelings on some level. But their adoptions, and mine, served to mitigate them, and our adoptive parents rescued us either from well-intentioned shelters, the foster care merry-go-round, or from much more compromising situations, and paved the way for us to realize our potential as productive citizens. Generous folks like you have helped defray the costs of adoption allowing state and county adoption agencies to provide homes for children so deserving of them. Please give with your hearts tonight, ladies and gentlemen. Your honorees and I are proof that your gifts can and do make a difference. Thank you, and may God bless you."

A round of applause erupted for the four guests of honor, all women: a heart surgeon, a homemaking mother-of-three, a kindergarten teacher, and a former Dallas Cowboys cheerleader, all assembled for the black-tie event by this popular first-term U.S. senator. After her speech the senator worked the gathering, on the stump as much for her campaign as she was for agency donations. She pulled aside Darlington Beckner, the local county adoption agency's director, who was also a practicing minister. She had him light her cigarette.

"How do you like your new pen, Pastor Beckner?"

He patted his vest pocket. In it was a diamond-encrusted Montblanc, a gift from the senator's pro-life campaign contributors, inscribed with his initials and the group's slogan: *Let them live, and we will help them thrive.*

"I like it very much, Senator. Thank you."

She clinked her drink glass with his. "I've been told someone wants to thank you personally for all your hard work this year, Pastor."

"How wonderful. Who?"

"I don't have any details. The hotel concierge will be along in a minute to fill you in. Now, if you'll excuse me…"

Upstairs in one of the hotel's luxury suites Mitzi, fundraiser honoree number four, the alleged former Dallas Cowboy cheerleader, was performing an act that Pastor Darlington Beckner knew broke at least one Commandment and countless other Bible admonishments. Influential religious leader, community organizer and adoption agency head, the forty-two-year-old devoted father of four was going through a tough stretch, his wife estranged, a divorce in the offing. Mitzi, naked from the waist up, was thanking the hell out of him. Seated on the edge of the bed, his tux pants off and out of the way, he had a close-up view of her bobbing head, her hair a soft, ash blonde, just like the hair of his lovely wife. At best, Mitzi had been a Cowboy cheerleader from the early seventies. At worst, she'd been a Cowboy cheerleader never, more likely a high-priced whore who filled out the formal gown nicely. Against his better judgment, a judgment significantly more impaired than it was an hour ago, Darlington had succumbed to the temptation and was along for the ride. Just a few more seconds.

The closet doors burst open; Mitzi didn't flinch. Two cameras flashed, then the photographers behind the cameras spilled out from their hiding place. Darlington recoiled, Mitzi disengaged herself. She pulled up the top of her gown and stood to leave.

"They want a name, Reverend," Mitzi said. "An adoptee who came through one of the county's agencies. She'd be about fifteen now. Someone will be in touch."

TWO

**Thirty-one years later
September 2016
Desoto, Texas**

T. Larinda Jordan stepped inside Shiloh Southwood Tabernacle United, a white stucco one-story church that pastor Darlington Beckner had led for the last thirty years. The locals called the church "Shoebox Methodist" because of its low, rectangular stature, with no steeple, only a small cross nailed to the wall above the front door. Larinda wasn't local and wasn't Methodist. She'd been raised an Oklahoma Catholic. One time not too long ago she'd been a cloistered nun. She entered the morning church service late, and she intended to leave early.

Larinda slipped into the last row of folding chairs, joining two other patrons. She was going for invisible in a high-necked white blouse and an eggshell white skirt of respectable length with embroidered white flowers. A short, unbuttoned denim jacket hid her toned, athletic upper torso. Flats lessened her height, makeup lessened her freckles, transitions lenses suggested dull gray eyes, and a blonde ponytail sold her as a college undergrad, reducing her age by ten years. The only thing difficult to hide was her bandaged left palm; the scabbing itched. A light fingertip massage provided relief until she was able to will the discomfort away.

She mouthed the words of the hymn in progress because she knew them, but she didn't sing. She scanned the congregation. It was mostly Native American parishioners, many elderly, a few children, all dressed in light jackets, sweaters or pullovers, geared to ward off the autumn chill. But she cared little about the parishioners; her focus was the church's pastor, now at the podium. A white male in his seventies, thin and vulture-like with a hunched back and a black comb-over, his eyes were a radiant light blue, their sparkle noticeable even at this distance. His hands rested flat on the lectern as he delivered a reading from the New Testament.

He matched the picture they'd given her.

A boy two rows ahead, a fidgeting pre-teen, scanned the congregation. Larinda lowered her head and tucked her face into a hymnal to blend in. After a moment she risked a peek to find him staring at her, his look judgmental, effeminate, with batting eyelashes. His mother whispered to him until he faced forward. The mother left behind a self-conscious smile for Larinda as an apology.

This was the kind of kid who saw more than he let on. The mother or the son or both could be a problem, but she wouldn't worry about that now.

Larinda waited in the church parking lot in a forest green, older model Ford Explorer, her binoculars raised. The midafternoon sun heated the car, forcing her to remove her jacket. Visible through the church's barred windows, Pastor Darlington Beckner flipped through hymnals in a sparsely furnished sunlit anteroom behind the altar, smoothing out the rabbit-eared pages, straightening the piles. This was taking longer than she'd expected. Regardless, she would not sully the sanctity of a church.

Pastor Beckner hobbled to the door on aged legs. He exited the anteroom, her binoculars following his progress down the center aisle on his way to the back of the church now empty of parishioners. Window to window, pew to pew, she had an unobstructed view of the small church's interior because there was no stained glass. He reached the vestibule at the church's entrance.

The Bible passage he'd read at the morning service had stayed with her, as had his grandfatherly demeanor while he delivered it. Matthew 19:14: "Jesus said, 'Let the little children come to me.'" The passage was a sign that this was right and just.

A dirt parking lot separated the church's entrance from her SUV. Shoebox Methodist was a repurposed municipal building, the stucco exterior whitewashed but not adequately, some fluorescent colored graffiti showing through. Rust stains dripped from the corners of its ancient iron window frames. One other car was in the lot, a late model Dodge sedan. The pastor exited the church, pulled the heavy front metal door closed behind him, making sure it latched. He paused, lifted his face skyward, breathed in the sunlit September air.

Old age and the recent passing of his wife had softened Pastor Beckner's conservative leanings, The Faithful had explained to her. He was now on the wrong path. His recent actions said he'd lost his own gospel, and this made him dangerous. The timing wasn't a coincidence. A new Texas law now forced women to view an ultrasound of their fetuses before they were allowed to have legal abortions. Planned Parenthood appealed the ruling to the U.S. Supreme Court. In two weeks, on the first Monday in October, the new Supreme Court term would begin, and the Texas case *Babineau v. Turbin* would be argued. If The Faithful had anything to say about it, the Court would validate the original Texas decision, and this validation would eventually be used to leverage overturning the 1973 *Roe v. Wade* decision in its entirety. The Court's opinion was in the process of being reshaped, considering the recent confirmation of a new Supreme Court associate justice.

For the past thirty years The Faithful had followed Darlington Beckner's every move. He'd never tried to contact anyone of political, municipal or jurisprudence consequence in all that time. Not the liberal politicians, not the police, not the media. His marriage was dead back then. Over time it resurrected itself to become rock solid. And if he'd felt the urge to confess to his wife his one and only extramarital transgression, The Faithful was fairly sure he hadn't done so. He'd been a good Christian, and they'd seen nothing that merited his elimination. Until now.

His wife's passing had been sudden. With it, apparently, came a need for him to divulge his miscarriage of duty when he was county adoption agency director. His sin.

His first misstep had been to contact the FBI. The Faithful had the reach and the resources to know these things. His second misstep was booking tomorrow's flight to D.C., where they expected him to fess up to his dereliction, his betrayal of the peoples' trust: he'd provided stolen information, from records sealed by law, about a certain closed adoption.

The Faithful had explained this to Larinda without volunteering other specifics about their agenda, to provide the context she needed to understand that if his confession reached the wrong people, it would be a bad thing. Pastor Beckner was now a new threat to the war on the unborn, a war that was close to being won. Eliminating him would neutralize this threat. Exactly how and where he fit into this equation, Larinda didn't need to know, and the good Christian that she was, she hadn't pressed them on it.

The Faithful. Her confidants and spiritual guides for most of her life in Texas, composed of ministers, town elders, captains of industry, televangelists, congressmen, and a senator. They were also her clandestine employers, on a contract-by-contract basis. Their text message to her that morning: "C.H.: Your new penance is to fix this. The Lord be with you."

C.H. "Church Hammer." Larinda's handle. She was a soldier, a righter of other people's wrongs, in the name of Jesus Christ.

The pastor unlocked his car. She waited until he climbed inside. The mess would stay contained that way.

"Pastor Beckner," she called, approaching his car on foot, her dimples accenting her warm smile. "A moment of your time, please." Her smile widened as she speed-walked her way closer.

He powered his car window down, her smile contagious. "Of course, miss. What can I help you with?"

At ten paces from the car she raised her arm, ready to shake his hand. Traffic coasted by on the street next to the lot. He made eye contact, was still smiling. He reached his hand through the window to clasp hers. At three paces the small ballistic knife strapped to her wrist inside her denim jacket sleeve ejected from its compressed air sheath with a quiet *thokkk*, the short blade entering his neck above his Adam's apple like an arrow, severing his vocal chords. He gripped his throat, a gurgling crimson leak springing from his neck and gushing through his fingers onto the steering wheel and windshield, asphyxiating him in his own blood. She clapped his shoulder like an old friend and scanned the empty parking lot for inquiring eyes, satisfied there were no witnesses. She removed the knife from his neck and wiped the blade on his shirt.

"That was a wonderful reading today, Pastor. Thank you, and may you rest in peace."

Jane's Baby

Before turning away, she reached into his front shirt pocket for the jeweled pen she noticed during his sermon. A trophy, or it would be, as soon as she wiped off the blood.

The police found her six days later.

Teresa Larinda Jordan, in jeans, track shoes and a loose pullover sweater, sat in a holding cell waiting for someone to post her bail. The charge for now was possession of prescription drugs in other people's names. She no longer considered herself a Teresa, answered instead to Larinda, not a saint's name, because she was no longer worthy of a saint's protection. She made the change when she was twenty-one, not long after agreeing to the decision that could send her soul to hell: to abort a child, an abominable wrong. There had been intense pressure from her grad student boyfriend, but this was no excuse. For her, the impact of terminating the pregnancy had been overwhelming. The impact to her boyfriend: nothing whatsoever, far as she'd been able to tell, that is until she killed him for being so cavalier and fed his body to her parents' hogs. Her first execution.

It stank in the jail cell, pungent as urine-soaked rotting meat. Most of the questions they'd asked her were about Pastor Beckner's murder, her arrest prompted by statements from the boy in the Shoebox Methodist congregation who'd taken an interest in her. That Indian kid. In an interrogation room, her court-appointed attorney read her the boy's statement.

"He said to the detective, and I quote, 'You don't wear white after Labor Day.' He busted in on his mother and the detective interviewing her at home, did the whole finger wag, no way girlfriend urban thing for emphasis. Then he added, 'I don't care what Emily Post says is acceptable now. Wearing white after Labor Day is abhorrent. If you take notes on anything, Detective, take a note on that.' The kid's a little different."

A twelve-year-old Indian kid who sounded like a queer socialite from Manhattan. Where did these kids learn this behavior? From the atheist liberals, of course.

No evidence could place her at the pastor's car, and no murder weapon had been found yet. They knew what it was, the police told her attorney. A knife or some other sharp projectile, based on the puncture wound to the neck. The cops did have an interest in the back of her hand and her palm, which showed scabbing in both places. They took a blood sample.

"From a nail gun," she'd told them. "I'm a journeyman carpenter." Closer to the truth than they needed to know.

All interesting stuff, her attorney had commented to her accusers, but how did any of it attach his client to the pastor's murder?

The connection: she was a non-church member who picked that Sunday to check out the church's service as a potential new parishioner. A coincidence, and detectives didn't like coincidences. That, plus the odd kid who identified her also knew where the white-on-white embroidered skirt could be purchased on summer clearance, the kid had emphasized, which led the cops to a certain women's clothing store, which produced a corroborating physical description from a sales clerk. Store video footage gave them their "person of interest," and local news stations blasted the airwaves with it. Anonymous tips brought the police to her doorstep.

Fingered by a crossdressing Indian kid who knew his women's clothing stores. She couldn't have planned for this.

The search of her apartment produced no incriminating evidence regarding the homicide. What they did find were fourteen filled prescription bottles of OxyContin, all current, only one with her name on it, some open gauze packages plus, oddly enough, a novice nun's habit, complete with a white wimple. The murder case remained open but there wasn't enough evidence to hold her. The charge for illegal possession of a controlled substance was the only charge that stuck. But this would allow them to keep an eye on her. The judge assigned bail and scheduled her hearing for tomorrow, Monday.

As a transplanted Tulsa, Oklahoma Catholic schoolteacher turned cloistered nun turned itinerant Dallas carpenter, she'd never been arrested before, this despite three executions she'd committed in the eighteen months since she'd pledged her devotion to the cause.

"Your bail's been posted, Larinda," her attorney told her, his Texas drawl thick. A turn-on if she were still into sex, but only if he were a Christian; he looked like a Jew. No different than the moneychangers Jesus cast out of the temple.

Jane's Baby

She had few friends in Texas; friends were distractions. She had The Faithful, and they had arranged her bail. Regardless, whenever and wherever her hearing would be, she decided she wouldn't be there.

"Thank you for the information, counselor."

She'd now find the mouthy little faggot Indian kid and his mother and kill them both.

THREE

Judge Drury left Shreveport twelve hundred bucks richer and rid of his bounty, a bail-jumping child pornographer-pedophile from Philly now in the hands of the Louisiana state cops. A short chase outside a Starbucks near a playground, no shots fired, dog bites to the bounty's face and arms from his deputies and, unfortunately for the bounty, three fingers shredded by canine teeth, both thumbs included. Not a planned outcome, but Judge loved the karma. If his bounty ever decided to get back into child pornography, pleasuring himself would be a challenge.

He arrived a little after eight p.m. in Arlington, Texas, at AT&T Stadium, home of the Dallas Cowboys and this week's Monday Night Football game. Two hundred miles, Shreveport to Dallas, in less than three hours. His Marine buddy LeVander Metcalf had called in a favor and scored a game ticket so Judge could see his Eagles play Dallas. He'd already checked into a pet-friendly B&B on a Texas farm, but it was always a risk leaving his two deputies somewhere. Not a risk for them, they were well trained; the risk was to him. For this reason they were with him in the stadium parking lot, resting in the van before he headed inside without them. A cool night, the late summer heat not a consideration. They had their orders, were well fed, watered and walked, with the windows cracked; they would be fine.

Well-fed, watered, walked, with the windows cracked.

Too many w's. Unintentional, the alliteration, but Judge's subconscious rarely missed it. He powered the windows up and gripped the steering wheel tight with both hands, an episode coming on, white-knuckle tight, tighter than a frog's ass, tighter than a...

"Wombat wiener, winkin blinkin nod your noggin, donkey dicking daisy duck, cluster fuck, flop your jock, jackbooted jiffy-lubed, snipper snooper SNIPER SNOT..."

Jane's Baby

Maeby, his brindle boxer terrier deputy, nudged his hand with her nose, for his comfort, not hers. His German Shepherd J.D., short for Judge Drury, stayed relaxed in his large crate in the back, unimpressed by his master's X-rated rap. Yes, he'd named his German Shepherd deputy after himself; Judge's Marine narcissism had gotten the better of him. J.D. was a shelter puppy that was now a highly trained attack dog.

The Tourette's tirade eased, then it powered off. He ran his hand over Maeby's smooth coat then her silky ears, then he patted her head. She retreated to the floor in front of the passenger seat. Dogs situated, windows ajar, and Tourette's episode number five thousand or so behind him, he was overheated from the rant but otherwise good to go.

The football game sucked, from Judge's perspective. His seat was in the nosebleeds with the drunks, so high up his shaved head got color from the intense stadium lighting. A jungle up there, just like the nosebleeds in Philly. No-man's land for a visiting team's fans, and for him especially, if something stoked his disease.

Judge's afflictions: coprolalia and copropraxia. For the uninformed, this meant compulsive profanity and obscene gestures, respectively.

Respectively. A word he had little use for in his vocabulary other than to describe these subsets of Tourette syndrome simmering just below the surface. Proof that God or whatever other supreme being out there did have a sense of humor, considering Judge was fifty-seven years old and a Marine, and having TS had, so far, not been a picnic. Thirty plus years and out. Such hilarity at his expense, living with this affliction for every one of those years in the Corps. Back at you, God. As hilarious as fuck.

Ten minutes left in the game with no issues so far, Judge was just another white face in a section loaded with them, all except for the one guy in the seat behind him. Judge's Eagles were stinking up the joint, and this Dallas fan was verbally wailing on them big time. Black guy; a little shit. Seriously little. A midget, decked out in an outfit from the Old West. Brown leather children's chaps, leather vest with fringe, a black sequined ten-gallon cowboy hat. Small body, big mouth, with one of the tallest hats Judge had ever seen. And drunk, with no idea that the guy in front of him, Judge, was an Eagles fan, and Judge wanting him to remain ignorant of that fact. This Dallas fan's glee at the game's lopsided 37-17 score made Judge want to puke.

Black midget: "Nice arm, Ramsay! You a gopher killer, boy? The gophers here in Texas are really big, son. Not like the ones in Philly. Gotta throw harder'n that to kill a Texas gopher, boy."

The object of his derision was a rookie Eagles quarterback with a strong young arm that could throw bullets. With the tough Cowboy pass rush, too many of his bullets had misfired and landed at his receivers' feet or were intercepted. Judge needed to stay in control, except, in his head.

...gopher dwarf, hogwart smurf, nigger nigger suck my trigger...

The midget was shouting now. "How's that, you Philly cheese-shits! I got your cheez-whiz hanging, right..." a crotch grab, "here!"

...gopher-fucker, stiffytucker.

Judge kept it together, thoughts only, nothing verbalized, stayed tight, his meds and him on top of it, no fallout, everything okay.

Judge Drury hated the Cowboys, which made the beating his Eagles were taking particularly painful. He'd hated them since 1967, when the Cowboys' Lee Fucking Roy cheap-shotted Timmy Brown, a star Eagles running back, in a lopsided Cowboys' home game like this one here. An elbow from Roy under the faceguard, after the whistle, fractured Brown's jaw. Judge was eight years old when that happened, and he never forgot the Philly newspaper stills of the hit. Timmy Brown's head went one way, and Judge swore the photos showed bits of his teeth go another. Fuck you, Lee Roy. Going on fifty years of fuck you, you cheap shot Cowboy SOB.

Judge's phone buzzed. A text message from LeVander, an Iraqi War Two vet like himself, and Judge's closest friend from the Corps. LeVander became a bail bondsman and Judge became a fugitive recovery agent. A perfect match made in each other's respective hells.

Jane's Baby

—Yo Judge. Jarhead buddy laid off some money. A bounty skipped her hearing today. Drug charge.

—Not interested. At the game.

—Here's her info. Not a hefty reward but easy money. You can bring her in tonight.

The next text message showed her mug shot. Attractive face. Brassy blonde hair. Some freckles.

There was always a catch, taking favors from LeVander, with him a persistent SOB about it.

—Negatory. Go Away.

—Dude. A woman schoolteacher from Oklahoma. Piece of cake.

—You greedy fuck. You picked it up because I'm down here & you think I owe you. Answer's still no, I'm busy.

—Eagles are getting mugged. Game's a dog. Avoid traffic, return my favor, earn some $. Ticket wasn't cheap.

Always about the favors.

—Screw the favor. You gave me a bogus ticket.

—Wtf you mean bogus ticket?

—Eagles are losing. You gave me a losing ticket.

—Fuck you Judge you wiseass. You have a trust fund, I don't. I need to earn a living.

In his text returning frenzy he almost didn't hear it, someone screaming "Cowboys bite it" in an infinite loop. Quick lip work, fast and irritating, like the fine print disclaimer for a car commercial. Soon, more of the same...

"Cowhumpers DALLAS SUCKS bite it bite it bite it...Texas wieners, lonestar boners, boner eaters, E-A-G-L-E-S, EAGLES!"

God damn it, the screamer was him. Shit.

He shoved the phone into a shirt pocket so he could free his hands to find and stroke the rabbit's foot talisman he kept on his belt loop for times like this, then he readied himself for whatever blowback that was queuing up from surrounding Cowboy fans.

What he got were arms around his neck in a chokehold, someone going for a takedown from behind, already airborne and on his back...kid's arms that jerked up against his windpipe in a sleeper-hold wrestling move, then a fist to his cheekbone, then snarling, snapping teeth in his ear.

...beer, he smelled beer on his breath, not a kid...

The little black guy in the cowboy outfit bit him, sank his teeth into his left ear, ripped at it like it was a turnbuckle, went all Mike Tyson on him, was now screaming.

"People...from Philly...SUCK. You...SUCK..."

If he was shouting, he wasn't biting. Judge's move.

He ripped him off his back with one hand on his shoulder and whipped his little body forward until they were face-to-face. Judge snarled back at him. "Calm...the hell...down, sport. My bad. I got carried away. Sorry. My Tourette's..."

He didn't get to finish the sentence. Judge spat out more verbal diarrhea as his latent mind-fuckery arrived in full force, spraying the little guy's contorted face and ending with:

"...smile and say midget. Middd-jettt! Nigger nigger midget trigger..."

Stadium Security descended on them from both sides of the row. Judge's mouth quieted. His attacker was drunk and Judge wasn't, so he knew better than to resist the guards wading through the fans to get at them; they had tasers and shit.

Judge raised his arms straight up, readied himself for a full surrender. The attacker took advantage with a leveraged punch to Judge's balls. Nothing small about his hands, damn it. Judge doubled over, felt his stomach lurch, but was able to suck the pain back so it didn't explode out the top of his shaved head.

"You! Stop!" a guard barked at the sneak-punching little SOB. "Don't. Move..."

The guards advanced, tasers out. The closest one spoke to the attacker in a calming voice. "Relax. We get it. You hate mouthy Eagles fans. Relax, son..." He reached the two combatants. "Easy there, son, easy..."

Words to soothe the savage beastie. The little drunk was having none of it. He nailed the guard in the chin with a short, jack-in-the-box right. The punch sent the guard onto his ass into the next row. Three other guards pounced, and they all

Jane's Baby

commenced stunning the pint-sized cowboy in his neck and chest, the high voltage jolts whipping his small body into spasms bad as a writhing flounder on the end of a fishhook. When the spasms stopped he curled into the cramped space under a now empty stadium seat while Security reached in again and zapped him repeatedly, so many times Judge expected his hair to ignite. He was taking a beating, and he wasn't so drunk that he wasn't feeling it.

"Please, guys!" he pleaded, his hands up, his words staticky, "n-no m-more. Owww. Stop...sorry..."

The shocks his compact body took, he'd have permanent damage if they didn't stop, so Judge waded his batshit-crazy six-three self in, went ballistic on their asses, ripped them off the little guy with a flurry of body slams, head and body shots, trying to keep them from killing him. An impressive burst of adrenaline and machismo on Judge's part, but it didn't last. A taser laid him out against some empty seats, then he dropped onto the sticky stadium concrete floor and twitched uncontrollably next to his semiconscious miniature assailant.

In the stadium's "police room" located on the event level, Judge still tingled from the taser with a bad headache, a bloody lip, and some bruised ribs, plus his balls still hurt.

"You. Mister Clean. Stand up."

When Judge didn't get the reference, a security guard, this one upwards of six-five, assisted him with two meaty hands under his arms and a swift clean and jerk move that lifted Judge onto his feet. The guy behind the desk was on a power trip, barking like he was a courtroom judge. At best he was a cop sergeant.

"I see from your IDs you're an ex-Marine, Mister Drury."

"Former enlisted," Judge said. There were no ex-Marines. Once a Marine, always a Marine.

"Yeah, well, whatever. You're lucky there were witnesses to Chigger's assault. You're also lucky none of those witnesses didn't go after you the way Chigger did, hearing how you bad-mouthed our football team."

'Chigger?'

"I'm sorry, your Excellency," Judge said, meaning no disrespect. Well, maybe meaning some, knowing what his thugs had done to the guy who jumped him, juicing him up so bad he could have powered the stadium scoreboard. "The other guy, Chigger, he okay?"

The official's glare said the sarcasm had earned him no favors. "'Your Honor,' to you, son. Chigger is sobering up. We'll process him next. He's a local sports writer with nine lives, although he's drinking most of them away. I'm gonna give you a break, Mister Drury, you being an ex-Marine and all. You gave the Security team a good workout. Charges won't be filed. You're free to go."

Not an 'ex,' Bozo. USMC Former Enlisted, you pointy-headed fuck. A grip of the rabbit's foot helped Judge let it go. "I want to see the other guy. Your Honor. Please."

"Not going to happen. We're busy. Albert, escort our Eagles fan friend here to the nearest stadium exit."

Albert was the six-five, plus-sized giant whose acquaintance, and that of his taser, Judge had already made. Albert gestured at him with an after-you and Judge complied.

Judge checked on his canine deputies, gave them quick walks and returned to the stadium exit where Albert and another security guard had deposited him. The cloudless, starry autumn night wasn't getting its due, losing out to blazing stadium lights that blasted the heavens at two in the morning with searchlight-equivalent candlepower. Judge seated his ass on a chilly aluminum bench, leaning away from the tender spot where the taser probes had connected, his headache almost gone. Ten minutes later, his eyes still on the stadium exit, he played with his phone, starting to think this wait was a waste of time. He read texts queued up from LeVander during the game:

—Schoolteacher was more than a pill-popper. Only charge that stuck. Got 2 addresses for you.

The bounty's apartment was one, in a Dallas suburb. The other was a trailer park in Glenn Heights, a half-hour from Arlington:

—People who ID'd her live there. They say she killed their church pastor. Not enough to hold her on it.

Jane's Baby

—Stop at the trailer park, ask questions, let them see your shiny dome, have them meet your cool dogs.

She'd skipped bail, but who skips bail for possession of bogus prescriptions? Had to have been for something more serious.

The lights inside the stadium dimmed to half-strength. The lighting for the exit in front of him switched off. The exit's long hallway went dark, turned opaque black, thick and heavy as a stage curtain. Except they still had a volunteer from the audience, Chigger, in the bowels of the building somewhere.

"...chigger-swigger, nigger-dwarf, earwig snort, cowboy jig, jiggy with it..."

All whispers through Judge's pursed lips, with no one there to witness them.

And then, showtime. His pint-sized assailant stumbled or was pushed out of the darkness and fell onto all fours. No black sequined hat, but the rest of his cowboy outfit was intact. He struggled getting to his feet, brushed himself off, then swept a tangle of black and gray dreads fit for a Rastafarian maestro out of his eyes. At full height in his cowboy boots he was at best four-foot-eight. The boots had spurs, something Judge had missed earlier, and was thankful he hadn't learned about them the hard way. The little guy squinted, the bright light from an overhead lamppost offending his previously light-deprived vision, or maybe his hangover.

A tossed black hat split the darkness from behind him, spinning out to hit him in the back of the head. He wobbled, picked it up and dented its sparkled ten-gallon top before he placed it on his head. A slight tug on the brim just above his forehead snugged it up. Calm and unfazed, his squint got more severe as Judge approached. Judge was calmer too, now that he saw they hadn't maimed or killed him. Coming face-to-face, sort of, his attacker's head tilted up, Judge's tilting down. They assessed each other.

"Owen Wingert. Dallas Morning News sportswriter. One helluva fight, huh?"

"One helluva fight. Gunnery Sergeant Judge Drury, USMC, Former Enlisted."

Bare-knuckled combatants always shared a certain camaraderie with each other after the fight was over. Judge first learned this growing up on the streets in Philly, where fistfights were common, even between best friends. And where some friendships grew from battles between sworn enemies.

"I appreciate what you did for me tonight, you going all superhero on them. No one's ever jumped in like that before. Wasn't needed, but I appreciate it."

"Certainly looked like you needed it. They were zapping you pretty good."

"They know when to stop. I don't, but they do. Sorry about the groin shot. You left yourself open."

"I didn't leave myself open. I was surrendering to Security. Hands up means white flag. 'No mas.'"

"No such thing as surrender for guys like me. Surrender only means getting a worse beating." They began their trek to the far reaches of the parking lot. "So it's Tourette's, huh?"

"Yep. Sometimes the medication works, sometimes it doesn't."

"How the hell did they let you in the Marines?"

A direct little SOB, Judge had to give him that. "Friends in high places." Better word would have been "acquaintances." Judge's father was responsible, but he was never a friend. Best word, prick.

Owen was late thirties or early forties, seemed easygoing enough and well adjusted. Judge went for cute, addressing the other elephant in the room. "So it's dwarfism, then."

"Close enough," he said, staying deadpan. "'Midget' is more accurate. My affliction's medicated, too." He pulled out a flask, took a hit. "Medication success rate one hundred percent, long as I stay that way." He offered Judge some and Judge declined. He took another hit, then got panicky. "Shit. What time is it? I've got a column to write."

Judge checked his phone. "Two forty-five. You all right getting home by yourself?"

"I could use a lift," he said. "I have no idea where I left my horse."

FOUR

The Palace Motel clock rearranged its red LED dashes. Two-forty-five a.m. Larinda watched the five become a six, the six a seven, then an eight...

She was wired, her adrenaline still pumping. A busy day yesterday. Productive, with one threat to the cause eliminated. The next threat, this one to her personally, needed addressing, and this was keeping her awake.

She'd been told to disappear, to use an alias, as in make herself a ghost and leave town. The ID by the mom and her kid at the church made her a person of interest in the pastor's murder, her appearance just before the murder too suspicious. It made The Faithful nervous in addition to the cops.

Out of bed now, face down and horizontal to the floor, her toes flexed, she locked then unlocked her elbows. Background noise drifted from the TV while she pounded out her pushups. An early morning farm and ranch report showed a farmer milking his cows, the flat screen's volume turned up to drown out neighbors who were bouncing off the adjacent wall, fornicating themselves silly. The cheap motel carpet smelled of mildew and wet dog fur, and it tickled her nose on each downward thrust as she counted out fifty intense pushups, "...twenty-two for Jesus, twenty-three for Jesus," her stress soon dissipating, "...forty-nine for Jesus, fifty for Jesus. Thank you Jesus, my Lord God and Savior."

Larinda relocated a Tec-9 mini semi-automatic handgun from the motel end table to the front pocket of her backpack. She pulled on a black windbreaker, flipped up the hood and slipped the backpack over her shoulder. With the farmers' cows milked, a TV news anchor slid in behind the dairy report, producing more white noise.

After she eliminated the people who could identify her, she'd abide by The Faithful's wishes and make herself scarce. But her definition of scarce and their definition differed. To them, scarce meant a motel in Minnesota scarce, or a campsite in Idaho scarce. Her gut feeling said it was even worse, that they'd prefer her to retire from the business. Their need for her and her services, her dedication, her religious zeal, her willingness to do whatever it took to save babies: was this all winding down?

No. Never. As far as she was concerned, more work was needed. Plus her sin needed more penance. Much more.

To her, scarce meant become invisible, blend in, hide in plain sight while staying enough steps ahead of getting caught. Regardless, their need for her scarcity wouldn't sway her from shadowing a certain newly appointed Supreme Court justice. The confirmation hearings, live on TV, had delved deeply into the prospective justice's background. The justice vocalized her liberal leanings as a college student, including blasphemous ideals like pro-choice and feminism. She was a widow, but she was unworthy of the marriage that had made her one, to a conservative Christian Republican husband and military hero. The new justice included pagan Indian spiritualism among the religions needing protection by the Constitution. Between cable news coverage and contentious analysis of the hearings, Larinda's faith was being soundly trampled every night on the evening news. Her beliefs were not debatable issues; they were God's word.

With Pastor Beckner out of the way, the newest loose end was now Associate Justice Naomi Coolsummer, an Indian. Larinda hated Indians, a few generations of family hate preceding her own. The Faithful hadn't approached her about neutralizing the Supreme Court justice, but did they really need to? Sometimes the targets were obvious. This one would be a freebie.

A droning TV anchor voice suddenly grabbed her attention. "In a few weeks, the first case on the docket for the new United States Supreme Court term will become the most controversial case it will hear in over forty years."

Larinda lowered the hood for her windbreaker, stared at the screen.

"A case birthed in Texas, argued, decided and won by the State," the reporter continued, "that Texas women who seek abortions would now be required by law to view ultrasounds of their fetuses before terminating their pregnancies."

Jane's Baby

The decision had been appealed to the U.S. Supreme Court. Its defense in that venue, per the reporter, "was primed as an opportunity for the Court to revisit and rule on, in its entirety, the legality of terminating pregnancies that had resulted from the right-to-privacy landmark *Roe v. Wade* ruling."

Killing babies. The thought made Larinda's stomach turn.

"And front and center to this debate is the newest associate justice of the Supreme Court, Texas' own federal judge Naomi Coolsummer. Here are some highlights of her confirmation hearing in front of the Senate Judiciary Committee."

Larinda moved closer to the TV.

"I grew up in modest circumstances in Austin, Texas…was adopted…I'm a Native American of Caddo Comanche extraction.

"I've been a prosecutor, a private litigator, a trial judge, and an appellate judge.

"…President William Jefferson Clinton appointed me to the United States Court of Appeals for the Fifth Circuit. President George Walker Bush appointed me to…

"My nomination to the U.S. Supreme Court by President Alfreda Helen Lindsay is the finest and most humbling moment of my career…"

Then came an excerpt of the U.S. Senator from Texas Mildred Folsom's comments and questions to the appointee: "…your agile legal mind…judicial integrity…You are, however, a chameleon. Someone has to mention this, so it might as well be the senator from your home state. You were an abortion advocate, then a volunteer abortion clinic assistant. You exhibited social activist behaviors as a college undergrad and at the OU College of Law. You came across as anti-religion, or at a minimum as an atheist. How do we reconcile this biased collegiate background to the fair and impartial judge we've seen render unbiased decisions in our district? A judge I truly admire, mind you, and one I would truly like to support…"

"Senator, I am not an atheist, nor am I anti-religion. I'm Native American, which is quite the contrary. Native American religions focus on nature, the landscape, animals…and I do not let my personal beliefs interfere with the law. My decisions have always served justice, never individual interests. I apply the law based on the facts at hand…the Constitution's statutes…justice…"

"And after I apply God's law," Larinda said to the TV screen, "your application of the law won't matter."

She tossed yesterday's church-going clothes into a gym bag, turned off the flat screen, grabbed the pocket change scattered atop the motel's rickety bureau and left the room key. She wouldn't be back.

She climbed behind the wheel of her SUV; it was three-thirty a.m. She'd need to find new transportation. Her targets lived in a trailer park in Glenn Heights. This info, plus their names, she'd gleaned during her interviews at the police station. Her young, court-appointed attorney had block-lettered her accusers' address on his legal pad. A rookie mistake.

Larinda checked one of her Tec-9s, switched out the ammo, inserted copper R.I.P. bullets into the clip. Radically Invasive Projectiles, her choice for this hit. R.I.P.s shredded solid objects; drywall, plywood, sheet metal, and they expanded in different directions while their trocar petal shrapnel spun on its way into and through the target. They were advertised as "the last bullet you will ever need," and very effective for human tissue destruction.

Two hours of total darkness to work with. She knew an all-night diner and truck stop near Ft. Worth where good folks with a disdain for seat belts, democrats, and atheists left their cars and trucks unlocked while they ate. She'd acquire another SUV, swap out her payload and do the deed. She'd get on the road to D.C. soon after.

Naomi lay awake in bed in her high-rise condo apartment in Austin. Reed had come to her in a dream again.

"Let go, Naomi," Reed said. "It's time. Let me go."

Reed Guest, her Texas high school sweetheart, and her soul mate. Today was the six-year anniversary of his death.

Reed served in Desert Storm while Naomi earned her BS in pre-law. He returned, earned a BS in Military Science and graduated from Officer Candidate School. She graduated from Oklahoma's School of Law and returned to practice in the Texas tribal court system. He learned to fly Black Hawk helicopters into war zones, served three tours of duty. She entered the federal legal system as a prosecutor. Distance and time apart had been a challenge for them, but their companionship and marriage proved unshakeable. Theirs was a bond that could have been broken only one way.

His goal, his brass ring: attain the rank of colonel. He'd finally earned it during his Iraqi Freedom tour, but he didn't stay stateside, didn't stay alive, long enough to receive it. A hero, killed in action soon after his deployment to Afghanistan. Since then she'd never shared her bed with anyone else.

"Reed. My Reed…"

His name on her lips was a soft release into the bedroom's stillness. Her son and daughter, students at the University of Texas at Austin, lived on campus, were a year apart in age, the best of friends, and emotionally close to her. But as adults they now needed her less, when she now, perhaps, would need them the most.

Her professional life's pinnacle, her grail, would be life altering, potentially world changing, and border on godlike, answerable both to current and future generations. In a moment of self-pity, in the dead of this interminable night, Naomi heaved a heavy sigh, feeling overwhelmed and alone.

"I miss you, Reed."

Missed him cupping her chin, missed his soft, playful pinch of her full face and her round cheeks, a plumpness he adored best when she blushed, the blush dusting her cocoa complexion with a dash of rose, her face framed by straight black hair, and her hair, during their lovemaking, tickling his chin, his neck, his chest, and then his stomach and other regions south. Oh how she melted inside his embrace, could rest there while he soothed away her insecurities, would let her speak of her doubts, her fear of clerking for the tough judges, of taking the Texas Bar, and her concern that her efforts as a prosecuting federal attorney weren't making enough of a difference.

As the first Native American woman seated in the federal judiciary in Texas, at five-ten she was physically imposing and took no prisoners. And now, Naomi Coolsummer-Guest, Naomi Coolsummer to the public, age forty-six, had become the first Native American confirmed for a seat on the U.S. Supreme Court.

Her husband was gone, and her kids lived on campus. Her adoptive parents were in assisted living, both with early stages

Alzheimer's, Naomi their only child. Leaving her parents behind, even with the excellent care they received, was so incredibly tough, and the reason she delayed her relocation to D.C. until the last weekend before the start of the fall term.

She fluffed her pillow. She needed to salvage a few hours of sleep. A big travel day today. A U.S. marshal would pick her up to escort her on her flight, Austin to D.C. He was to remain assigned to her until she moved into her Georgetown townhouse.

Sinking farther down, inside her dreamscape, a snippet rose up, of her as an infant gazing skyward, falling, no, tossed, from an open window, a woman wringing her hands above her, the woman's hands and arms growing smaller as Naomi descended in a free fall from floor to floor. The woman's arms and head disappeared, her hands still on the sill, then her head reemerged for one last, featureless peek, a blurred dark speck that lingered then pulled back inside, gone.

The child discarded, the deed done.

Her biological mother: Was she still alive? What about her biological father? Did she have any siblings?

"I'm so proud of you," her husband Reed said, returning to her subconscious. "Don't go it alone, Naomi. Open your heart a*gain. You deserve it. Share…"*

FIVE

"There she is," Owen said, pointing.

His horse was a late model Boss 302 Ford Mustang, with a custom paint job in Dallas Cowboy navy blue with a wide, silver stripe from the grill to the rear bumper. At three-thirty in the morning, it was the only car left in the stadium's section fifteen parking lot. They pulled up next to it. "Just needed to make sure she's okay. Say, wanna do me a favor?"

Owen was sober enough to know he wasn't sober enough to be driving. Judge keyed in the cross streets for the lot, Web and Slaughter, to his van's GPS and waited for Owen's input, as in where the hell he wanted him to drop him off.

"My spread's in Oak Leaf, Texas. About a half hour."

The GPS agreed on the ETA. It also showed the location was near Glenn Heights, home to the people who identified LeVander's bounty. Both out of the way to Judge's B&B, but not by much.

A long haul to the stadium on foot from here. For his new friend, the equivalent of a marathon, acknowledging his, ah, short stride. So why park all the way the hell out here?

"I take the shuttle, wise guy."

The little fucker had read him. In Judge's head...nigger midget jigger widget...

Behind the driver's seat Maeby raised herself to all fours, went on alert, stood tall enough to lay her chin on Judge's shoulder. Anticipating his TS mood swings was a sixth sense for her. With her chin there, Judge choked this one back.

"Press credentials don't get you anything closer?" Judge asked.

"Sure, if I still had 'em. So would season tickets. Because of out-of-town shitheads like you, no offense, I wore out my welcome. Now I'm stuck looking online for ticket resellers for any seat I can get."

"So that was all bullshit about how you write for a newspaper?"

"No bullshit. I've got a friggin' column, and it's a good one. 'Chigger Bytes.' Lost my press credentials, but I still have the column. They don't want me near the affluent ticket holders. Or the press box. Too many out-of-town writers. It seems I have anger management issues."

He sniffed, an ambivalent little sniff like movie tough guys did when they paused for effect; a nose-noise equivalent of a 'ya know.' "Add a coupla beers and it's like, whoa Nellie, gasoline on a fire. I'm Cowboy silver and blue, through and through, pardner, know what I'm saying? They all just need to shut the fuck up about my Cowboys."

He was fading, bordering on passing out, then rallied: "Or I'll shut them all up, every one of them. The bastards all just need to shut the hell (errrrp) up." The smell of semi-digested burritos and beer capped off a huge guttural belch.

Maeby stood again and J.D., his eighty-pound German Shepherd, creeped out of his crate with a low growl, both now interested in Judge's manners-challenged passenger.

"Ever think of seeing someone about the anger, or maybe AA?"

He didn't get an answer. Owen was busy absorbing what was in the cargo area behind the van's bucket seats. Passing headlights and an occasional utility pole lamp gave fleeting glimpses of Judge's onboard tools and other occupational necessities. Slanted shadows were not the way people needed to see the inside of this van for the first time. Secured to the walls, the ceiling and the floor were leg irons, handcuffs, waist chains, some Kevlar vests, police batons, a short-stock shotgun and other weaponry, plus dog paraphernalia: leashes, harnesses, muzzles, and a dog crate large enough to hold a human being. There was no barrier between the seats and the cargo area, so to an unsuspecting passenger the space looked like a walk-in kink-fest closet. The two military-trained dogs didn't soften these images.

"Kee-rist, Judge, what the hell you got going on back here?"

"Grrr." The German Shepherd was sticking up for his master.

"My job is what's going on. I'm a fugitive recovery agent."

"What the hell's a...?"

Jane's Baby

"A bounty hunter. Like Dog the Bounty Hunter, but with real dogs as deputies, not big-boobed brassy blonds."

Too many b's. Shit. A grip of the rabbit's foot calmed him.

"Cool," Owen said. "Let's go do some bounty recovery hunter shit. My news column can wait. Cowboys won, Eagles sucked. Whaddaya say, Judge?"

"Look, Owen, you're going home, and I'm heading back to my B&B so me and my partners can get some sleep. Four miles to your place, then I'm done."

Owen's head slumped before Judge finished speaking. Moments later his mouth drooled, the shoulder belt the only thing keeping him from sliding to the floor in front of the seat. They stayed on this road for another three miles, a straight run, then one turn. Tonight had in fact been fun, Judge mused, except for the Eagles loss. LeVander would eat up this little interlude with one Mister Owen "Chigger" Wingert when Judge told him about it tomorrow, on his way back to Pennsylvania.

His passenger commenced mumbling. "...you don't bounce till you hit the ground..."

"Come again?"

His head tilted right, stayed buffeted by the window. He settled back into a snore, then, "...ain't hit bottom yet, you high and mighty sons-a-bitches. (zzzzz.) Ain't fucking ready. No AA till I hit bottom. Then watch this mighty midget bounce like a fucking superball, y'all..."

Drunk guy gibberish. Judge and his deputies settled back into the drive, passing through Glenn Heights. He had no interest in LeVander's schoolteacher bounty this time of night. Maybe he'd stop back tomorrow to interview these people to learn about her. Next town up was Oak Leaf, their destination, and the end of Judge's time with Chigger, but something on the right caught his eye, a bright flash.

"What in the fuck was that?" Judge mused aloud.

A hundred yards off the road, the nighttime horizon tore open. Three short yellow-white muzzle flashes silently ripped holes in the veiled darkness, silent at least to Judge, but he was sure he'd seen them, the occupational hazard of midnight watches during multiple tours of duty as a Marine. He powered down the passenger window. Owen's head skittered against the glass as the window disappeared into the door but he stayed unconscious even after its retraction. More short bursts, again with no noise. No matter, Judge knew nighttime gunfire when he saw it. He made a sharp right onto a two-laner and put the pedal to the floor. The van fishtailed through an entrance to an RV campground and trailer park, Judge concentrating on the spot on the horizon where he saw the gunfire, straight ahead, maybe five hundred feet away now, looking for any movement or more gunplay.

Ba-BOOM.

An orange fireball erupted like propane stoked to fuel a hot air balloon, a short burst that blasted skyward then expanded at its base. A mobile home engulfed in flames, and holy shit it was propane. All the trailers had propane tanks for heating and cooking, including those next to the one burning. He jammed the brakes, stopping in front of a camper two sites away from the burning home. This close in Judge realized the newest danger, the back half of the trailer park heavily forested. People needed to get out of their trailers, move to a safe distance.

"Owen!" Judge shoved his passenger's shoulder. "Chigger! Call 911!"

"What the fuck..." Owen was fully awake, no choice otherwise, shocked sober by the blast. His eyes mirrored the flames.

The home site was on fire, the exploded propane tank still showering debris onto the dirt and leaves behind the trailer like sparks from a welding gun, the leaves igniting. Out of the van, Judge trotted toward the screams coming from inside the trailer, scanning the perimeter as he closed in. Sirens gained strength in the distance. The mobile home was, had been, a creamy white aluminum, with two white picket fences, low to the ground that lined a walkway of red and brown pavers, and led to the front door. The door's perimeter was the only part of the trailer not scorched. Little hope for anyone inside. Judge wrapped his hand in his tee shirt to try the doorknob despite what the burning metal might do to him. A jagged line of holes distracted him: bullet holes, punched into the trailer's white metal hide and running forward from the trailer's scorched rear section to its front door, the fire still moving, eating past them, nearing the door. The door burst open. A young girl stumbled out, her chest bleeding, her hair on

Jane's Baby

fire, her face scorched black. In her two-fisted grip was a dead-weighted woman, the girl dragging her by the woman's shirt.

"My mother...help her..."

Judge grabbed a waistband full of pink polyester pajamas in one hand and a fistful of gray adult sweatshirt smeared in blood in the other. He back-peddled, dragging both victims down the walkway, heat radiating from them, could smell their charred flesh, wouldn't look closely at them until he'd pulled them far enough away from the advancing flames. They reached the street. Owen bent over and heaved his tortured stomach as Judge got closer to him then stepped quickly in his direction, but his vomiting stopped him again. The adult's face and chest were charred and slimy and hot to the touch, like she was burning from the inside out. Judge knew CPR but quickly realized he'd be of no help to her; no one would.

He moved over to the young girl, her pink pajamas on fire. He ripped at them, needed to get them off her body, to put the flames out...

Christ, I'm wrong, he realized. The kid dragging the mother was a boy, and he was bleeding near his waist, from a gunshot wound.

His arms flailed, were grabbing, searching, soon found Judge's head, his hand connecting with his mouth. He gripped Judge's lower jaw and pulled him down into his face, beneath his seared, blistering scalp. Smoke left his mouth as he tried to speak.

"...we saw her...morning service. She killed...our pastor..."

He passed out while Judge administered CPR. *C'mon, kid, stay with me...*

A push nudged Judge's shoulder, someone trying to get his attention, the person grabbing at his shirt, then pushing and shoving him.

Screw that, this kid is dying!

"EMTs are here. Judge! Stop!"

Owen was spitting his words, buzzing about Judge's face, this insect, this fucking Chigger insect buzzing in his ear goddamn it, not letting him do this. Steam shimmered from Judge's bald head, and in a throat raspy from the smoke the verbal bile accumulated, the Tourette's, looking for release.

"Get off him, Judge! The EMTs, let them do their job."

Fuck no, we're doing this, c'mon kiddo...
...can't...hold it...in...

"...burning...Cunt! Cunt balls...everybody smile, everybody say mid-jettt! Middd-jettt!"

Two men dragged Judge off the boy while a third took over the CPR. They settled Judge on the grass, draped a blanket over his shoulders, gave him some bottled water. He further calmed himself by gripping the rabbit fur attached to his belt.

Ambulances, fire trucks, the police chief, some deputies, and horrified trailer and campground residents, all were at safe distances from the rectangular bonfire that had once been a single mobile home, sparks shooting out like a roman candle in all directions. The fire trucks drenched the trailer skeleton and the dead leaves and tree fires surrounding it, keeping anything else from igniting.

The woman was dead, maybe from the fire, maybe from a bullet hole in her right cheek. The blood soaking her sweatpants indicated she'd also been shot in the lower half of her body. They slid her into an ambulance, Judge watching them work on the naked boy, watched them connect him to fluids, wrap him in moist towels, prepare him for transport. He regained consciousness, the EMTs trying to reassure him, comfort him while he screamed in agony, and then the screams stopped. The woman emergency tech began the CPR drill again, this time with reduced enthusiasm. The tech shot Judge a look, followed up with a shake of her head no. They loaded the boy into a second ambulance, the tech still doing chest compressions. Judge's disease stayed active, speaking its half-truths.

"...silent night, holy fright, grab your ass, hold on tight. Silent night."

Owen spoke. "You say something, Judge?"

"The shooter. The gun had a silencer."

When the garbled TS crap retreated Judge shook himself out of the blanket and sucked the bottle of water dry. Another bottle magically appeared in his hands. Two ambulances kicked up gravel as they hurried their way toward the RV park exit. Judge addressed Owen.

"I saw the shots from the road but heard no report. They were from a semi-automatic with a suppressor." The ambulances' sirens waned but their flashing lights stayed visible along the horizon, few trees obstructing it, as the vehicles sped up the road. "My guess is the guy intended to hit and run without the histrionics of a fire."

Judge told the police chief what he knew, gave his name, his USMC rank at retirement, let the police know he was a fugitive recovery agent and that he was carrying, and he let them take his weapon. No mention of his other guns in the van, and they didn't ask to search it after they heard from other residents about Judge's attempt at saving the two victims. He let the chief know where he was staying, and that he planned on leaving tomorrow for a return trip to Philly, once he got some sleep.

"You with Chigger?" the police chief asked. Owen's ten-gallon hat put the cop's Texas Stetson to shame.

"Yes. I was driving him home."

"Right. From the Cowboys game. Cops at the stadium alerted us about his episode in the stands. You sober?"

"Yes."

"Fine. We appreciate the car service. Stop by the station tomorrow for your gun. We'll need to have someone run ballistics. A formality. Tell me again what the kid said to you."

"The kid said 'she killed our pastor.'"

"Thanks," the police chief said. "You're good to go for now."

Owen was of little help to them other than vouching for Judge. But right about then was when Judge got it, that Owen was a local celebrity or some other such shit, like Oak Leaf's town drunk and pet and crier all rolled into one.

They cruised toward the trailer park exit. Owen went for his flask again.

"Christ, how much does that thing hold, Owen? Why not give it a rest. It's six in the morning. Don't you have a column to write?"

He twisted the top back on after a huge gulp. "Not booze. One of the campers dripped coffee into it. The column's almost written in my head. It starts with the football game, ends with the fire. Sports recap plus human interest. By tomorrow afternoon you'll be an Internet sensation, Judge. 'Eagles Fan: True Dallas Hero.' Oh, the irony. Your friends in Philly will never look at you the same."

This small man knew little about him, little about his cultivated friendships that, aside from his Marine buddy LeVander Metcalf in Allentown and one very special woman in upstate Pennsylvania, did not exist. Regardless, Judge had an ultimatum for him. "Leave my name out. Say 'anonymous Eagles fan.' No other identifiers. Got that?"

"But..."

"I don't need any more friends, Owen, especially in my business. The less people know about me, the better."

"C'mon, dude, Philly fans could use some good press. Calling you 'anonymous' almost makes it sound like it didn't happen."

"Then it didn't happen. No name."

At the RV park exit the headlights flashed across a rectangular, gold-embossed wooden sign surrounded by a rock garden.

Leaving Hi Ho RV Park. Come back soon. Hi ho! Hi ho!

The coprolalia part of Judge's TS kicked in, wanting out with a vengeance. His mouth geared up, poised to sing selected portions of the fucking Seven Dwarfs song, 'cause his subconscious for some reason knew them. Maeby again rested her head on his shoulder. Judge pinched his rabbit's foot, started massaging it. The internal tempest subsided.

"A few miles will put us in Oak Leaf," Owen said. "Make a right at the first intersection. My place is on a side road, on five acres."

A straight, lonely Texas road at dawn, the silence broken by Owen humming a tune Judge recognized. Unmistakable, it was soon banging around inside his head, messing with his Tourette's for Christ sake, pressing all the buttons: "Hi-ho, hi-ho, it's off to work we go..."

With that Judge lost control, his mouth babbling like a stuttering auctioneer:

"...we dig dig dig dig dig dig dig dig dig..."

Owen joined him, nailing the lyrics as they both serenaded an empty Texas two-laner at sunrise. That was when Judge decided he liked this guy.

"...we dig dig dig dig dig dig dig dig DIG DIG DIG DIG..."

Jane's Baby

They entered Owen's driveway, and facing them was a sprawling ranch home, u-shaped, with a circular drive and a dusty-brown front lawn, very little of it green, a sagebrush, tumbling-tumbleweed kind of dusty, hardened and rocky. The house design fit the other few homes they'd passed on the way in, but the condition of Owen's property didn't. All were on Texas-sized lots, five acres plus, he said, but the other front lawns were well maintained and lushly landscaped. Owen's rancher looked fairly new save for some missing shutters and roof shingles. Closer in to it was an uprooted blue and silver mailbox and its crushed wooden post, the mailbox and post both jutting from the center of tire tracks burrowed into deep mud that had hardened. The tracks ended a few feet from the home's front porch overhang. Still in evidence in the grip of the hardened dirt was a pickup truck, its mud flaps caked in baby-shit brown. The truck was a custom paint job, a navy blue with a silver stripe, same colors as the Mustang and the mailbox. A late nineties Ford, and from the looks of it, late nineties was also when it became a permanent lawn ornament.

The sun peeked over the horizon. The van reached the end of the long driveway and curled around near the house's front overhang. Whatever statement his abandoned truck was making sidetracked Judge's need to retrieve a text he'd just received. Owen spoke up.

"Welcome to Casa Chigger, home to Owen Wingert, beloved Dallas sportswriter. Also, for some reason that escapes me, the scourge of Oak Leaf Farms per my odious neighbors. Well, this has been quite the eventful evening, Mister Drury, and I'd invite you in but I'm afraid there's not much of anything to consume other than alcohol, and with you needing to head out today…"

The text came from LeVander. It led with exclamation points, then…

—Find that schoolteacher bounty NOW, Judge!

"Owen, Chigger, gimme a sec."

—Change in her status. My Dallas connection says they now like her for 3 murders, a church pastor, a woman and her kid. Assassinations, maybe arson. Just happened.

—Where?

Judge keyed this, but he already knew.

—An RV park. Hi-Ho RV park, town called Glenn Heights. Local law is talking reward money.
—Fuck the money LeVander. The murdered kid died in front of me. Tell you about it later. Screw what I said before. I'm in.

Judge put the phone away, addressed Owen. "I'm not going home today."

SIX

Larinda entered the Texarkana, Texas, city limits, around seven thirty a.m. after three hours on the road in a newly acquired silver Dodge Durango with switched plates. A few minutes more on Route 30, she'd cross the state line and enter Texarkana, Arkansas.

The R.I.P. bullets had been too effective. Her intention was to walk the perimeter of the trailer in the dead of night with her Tec-9s, strafe the section with the bedrooms, blow open the front door and go inside. Except the bullets had shredded a propane tank gas line. Too much collateral damage and too much attention.

She needed to make sure the woman and boy were dead. In the shadows, away from the huddles of horrified trailer park gawkers, the circus got underway when a hero showed up in a van with barking dogs: a put-together guy, bald, maybe military, who joined the action by dragging the big-mouthed little queer and his mother away from the fire. Larinda waited, saw the EMTs work on them then shake their heads no to both. A fortunate outcome for the EMTs. Without the headshake, Larinda would have had to follow the ambulance and take them all out.

The U.S. marshal produced his badge at Naomi's condo door, raised it to the eyehole and announced himself. "Deputy U.S. Marshal Edward W. P. Trenton, Your Honor."

Naomi straightened the top half of her most comfortable travel ensemble, a conservative business suit in charcoal. She glanced at a wall clock, then the mirror. Ten a.m. The marshal was right on time.

Mr. Trenton was tall and wide, the eyehole showing the lower half of his face while it exaggerated his width, spreading it east and west inside the high rise's hallway.

Naomi's first reaction when she opened her door was he would have trouble fitting into the seat on the plane, even in business class. Zippered up to his chin, his blue windbreaker sported a U.S. Marshals Service five-pointed tin star emblem left of center. His tan slacks strained at his thighs. She didn't know how much of what was under the windbreaker was him and how much was weaponry, but he was bulky. A weathered, copper-brown Native American face disguised his age, which looked to be anywhere from late thirties to early fifties. Her eyes lingered, entranced by him and his one earring, a small, black bear claw. She wondered if they'd assigned him to her because of his ethnicity. She opened the door wider.

"My goodness, Mister Trenton, where are my manners? How nice to meet you. Please come inside."

"Thank you, ma'am." He removed his tan Stetson to enter her home. Naomi was tall, and yet he towered over her. His bulk filled the vestibule, leaving a lot less room in there for their shared presence. She gestured, and he proceeded down the length of the hallway. He stepped aside at the end to let her pass.

"Your Honor...ma'am..." Mr. Trenton kneaded the brim of his Stetson, taking it on a nervous spin. "I want you to know I asked for this detail, and I'm honored I was chosen."

"I see," she said, smiling. "I too am honored, Mister Trenton, and humbled. It will be rewarding to serve you and the rest of the American people. Thanks so much, in advance, for your help. I hope I won't be too much trouble."

"I expect you won't, ma'am, and I'll make sure no one else will be either." With this, the sparkle of hero worship in his eyes switched off. Replacing it was expressionless, all-business, bodyguard brown.

Her baggage was ready to go, four large luggage pieces plus one trunk and a carry-on, all on wheels, some of which maybe should have been shipped. Her intention had been to have a law clerk assist them for their ride to the airport, but the Marshals office said no, they would handle the arrangements. Deputy Marshal Trenton looked large enough that, with her help, the two of them would have been able to handle her stuff with a few trips, but apparently that wasn't how this was going to go.

"There's another marshal waiting downstairs, ma'am," he said. "He'll accompany us through the boarding process." Mr. Trenton barked into a two-way handheld radio. His associate's response was immediate: "Roger that, Toes."

"Roger that, Vernon." Mr. Trenton addressed Naomi. "Ma'am, Deputy Marshal Vernon is on his way up to help with the bags. It's best we keep one arm unencumbered."

She nodded, but she was still processing the exchange. One word of it, to be specific: *Toes*. A Native American name perhaps. She'd save her question for her getting-to-know-you chat onboard their three-hour flight to Dulles.

SEVEN

"Forget the drink," Judge told Chigger, his host. "I gotta go. My stink is starting to offend my dogs."

He had faxes to read and a murder suspect to find, a shower to take, and forty winks to catch. Plus, "My partners need to eat."

"There's food in the house, somewhere," Owen said. "Look. Judge. I know my way around Dallas. I can help you find your bounty. Stay for one drink."

Owen reemerged from his house with a bottle of Jose Cuervo, some shot glasses and an institution-sized bar of Hershey's chocolate. He poured and they sipped, the two leaning against Owen's abandoned truck lawn ornament. They sipped some more. They were big shot glasses. Owen opened the candy, broke off two chunks. Instead of handing one to Judge he raised his arm, was about to toss them to Judge's canine deputies sitting at attention near his front door. Judge grabbed his hand.

"Damn it, Owen, no chocolate for the dogs. It's toxic."

"Huh. Wow." A slight nod of his head. "That explains some things."

Maeby and J.D. lingered near his open front door, seated next to each other on their haunches like they'd just filed in for morning reveille. Hungry eyes, the both of them.

"Look, I've got no problem if they want inside the house," Owen offered. "Nothing in there they can hurt. We'll head inside in a few, rustle something up for them."

Maeby sniffed, anticipating an order, her sawed-off terrier tail and her butt both wiggling double-time. J.D., his pointy Shepherd ears making him a full head taller than Maeby, sat motionless as a Marine boot recruit.

"No chocolate bars on the floor?" Judge asked. "No open D-Con boxes or anything?"

He chuckled, thought a moment, said no to both. Judge focused on Maeby, made eye contact with her, told her with a head nod it

Jane's Baby

was okay to go inside. She vaulted through the open front door into the house. J.D followed, his filthy leather leash attached to his collar trailing him.

"Why not take off the leash?" Owen asked.

"It keeps him from getting nervous, like a security blanket. Less nervousness means less aggression, fewer accidents." Since they were sharing, "Why the cowboy outfit?"

"Yeah, well, why not a cowboy outfit? I'm supporting my team and it gets me on TV. Plus it's sentimental. See, I once auditioned for Wrestlemania…"

Judge heard about the outfit's history, how Owen had channeled midget wrestler Cowboy Bob Bradley from the fifties.

"Called myself Cowboy Black Bart. Cracked my skull open during the audition. They didn't pick me, but they let me keep the outfit." He sipped, smiled, his eyes losing their focus while savoring a memory. "I was also a rodeo clown for two years, and I tried midget bowling, too. It's actually safer. You get to wear a helmet."

Wrestling, rodeo clowning, and midget tossing. Owen was a walking cliché.

He sipped more, stayed maudlin. "Now that I think about it, it wasn't just a few years back. More like twenty. Wow. What an idiot. Live and learn, huh? In my defense, back then I figured I'd be dead by now."

A societal misfit with a death wish at a younger age. Judge had no problem empathizing.

"Then I took me some readin' and writin' classes, learned me some news reporting skills, and the rest is local sports-writing history. So tell me about this woman you're after."

"A former schoolteacher from Tulsa." Judge mentioned her bogus prescriptions for controlled substances, and that she'd jumped bail, "and now this thing with the Native American kid and his mother at the trailer park, and the murder of a church pastor."

"Like I said, Judge, I know my way around. When you pick up your gun today we'll get more info from the Chief of Police."

A commotion inside the house turned Judge around. Through the front bay window they saw a brown blur hurdle an end table.

A large black blur followed, knocking over a lamp. The first blur was Maeby. The second wasn't J.D., it was a cat. A huge one.

"That's Bruce," he said, chuckling into his near-empty glass. Maeby bolted out the front door, snorted, all fired up; she headed back in for round two. She was the best Marine military working dog partner Judge had ever had, even though she was on the smaller side. He pushed off from the truck, called her name, then heard something else inside crash into pieces.

"That," Judge said, "is my cue to check on her." They headed inside.

If the outside seemed like a bizarrely sculpted shrubbery garden, the inside was something completely different, like a fun house at a carnival. Low wall hangings and a mirror all hung on for dear life in the living room, and a jagged crack in the room's drywall ran floor to ceiling, from either a foundation problem or an earthquake. A footless sofa, two legless wing chairs, multiple step stools. A huge litter box sat on the tile floor in the utility room, something Judge smelled before he saw. In the kitchen the cabinets, counter and an island table were normal height, with a kick stool with wheels at rest in front of the sink. J.D. was eating from the cat's bowl.

Maeby bolted past them into the family room and snapped at a wall shelving unit with home theater speakers, the topmost shelf no more than four feet off the floor. The cat hissed from his perch there, the shelf's low height another shrimpy-person room feature, the shelf looking even closer to the floor because of the tall cathedral ceiling. Maeby, with the spring of a kangaroo, leaped for the cat and knocked a speaker down. The cat bolted, exiting the house through the partially open sliding glass door, onto the patio. Maeby scratched at the slim opening, smacked her lips and grunted, her standard plea for wanting out.

"Don't do it," Owen said. "It's crazy out back."

He heeded Owen, grabbed Maeby's collar, and commanded her to shush. She relaxed, which gave him time to absorb the surroundings. Whatever was outside, it couldn't have been much crazier than in here.

Owen was a hoarder, at least in this expansive family room, which showed like a small movie theater at a local twenty-screen Cineplex Judge knew back home. A path led to the sliding glass

Jane's Baby

doors, and a narrower path led to an entertainment center with a large flat screen and a home theater system, but that was the only area where the floor was visible. Next to the wider path, a sofa with only one of its cushions empty of debris left room enough for one person to sit. Or, if you were Owen, maybe room to lie down. Everywhere else were keepsake dolls in display boxes. Madame Alexander Collectibles, on shelves, in leaning box piles, toppled box piles, empty box piles, plus a mass grave of doll carcasses and body parts that reached almost to the cathedral ceiling in a far corner, looking like a pile of zombies clambering to get over the castle wall. Behind the fireplace screen and looking out at them, mixed in with some charred wood, were unboxed Cinderella dolls, their faces caked in soot and pressed against the glass, their eyes open and terrified. Boxed Dorothys, Glindas, thumb-sucking babies, Dallas Cowboy Cheerleaders, lollipop girls, Belles, and a Scarlett O'Hara were scattered throughout the room scape, their white, black, brown, yellow, and Smurf-blue faces all frozen in patented doll pouts.

"Mom's stuff. One of these days I'll get rid of it. And no, she's not mixed in there with it. Her ashes are on that shelf over there." He pointed to a shelf low on the wall, nearest the floor. From what Judge could see she had company, four urns in total. "Hers and her cats."

There was doll hoarding in evidence here, and then there was food hoarding, with the overpowering smell possibly attributable to recent cooking but probably not. Pizza boxes, liquor bottles, Arby's wrappers, Wendy's wrappers, Mickey Dee's, Burger-Whop. Maybe Owen wasn't the doll hoarder, but he did live like a pig.

"Ball Park hot dogs in the fridge. How about I throw some on the grill for them? The coast looks clear, so we can go out back now."

He fired up the barbecue on the patio. Judge wasn't worried about Maeby accosting Owen's cat, either inside or out, nor was he worried about the abandoned-lawn-tractor-Maytag-appliance-automobile graveyard that started a few feet beyond a paver patio overgrown with weeds. Owen lived in what could have passed as the equivalent of a combination amusement park, petting zoo and Texas safari. What most concerned him were the large animals whose shapes were visible on the horizon. Left of center a hundred-plus yards away, beyond a cannibalized Chevy Camaro, were grazing cattle. Right of center, in a separate fence enclosure next to the cattle, was a bull, a big one, gray, with massive white horns. Judge shielded his eyes and squinted to get a better look.

"Don't worry about my neighbor's cattle," Owen said. "They're all fenced in. The bull...he, um, sometimes isn't."

"How's that happen?"

"He rushes the split rail fence every once in a while, sometimes busts through it. It's electrified, too, on both sides of the wooden rails. I've found him out back here, goring my old John Deere riding mower. One time I caught him mounting the rear of the Camaro, all pecker-happy. Whenever he gets loose I get my neighbor on the line and he sends his cowhands over here pronto. So far, no damage to the house."

Not like anyone would have ever noticed. Under Judge's breath his Tourette's had gained a foothold, an oldie-but-goodie.

"...wooly bully, wooly bully, wooly bully. Watchitnow, watchit..."

He picked up J.D.'s leash, pulled him into an embrace. A quick pet of his furry head; Judge's anxiety dissipated.

Maeby wandered the yard unleashed in search of Owen's cat Bruce. The smell of wieners on the barbecue drew her back to the patio. She and J.D. sat side-by-side in observance of the sizzle and pop coming from the grill, with Owen as chef.

"The bull's name is Señor Quixote," Owen said, rearranging the grilling meat. "A rodeo bull sent to stud. He's my buddy."

"Your buddy?" Judge said. "Interesting."

"Well, more of a love-hate thing but yeah, we're buds. Like I said, Señor Q's not intimidated by high voltage. Me neither, as it turns out. When I'm drunk."

Ah. The tasers at the football game. Given the number of times they'd zapped his small body with no apparent side effects, Owen had to have been more of a freak than met the eye. Or maybe the dead brain cells he'd accumulated from his drinking acted as insulators.

"Bull riding," Judge repeated. He drilled a stare at Owen's distant bull friend, grazing in his pasture. "The most dangerous eight seconds in sports. Or so they tell me."

"And they would be right," Owen said. "Very violent. Even worse when a rider isn't thrown. The ride ends, the horn goes off, the rider bails. Not a favorite time for the bull, 'cause he knows he lost. The horn can trigger some major acting out. Real ornery fuckers at that point. Here. Check this out."

Owen retrieved his phone from his pocket, held it out so he could see the keypad. He shot his guest a look. "My ringtone is from my rodeo clowning days. This key right here. It's a crowd pleaser. Great alarm clock, too. Be ready to get your dogs in the house."

He eyed his bull buddy in the distance, poised his thumb over a phone key then pressed it. A tinny air horn blast exploded from the phone, something obnoxious fans used at sporting events like hockey and basketball games, and reminiscent of televised rodeo events where a horn or buzzer signified the end of a bull or bronco ride, that it was time for the rider to disengage, and try to stay alive while doing it.

The bull raised his head at the noise, snorted, bucked his eighteen hundred pounds and rear legs skyward a few times, then took a run at the fence, looking generally pissed. He retreated after breaching one of the fence rungs.

The back of Owen's arm found its way across Judge's waist, ready to push him back through the door and into the house. He lowered it, the threat neutralized. "The high voltage wire stopped him. We're good for today. So who gets the first hot dog?'

He was going to a lot of trouble to feed the dogs when all they really needed were bowls of kibble back at the B&B. And Judge needed to get on the trail of the bail-jumping teacher-murderer.

Screw it, Judge decided. His deputies had been cooped up in the van all last night. A pound of charred wieners tasted better than dry Pedigree from a bag.

Crammed against one of the sliders, on the inside looking out, and with the crush of the family room doll pile pressing against it from behind, a cardboard box with a freakish-looking doll in it stood on end at floor level. Thin white face, almost gaunt. Glasses on the bridge of her nose. White doily collar above a black robe. A gavel in her hand. Next to this doll, also in a box, was a Madame Alexander Pocahontas.

"Owen. That doll there, in the glasses. Who's she supposed to be?"

"TV Judge Judy. Limited edition. Nine hundred bucks. Quite a coincidence right there, those two dolls side-by-side. Swear to God they've been next to each other like that for years, way before the Supreme Court nomination." He rolled the hot dogs over with the spatula. "These Ball Parks look good to go."

Judge had no idea what coincidence he was talking about. Owen retrieved two plates from under the barbecue and squinted at them. He rubbed each with his shirtsleeve like he was doing the dogs a favor and glanced at Judge for a reaction; Judge nodded.

Owen deposited six hot dogs onto each dish, lowered the plates to the patio. Maeby and J.D. pounced.

"Tell me about this coincidence thing with the dolls," Judge said.

"You don't know? A big deal around here, at least to the Indians native to these parts. The newest associate judge installed on the U.S. Supreme Court is a Native American, from Texas. First Native American ever to serve on the Supreme Court. You want any of these?"

Maybe Judge had heard that, what with there being a public hearing on her nomination. Federal, now Supreme Court associate justice Naomi Coolsummer, was in her mid-forties or thereabouts. "Pass."

Owen forked up a charred hot dog, blew on it, chomped off an end and chewed. He tore off a second bite. His mouth open, he chewed while he talked, leaving nothing to the imagination about what was going on in there.

"She'll be in session with the heavyweights when the fall term starts next week. She's young; hot looking, too. Plus, get this." An animated Owen shook the fork while he talked about a Texas abortion case on the Court's fall docket. "If there's any chinks in *Roe v. Wade*, this case could find them. Big-time judicial landmark case drama, coming right up. Gonna make history, dude."

An alcoholic hobbit waving meat on a fork knew more about current events than Judge did. His grade school nuns would be spinning in their graves.

Jane's Baby

Owen wasn't done. "She's a liberal, too. Replaced the conservative justice who just retired. I'm not expecting Roe to be overturned. She should maintain a pro-choice majority, but it'll make for some great theater. I also wanna get to D.C. to see some of the cases argued this year. Saw a few of them before. They're awesome."

A former rodeo clown in a kid's cowboy outfit who followed the Supreme Court. Something else was going on here.

"Let me get this straight. You're a sports writer who's also a judicial system groupie. How'd that happen?"

"Yeah. How about that." Owen eyed the remaining hot dogs on the grill, both looking crispy at this point. His stare had some weight behind it. After a few seconds it succumbed to unfocused blinking, his face sagging. One-Mississippi-blink, two-Mississippi-blink, three Mississippi...

He ripped the last three hot dogs off the grill in succession with his bare hand then winged them into the yard with bad intentions. "You want a drink? I could use a drink. I'm getting a drink." He reentered his house without waiting for an answer.

Judge wasn't sure what had just come over Owen, but something disgusting hit home for Judge. Charred meat. A wrong choice for food after what had gone down at the trailer park this morning. His stomach felt uneasy. Owen returned with a new bottle of tequila and opened it.

"Sorry about that. I get emotional when it comes to the courts. One Supreme Court case in particular. Roe. It had its origins here in Texas."

Judge waved off the tequila. Owen filled both glasses anyway, grabbed one, tipped it into his mouth, emptied it. His lips curled.

"My mother wasn't like the rest of the folks around here. She wanted abortion legalized. Wasn't 'pro-choice.'" He opted for air quotes. "That was too tame a position. She was pro-abortion, period. 'When it made sense,' she said. And she loved the way the word abortion rolled off her tongue, how its first two syllables defined its reason for being. 'Ab-HOR-shun.' She'd use it, her enunciation of it, with impunity around me when I was a kid, fucking teased me with it. Terminating unwanted children appealed to her, period.

"I was born the year the decision was handed down. Nineteen seventy-three. I didn't miss the significance of her teasing, even at an early age."

Heavy shit. Owen's mother sounded less like a parent, more like a special needs caregiver with a load of resentment. In contrast, Judge's mother was a saint when his affliction reared itself. His father, a U.S. Senator, was the dickhead.

"As it was, the Roe decision appeals to me regardless of Mom's ass-hattedness. Simple logic: the right to privacy, which is what the decision was based on. That, plus if you don't want to have the kid, then don't. Not a popular opinion in these parts. So what. Screw the religious nut jobs."

Even Judge knew it wasn't that simple. The age of the fetus came to mind. They'd shifted into drunk opinion territory again. Judge needed to leave before it got crazy. "Look, Owen, I'm gonna head out. Thanks much for feeding my dogs. Thanks for the drink."

"You wanna know why I know so much about the courts? I write about them. Yep. Got two columns. One on sports, the second a courthouse beat column. I taunted Mom by using a pseudonym for it. When she got to bragging to people about me writing it, I denied it was mine. Someone who wishes her kid was never born shouldn't get to revel in his achievements."

His cat light-footed it past the bull on the edge of the property. Judge was glad for the distraction. "Your cat's teasing your neighbor," he told him. The bull grunted then bucked up against an electrified fence post. It zapped him. He snarled then backed off, quieted. The cat strutted away. "My cue to leave, Owen, before your bull buddy decides to make a move."

"Señor Q, biding his time. You wanna know something else? She had the kid."

Owen was all over the place, but his rambling had Judge intrigued. "Who? What kid?"

"Norma McCorvey. The real Jane Roe in *Roe v. Wade*. By the time the decision came down she'd delivered the baby. A girl. Put her up for adoption. The baby's whereabouts, then and now, are unknown. The adoption was closed, so neither party knew the other. She'd be in her forties now. Still might not know who she is."

No shit. Judge couldn't say he knew this. Interesting, but it wasn't enough to make him stay. "Maeby, J.D., time to go, guys."

J.D. fell in next to the grill, his leash intact. Maeby had discovered the hot dogs Owen winged into this mini-landfill he called a backyard. She fell in after J.D., smacking her thin terrier lips.

"So here's how I can help you find this woman." He downed the second tequila shot.

Jesus, Owen, concentrate much? "And this would be who now?"

"Your bounty. I know the Glenn Heights police chief and most of his cops. I know cops in Arlington. Dallas, too, and most of the cops in between, for reasons you can guess. That covers a lot of territory. Let me go with you when you pick up your gun. We'll ask some questions, see what we can find."

Judge needed a shower, a few hours' sleep and time away from this guy.

"Give me your number. I'll think about it."

EIGHT

The business class seats on United's Austin to Dulles flight were more accommodating than Naomi had anticipated. Wide, with an extended leg rest, a swivel table, a personal entertainment screen, and headphones for streaming Sirius radio or any playlist she had access to. Her table was strewn with paper and two hardbound legal journals, and accented by a half-empty wine glass. She had multiple court briefs open at the same time, some in print, some on her laptop, the seat next to her unoccupied. She keyed in notes as they popped into her head.

Across the aisle, Deputy Marshal Trenton was managing his spacious but still somewhat imperfect personal space nicely. It was all him underneath his unzipped jacket, she'd decided, with massive shoulders atop a barrel chest and a Sequoia tree-trunk waist, which from her vantage point looked rock solid. One of the largest Native Americans she'd ever seen. He sipped an iced tea, checked his phone, then settled into a straight-ahead deadpan look apparently necessary for the job. Their flight attendant topped off Naomi's post-lunch rosé. They were about an hour outside D.C.

Naomi removed her earplugs and acclimated herself to the white noise of the pressurized cabin. She repositioned some paper, jabbed at her eyeglasses, stayed focused on her reading material.

"'Toes,'" she said, directed at Mr. Trenton, and knowing she'd said it loud enough. "That's an odd Indian name."

"Yes, ma'am. My associates take liberties." He spoke matter-of-factly into the seatback in front of him, no eye contact with her. "My Comanche name is White Paw, Your Honor." A respectful answer, yet it sounded a tad weary of anticipating a need to deliver more of an explanation.

Naomi recalled the email that introduced him as Deputy U.S. Marshal Edward W.P. Trenton. "'White Paw.' Wonderful. Are your middle initials a coincidence?"

"No, Your Honor. It's my middle name as well. There's more truth to the name than symbolism. It's because of a physical trait." He repositioned his right foot into the aisle, extended his leg for effect. "All the toes on this foot are white. A birthmark."

She studied his large black shoe, visualized how the birthmarked foot looked inside it: brown-skinned heel, arch, and instep, then five discolored toes, each splotched a milky white.

"My associates know no shame, ma'am. 'Toes' means no disrespect. Like White Paw, it makes me proud, Your Honor."

"As well you should be, Mister Trenton," she said.

His resume, shared by the Marshal's Office, had been impressive. Early life on a reservation, an athlete at the high school and collegiate level, a high undergrad GPA, some grad school work. Mr. Trenton had every right to be proud.

Naomi pondered her own resume and upbringing, a Native American both by blood and by adoption. Her looks and coloring, her maiden name, her middle class life with parents who embraced many aspects of their common heritage. All of this pointed to a healthy, nurturing, unapologetic childhood. Not in the old ways of the Comanche, but in acknowledgement that these old ways existed. Still, in many respects, she was incredibly fortunate to be where she was, because she'd had some breaks.

"You're new Supreme Court justice Naomi Coolsummer, aren't you?"

The question came from the attractive older woman seated two seats down in the same row, across the aisle. Her body was tucked into tight upper and lower ranch-boss denim blouse and jeans. She'd been quiet until now, probably because she'd been overly attentive to the constant stream of drinks she'd ordered. The "aren't you" came out "arren-chewww," her drawl probably Texan, and clearly alcohol-fueled.

"Yes, I am," Naomi said. "Can I help you?"

"Just checking you out online, honey. Reading about you in the Wikipedia," the woman said, "plus pa-roozing the minutes from your confirmation hearing. You're one smart Indian, I'll give you that."

In Naomi's junior year in high school a good-luck faucet had conspicuously opened in full force. She'd earned high SATs, but they were only borderline for the Ivies, yet Harvard and Yale both accepted her. Tribal councils, local and state business acquaintances, other private minority benefactors, they'd all acknowledged her as an overachiever, and a Native American one at that, so she decided to stay regional, opting for Oklahoma.

Mr. Trenton unbuckled his seat belt and leaned forward, to focus on the intoxicated speaker.

"You handle that McCarney, Texas, boy Gary Gilmore's murder case?" the woman asked.

A 1977 capital punishment case, the first one tried in nearly ten years after the death penalty had been reinstated. Gary Gilmore was a Texas-born criminal sentenced to death by firing squad and executed in Utah, where the murders he was convicted of had been committed. He and the case itself were lightning rods that fueled the capital punishment debate. Gilmore's case included two stays of execution by the Supreme Court, if Naomi's memory served her. The stays prompted two suicide attempts. Gilmore wanted it over. His final words, "Let's do this," had resonated with the media.

"Sorry, ma'am, but no. A different state, and it was quite a bit before my time as a federal judge."

"A pity what they did to him. The men he killed? Hell, they were probably Mormons. No big loss."

Nothing good could come from further conversation with this woman. Naomi leaned back in her seat to avoid it, her thoughts returning to her career. Other breaks, like assignments as lead litigator to a few high-profile capital punishment cases, had come out of the blue. She had continued to impress somebody, more than a few important, unnamed somebodies, as she built a star-power legal resume. But she'd been thankful for one thing among others: the politicos had stayed away during her ascension through state and federal judicial appointments. Their anonymity was a welcomed gift horse, even though she'd found this across-the-board, arms-length conduct a bit curious.

"Got another one for you, Judge. The Babineau baby case. How 'bout that one?"

Much closer in context, Naomi thought. "That one was during my tenure as a federal judge in Texas, yes, but it was in another district court, so no, not my case."

Jane's Baby

Women's rights, religious freedoms, children's rights, Native American rights. Her personal pro-choice and feminist beliefs were well documented from early on in her adulthood, considerably left of center and so very distant from the right-wing beliefs of local and state politicians, like revered long-term Texas Senator Mildred Folsom. The Babineau case: Texas women now had to view ultrasounds before they could terminate their pregnancy. It also posited that a fetus felt pain earlier than originally thought. Yet, unlike the politicians, her beliefs stayed compartmentalized, causing no personal bias and with no judicial impairment. Her associate justice appointment validated her success in this regard, a record she intended to maintain.

"Too bad," her questioner said. "It would have been a nice change of pace hearing about a redskin on the side of saving babies rather than stealing them, know what I mean, darlin'?"

Mr. Trenton got out of his seat, and with a few long strides he reached the offensive passenger, but by this time the intoxicated woman was asleep, her chin on her chest.

"Stop serving her," he told a flight attendant. "She's being verbally abusive to Justice Coolsummer. U.S. Marshall's Office orders."

When he returned to his seat, Naomi addressed him. "Mister Trenton."

"Yes, ma'am?"

"The skin gets thicker after a while. You for one should know that. Your intercession wasn't necessary. But I do thank you."

"You're welcome, ma'am."

"Would you mind if I called you Edward while we worked together?"

"Your prerogative, ma'am."

"Thank you, Edward."

It was a total of five hundred twenty-five divided highway miles and eight-plus hours on Interstate 40, from Little Rock, Arkansas, to Knoxville, Tennessee. Five hours into the trip, Larinda pulled into a Cracker Barrel restaurant in Nashville for a break, where she took time to pack a sterile gauze sponge into the gash in her left palm and triple-wrap it with gauze dressing.

She popped two five-milligram oxys, needed more, but she didn't indulge herself. Two kept the suffering at a manageable level, the pain a reminder of her pilgrimage earlier in the year, and the sin that took her there. Pain was good, pain was retribution, but an oozing bloody discharge as evidence of it wasn't.

She'd traveled to the Philippines during Holy Week for the crucifixion reenactment. Reverend Higby Hunt, a televangelist and one of The Faithful, had tried to talk her out of it. "God doesn't question your faith, or your dedication, child. With your repeated penances, how could he?"

Regardless, it was something she'd found necessary, out of her love for Jesus Christ and her need for contrition. Her search for absolution and grace was between her and her Savior.

She'd flown into Manila and gained audience with the Filipino cardinal on Holy Thursday. For show, like he did with the other sinners, he'd officially condemned her intentions to participate. She made a donation, was ushered by the locals to San Pedro Cutud. After another donation the local priests gave her the location of the reenactment.

Her feet had been washed in perfume. She received forty lashes minus one, the maximum allowed in accordance with Jewish law as was the custom, plus a crown of thorns, and later a veil to wipe her blood-streamed face. She both carried and dragged her cross in the street to a makeshift Calvary.

They placed her on the crucifix, tied her limbs down with red cloth strips, commenced nailing her hands and feet into the wood alongside the other Good Friday penitents, most notably Ruben Enaje, a carpenter like her, and the veteran of twenty-seven reenactments. Larinda bled profusely, but her greatest fear hadn't been of dying, it was of dying before she could recite her prepared prayers. Before she could request God the Father's forgiveness for her sins. With no memory of being taken down from the cross she'd walked out of a Philippine hospital two days later, on Easter Sunday, "resucitado" or risen from the dead, some of the Filipino faithful had decided. They called her "Babae Hesus," or "The Female Jesus."

For her, the early hospital release had been a question of necessity. Mind over matter. Regardless of the pain, which she welcomed, embraced, she had to get back to the States. Four of the five Holy Wounds, to her palms, her feet and ribs, took a few months to heal. The rib cage wound below her right breast was superficial, provided with much less intensity than the one Jesus had received, the one delivered to make sure He was dead. The others had nastier entry and exits, where large galvanized nails had been hammered though her flesh and had grazed bones on their way to exiting the body before entering the wood. The fifth wound, through her left hand, was still healing, a prolonged work in progress.

OxyContin, not using it as prescribed, which should have been a higher dose but for a shorter period of time, had gotten her into trouble. She'd chosen half the dose to keep the pain manageable while still forcing her, a sinner, to suffer, but she continued using it after the recommended period. It was now part of her daily routine. A dependency.

She had enough pills to accommodate her road trip, assuming eliminating new associate justice Naomi Coolsummer didn't take too long. After that, or if things didn't go as she planned...well, she'd worry about the after-that if the time came.

NINE

Judge liked Victorian B&Bs, the antiques, the architecture, the gaudy tile bathrooms with period fixtures, the frilly beds, and the high-calorie, pomp-and-circumstance breakfasts. It was how he'd met his girlfriend Geenie, a B&B proprietor when she wasn't filling in as a nurse, her inn tucked into coal country in a small burg in the Pocono Mountains. Meeting Geenie solidified his love for B&Bs. His love for her hadn't trailed far behind.

Judge picked up his key, apologized to the manager for his physical appearance yet offered no details. He retrieved Maeby from the van but left J.D. there to chill. He liked his crate. It was another security blanket for him, like keeping his leash on. He settled Maeby into their second-floor room. Judge's face was smeared in fire soot he couldn't scrub off, his jeans soaked in urine from the boy and his mom. Add tequila breath and a pervasive dead-body bouquet, plus a torn Cream Live! tee shirt, and it all conspired to sell him as homeless. Still, if he didn't eat breakfast right then, he wouldn't get to eat it at all.

The B&B's enclosed porch served as the breakfast room, its old-fashioned wooden floor-to-ceiling windows crisscrossed with hand-painted white grilles, the panes individually puttied into place. Small flat-screen TVs were affixed to the porch ceiling, bookending the seating area. A fresh fruit cup topped with homemade whipped cream awaited each guest at café tables set for two. The aromas of spinach quiche and seasoned potatoes drifted in from the kitchen. Everything looked and smelled fantastic. In contrast, Judge didn't. The couple at the café table next to him was unimpressed, the guy an older GQ type with sculpted white-gray temples, his tablemate a woman half his age with a dreamy-eyed, post-coital glow.

Consenting adults, Judge reminded himself.

'Unimpressed' was too positive a term. Mr. GQ Perfect Posture's jaw muscles started tightening. He was loading up,

Jane's Baby

readying for a confrontation about Judge's appearance. Absent his dogs, Judge was vulnerable. Upscale B&B, conservative patrons, with both flat screens tuned to a sermon by televangelist Higby Hunt, a blustery Texas preacher with a nationwide ministry. Okay, Judge got it, so maybe he could have asked the kitchen staff to put together a plate for him to eat upstairs. Too late. Out of respect, he ate quickly. This only added to the man's agitation, since it looked like Judge hadn't eaten in days.

"Looks like you had a tough night, fella," GQ said to him. "I'll give you one hundred dollars if you leave right now." His stare drilled into the side of Judge's head. If Judge had sideburns, or any hair for that matter, his head would have ignited.

Custom-fitted, tight white dress shirt, each collar bearing a "JESUS" stickpin in gold block letters, the guy and his health-club physique looked a tad precious, much more Lucille Roberts than Gold's Gym. Gold tips decorated his bolo tie, its etched, oval Western slide in gold as well. Above the collar was a body-shop tan and a silver-flecked blond mustache. In contrast Judge looked like he'd spent a night in a landfill and was in need of a hazmat scrub.

"One hundred dollars," GQ repeated. "Take it outside, and when I'm finished eating you'll get your money. How's that sound, old man?"

Good diction. A smirk-laden, condescending pal-o'-mine delivery. A presence. The guy had done this before and gotten his way. And whomever he'd suckered into the offer had never seen the money.

Hell, Judge was game. "So if I stop eating right now, and I wait outside, you'll come out when you're finished your quiche and give me some money? You know, champ, you're right. My bad. A poor choice on my part, ruining breakfast for the rest of these nice folks." Judge drained his coffee and pushed his chair back. "But as far as you and your girlfriend here are concerned," he stood, producing his wallet, "I couldn't give a shit." He slapped two one-hundred-dollar bills onto GQ's table. "To reimburse you for your stay. Old man."

The money next to the man's half-eaten fruit cup should have been statement enough, but Judge felt feisty. He dropped another bill onto the woman's plate.

"And for you, young lady, here's a twenty in case he didn't tip you for, you know, renting your cu...cu..."

He got stuck on the hard "c," which tangled his throat up, nearly choking him while he tried to hold back the rest of a mounting verbal assault.

"...cuh, cuh, cuh..."

His subconscious loaded up for an explosion of shit-talk, readying a barrage of streaming profanity set to sprint off his tongue into an abyss of deranged utterances unfit for human consumption, offensive to all within earshot if they got out.

"...cun, cun, cun-cun-cun..."

To those nearby, he presented as a stuttering adult trying hard to complete a sentence, not what he was, a guy with a severe potty-mouth disorder about to bust a gasket trying to dam up the diarrhea.

GQ's date was super pissed, which made GQ super pissed, which made him toss his napkin and get to his feet.

Judge powered through the pending barrage, defused it by locating his rabbit's foot keychain. He finally squeezed out the last word like he was passing a kidney stone.

"...companionship."

There. Whew. Judge smiled at him. All better now.

It might as well have been the c-word; the sentiment was the same. Mr. GQ's manliness got the better of him. The two men were now nose to nose, and they were gonna go.

From over Judge's shoulder: "Mister Drury! Please!"

A silver-haired man in a Kiss-The-Cook bib apron separated them with arms to their chests. The cook's younger partner, also male, pulled Judge aside. "I'm sorry, Mister Drury, but I can't have you upsetting our other guests like this. I think it best that you leave. We'll refund your deposit. I'm sure you understand."

It was as much a plea as it was a directive. The fear in the man's eyes made Judge back off, and he was about to apologize for scaring him when his partner's nervous glances past Judge's shoulder said he was less afraid of Judge and more afraid of Mr. GQ; the man's dress, his confidence, and his need to assert himself. This was a self-righteous conservative who could make trouble for this gay couple trying to make a living in Texas, the

Jane's Baby

straightest state in the Union, or so its residents wanted everyone to believe.

So be it. GQ got to keep his dignity and his balls because of Judge's read of the situation. He went upstairs to collect Maeby.

Saddled up in the van, Judge reached behind Maeby's ears and gave her a quick scratch. Finding another place to stay that was pet friendly on short notice would be a challenge. Nothing within twenty miles, and he was deathbed tired. Against his better judgment he keyed in a certain phone number. After many rings:

"…mgglumph…"

"Owen. Judge Drury."

"…orggg."

"Wake up, Owen."

"Leave me the hell alone, Evans. I filed the story. I accept your edits, whatever the hell they are."

"Owen, it's not your editor. It's Judge Drury, the bounty hunter. I need a favor."

"What."

"I need a place to stay for a few days."

"Fine. Door's open. I'm going back to sleep."

The answer he expected. God help him.

Owen's front door wasn't open. Judge walked his dogs, both leashed, around back. Deep-throated moos and other animal noises greeted them from the edge of the property. They also got an ominous snort from Señor Q, his black bull eyes following them. The monster looked bigger than he did yesterday, all eighteen- hundred of his pounds full of mean. The sliding glass door to the family room was ajar. With some effort Judge ushered his dogs inside.

No welcome from Owen, only snoring from another room. Judge cleaned off one of the couches and lay down. The dogs settled in next to him on the cluttered floor, exhausted.

Judge woke up, his face full of cat, until Bruce the cat retreated.

From his space on the couch Judge smelled bacon, then saw bacon, greasy undercooked strips of it silhouetted against an overhead light in the kitchen, dangling from each of Owen's hands until he released them into the dogs' patiently waiting mouths. Judge checked his phone. One-thirty p.m. A four-hour nap would have to do. Owen was now dressed in street clothes with bib jeans and a yellow tee. Much better than his Cowboy Black Bart clown outfit. Without the cowboy hat, his dreads were in full display. Not a bad look for him.

"You're going to make my dogs sick, Owen. They'll shit when and where you don't want them to. No more greasy bacon."

"How about you? Want some? I'll microwave another pound. I'm starving."

He declined and asked if there was coffee. Owen's chin directed him to a Keurig at the end of the counter. Five minutes and eight consumed ounces later, Judge was alert enough to remember he was a day and a half overdue for a shower.

"Guest bathroom is down the hall, on the right. Enough of the plumbing works so keep your mouth shut about the rest of it, capisce? I had a girlfriend a while back. It was her bathroom. We didn't part on good terms."

Judge grabbed his toiletry kit. Owen called after him. "Oh. And I think I got all the broken glass, if that crosses your mind."

Two white sinks, a dripping spigot. Brown hair, strands and stubs of it, in both sink drains; it was also on the floor, the light-colored walls, and the sweating toilet tank. A wide mirror spanned both sinks, with cracks spidering away from a bulls-eye impact at eye level. Shelves with women's cosmetics. And splashes and drips of glow-in-the-dark nail polish everywhere, the bottles not in evidence.

Jackson Pollock's bathroom, in 3-D. Judge planned on taking the quickest shower ever, and with his eyes closed.

"She did like my genitals," Owen volunteered when he returned from the shower, "after I validated the black myth for her. But you know the type, Judge. 'I love you, you're perfect, now change.' For some reason she thought she could make me taller. Or maybe she wanted me to quit drinking. Can't remember which. Either way, she lost. By the way, Frannie Kitchens called."

"And he would be...?"

"Glenn Heights Chief of Police. We've known each other since we were kids. You can have your gun back, you're cleared. Oh, and he liked my column this morning. I could have made you an Internet hero if you'd let me use your name."

"No thanks. You still drunk?"

"No, unfortunately."

"Good. Let's go get my gun and ask some questions."

Owen grabbed his sequined ten-gallon hat, snapped it onto his head, his dreads hanging to his shoulders. Judge stared him down. "You need to lose that. You look like a walking condom."

"Heard it before." He dented the top of the hat. This only solidified the penis image. "The hat's subliminal. Impresses the women. Shut up and drive."

TEN

The flight touched down at Dulles Airport. Naomi awakened to find her head cradled against a pillow. The pillow's placement was a good thing. Her neck would have been stiff without it. She'd thank their attentive business class flight attendant for her kindness on the way out.

But when they reached the exit there was no flight attendant to thank. Naomi strained to look past Mr. Trenton. Their attendant flipped open the overhead bin to stow Naomi's pillow away. She stopped short, a pillow already there. After an about face, the attendant stuffed the pillow in its rightful place, the empty bin above Mr. Trenton's seat.

Edward White Paw Trenton. An attentive, kind, and gentle giant of a man.

Naomi liked him.

"Washington, D.C.," Larinda said, speaking into her phone. "Motel 6. Yes," she answered when prompted. She made the reservation with one of the six or so credit cards in her possession, none of which were hers. At four p.m. in Knoxville, Tennessee, Larinda was still on Route 40 in the rain, a downpour, almost twelve hours after she first got on the road, but the rain was letting up.

Her intent: drive through to D.C. tonight, arrive around eleven, crash in a motel. Tomorrow she'd change her hair color again, scope out the area, and check into the process for gaining admission to the Supreme Court while it was in session.

The Court had its own police, and in the courtroom itself, security was prohibitively extreme. Outside the courtroom but inside the building, it was more tourist-friendly. Other than that, when a justice traveled on official business, the U.S. Marshal Service was engaged. But when justices circulated among the general citizenry, it was dial nine-one-one.

Jane's Baby

Incidents of violence against Supreme Court justices that she was aware of, because she'd looked them up: Ruth Bader Ginsburg, a purse snatching; David Souter, a mugging by two men while he jogged in D.C.; Stephen Breyer, robbed at his vacation home in St. Kitts by a machete-wielding intruder, then robbed again in Georgetown the same year. Wrong place, wrong time for all three of these justices, each act directed against them as general citizens, not against them as members of the Supreme Court.

And then there was Justice Byron White, deceased, who'd been far from a wallflower. "Whizzer" White in college, he was a football star who played professionally for Pittsburgh in the 1930s and 1940s. He served in WWII, returned home and graduated Yale Law. In 1982 he was attacked while he gave a speech in Utah. According to reports, the sixty-four-year-old Supreme Court justice "cleaned the attacker's clock." Gutsy and admirable, and certainly not a typical outcome from an attack on a senior. Regardless, soon after the attack, the U.S. Marshal Service began protecting traveling Supreme Court justices.

Justice White was also one of the two dissenters in *Roe v. Wade*. This, for Larinda, made him gutsy and admirable times two.

The newest judge was neither gutsy nor admirable; she was a disease. A heathen savage worse than an atheist. Assassinating her would be the first such act against a Supreme Court justice in history. No special thrill, no laurels, only the satisfaction that with this attack the Church Hammer would have smitten forty years of atrocious, immoral acts in the name of an abominable 1973 court decision.

The rain picked up again, pounding the windshield. She tapped at the brakes, negotiated the interstate amid Knoxville's rush hour traffic now complicated by severe weather. Her hand wound bled through the gauze again. At the next rest stop, she'd repack it.

Apartments, condos, townhouses, rentals or owned, the justices' residences were all within commuting car service distance to D.C., but there was little else Larinda knew about where they lived. The locations of their residences weren't publicized. She'd need help in determining her target's address. But it wouldn't come from any contact with The Faithful. She wanted the assassination to be a surprise to them. A gift, for all they'd done for her.

ELEVEN

Judge returned his Glock to the holster in the small of his back, underneath his tee shirt, the gun having suffered no observable repercussions from whatever ballistics were performed on it. The police chief seemed like a good guy but wasn't forthcoming like Owen said he'd be. He talked with them near his dispatcher's desk, inside the combination police station/town government building. The cops occupied the basement. It was around four p.m. Judge's dogs were in the van.

"No, Chigger. No access."

"Look. Chief. Frannie." If Owen weren't a little person, this would have been the point when he'd put his arm around his friend the chief's shoulder in full schmooze mode. Regardless, apparently his balls were just as big as he claimed. "A favor. Just let us see Miss Jordan's place. My buddy here has dogs. Trained military working dogs. They find shit people miss."

Owen had no idea what he was talking about but Judge let him muddle through it. Maeby was a bomb-sniffing expert and a tracker, Judge's partner in the Marines, and she was damn good at all of it. J.D. was an eighty-pound savage takedown artist, apprentice bomb-sniffer and tracker, but not military; a pound puppy both he and Maeby trained. His deputies were taught to restrain, maim and/or kill, and they'd done all three. But aside from bombs and bad guys, finding things police detectives missed, like clues, was a stretch.

"So you're saying my detective is incompetent. You're not helping yourself here, Chigger. You sure you're sober?"

A red-haired guy with glasses two desks away was keenly interested in Owen's response. "Your detective, he, ah, looks competent enough to me, Frannie, so no, that's not what I'm saying, but yes, sorry to say, I am sober."

The chief turned to Judge for confirmation about the sobriety. Not that he should believe a complete stranger, but Judge had been elevated to hero status because of last night's efforts. He nodded affirmation.

"Fine then." The chief eyed Owen's hat. "Lose that black phallus and I'll let you in my office." Under a whiney protest the high-rise black Stetson didn't accompany them inside, was instead parked on a credenza just outside.

Chief Frannie Kitchens' desk was polished mahogany, long and narrow, and clean except for two tight paper piles, one left, one right, and a pen and legal pad front and center. Starched navy blue cop uniform, ice blue eyes, with a gray-blond crew cut waxed and standing at attention just above his forehead. Judge didn't press it, but this guy had ex-military written all over him. Younger, maybe mid-forties, and in kick-ass shape. His hair and chiseled face gave him the look of a Butch or a Bull or a Bo, not a Frannie. Owen declined a seat, stayed on his feet in front of the chief's desk. Judge took the seat offered. They faced their host.

An autographed eight-by-ten glossy of Chief Kitchens standing with one Owen "Chigger" Wingert hung on the left wall, left of center, among many photos. In it Owen cradled his hat in his arm like in a photo from the Old West, his other hand shaking the chief's. At bottom: "Byte this, Frannie. Never losing the hat. Your friend, Chigger."

"You will stay out of our way," the chief stated rather than asked, emphasis on 'will.' "And you will cooperate, and you will share information. And you will not write about it in your column. Not until we make a collar. Otherwise, no deal."

"You have our word, Frannie. On my mother's grave."

"Your mother was cremated, Chigger. Her ashes are on your mantle. And you hated her."

"Fine, Frannie, whatever. We promise all of it, right, Judge?"

"Cross my heart."

The chief called ahead, then confirmed the address LeVander had already given Judge for the bounty's apartment in a Dallas suburb, plus the plate number for her Ford SUV. They also learned a local pastor had put up her bail. Chief Kitchens provided a list of aliases that appeared on the bogus OxyContin prescriptions the police had found at her place. No weapons were located, although the chief did share one peculiar detail about the murders.

"The bullets were R.I.P. bullets. Some nasty high-tech stuff that fragments into pieces once they poke a hole into body tissue. They blew holes through the sheet metal and the trailer's composite walls before they entered its interior. Expensive ammunition, purchased from a hunting accessories store in Dallas.

"One other thing. She left her teacher's job in the Tulsa Catholic school system to become a nun. Some time after that, she ended up in Dallas."

If it weren't for the proximity and timing of the three murders, with someone placing this person at the church just before the pastor was killed, Frannie said she wouldn't have been considered a suspect in any of this.

Soon as they exited the chief's office, Owen went off. "All right you bastards, who took my Stetson?"

His outburst got him two sets of shoulder shrugs from uniformed officers and another if-looks-could-kill death stare from the redheaded detective in plainclothes. The fourth cop, the dispatcher, was on a call. She thumbed him in the direction of the station's galley kitchen.

There it was, sitting tall on the kitchen counter, sheathed in plastic food wrap and lubed with olive oil and what looked like creamy Italian salad dressing on its dented top.

"Un-condomize that thing, or it's not going in the van," Judge told him.

"Fuckers. They're just jealous. They love me."

At the South Dallas apartment building Owen exited the van and Maeby followed him, loose. Judge leashed her outside the van. They left his Shepherd sacked out in his crate. The frogs around the modestly landscaped pond in front of the building quit their bellowing with their approach, Maeby's curious sniffing shutting them up. A lizard crossed the sidewalk in front of them and hustled into the greenery. Maeby perked up but stayed on task.

Judge had to grease the building manager's palm with a twenty before he would admit he got a call from the police chief on their behalf. He let them into Ms. Jordan's garden apartment a few steps below street level, to where it shared space with another apartment and the basement. Hers was a furnished one bedroom that let the sunlight in with four oblong casement windows at eye level, two in the living room, two in the bedroom.

A mouse bolted from under an end table, scrambled into the kitchen. Maeby was part terrier, and mice were like hors d'oeuvres to her. Judge tightened his hold on her leash. "Maeby, stay."

She strained, growled then relaxed, her attention settling on Owen. He smelled like a garden salad, from vinegar that had dripped onto the brim of his hat. No other damage to the Stetson, but the odor lingered.

Here was a sparse, utilitarian habitat, except for the expensive mountain bike leaning against a wall near the front door. The window treatments were cream-colored cotton with brown amoeba-shaped water stains. A pair of wooden shelves rested on two levels of milk crates, with a small flat screen TV in the middle of the top shelf along with a Blue-Ray disc player. No videos. If she'd had any, the cops had them now. One couch, one wing chair, one coffee table, one end table, all worn. On the end table, a Bible. Judge picked it up.

"Furnished don't mean with Bibles," the super said, answering a question before Judge could ask it. "She had a bunch of them delivered from Amazon."

Three thin, silk ribbon markers in different shades were sewn into the Bible's binding. The book was new. "Any idea why the cops didn't take this one?" Judge asked.

"Too many of them maybe? They did take a few. How many, I dunno. Like I said, she had a bunch delivered."

Judge paged through it. The pages the ribbons marked were all in the Old Testament. Maybe worth a closer look after they got through the rest of the place.

In the narrow kitchen, two metal chairs with vinyl-padded seats were tucked under a metal café table. In better condition it would have been a great nostalgic find at a flea market. Judge wandered in, started poking around. On the kitchen table, another new Bible. In the oak cabinets and drawers were plain white dishware, hotel silverware, Grape Nuts, Paul Newman spaghetti sauces, and some wheat pasta. In the fridge, probiotic yogurt and a capped container full of a green liquid from a juicer. On the counter was the juicer, unwashed, the inside smelling like a compost pile.

Jane's Baby

In the bedroom was an unmade double bed, a closet with a few tops and skirts, a pair of jeans, and a pair of athletic shoes. Also a long bureau containing spandex and underwear that included two bras, both 32B. On the bureau, another Bible. Packages of gauze and adhesive bandages sat open on the bathroom counter. Some blood in the sink; the cops would have taken samples. On the toilet tank, Bible number four.

The clothing and shoes and jeans inseam validated the physical traits listed with her mug shot. Tall and lean. Size ten shoes said she had big feet, her small bra size said she had sport tits. The gauze and blood indicated she recently had an open wound.

Little of this place had any feel of permanence. To Judge she seemed less a tenant, more a transient.

"How long has she lived here?" he asked.

"Six months give or take," said the super.

Judge grabbed a colored tee shirt from a laundry pile and let Maeby have a sniff. "Let's finish the tour," the super said and left the bedroom, Owen following. Judge lifted Owen's ten-gallon off his head, stuffed the tee underneath it, shushed him with a finger to his lips. Owen snugged the hat back up.

Back in the living room, Judge asked their host if there were any storage units in the building.

"Yeah, but hers is empty."

"Let me see it anyway."

They left the apartment, reached the end of the hall and pushed through a fire door. Inside, ten small floor-to-ceiling chain link cages were bolted into cinder block walls, all mixed in with the building's heating and hot water equipment and washers and dryers. A sniffing Maeby guided Judge to the cage with the bounty's apartment number on it. The other nine cages had stuff in them, some a lot, some a little. As the super advised, her cage was empty. They left the storage area and reentered her apartment.

Judge checked more closets, cabinets, drawers, under cushions and rugs, even inside the toilet tank. He found nothing incriminating. No undiscovered laptop or desktop computer either. Anything of interest she left behind was no doubt now in the possession of the Glenn Heights police. The only real oddity was her collection of Bibles.

He retraced his steps back to the Bibles in each room, flipped through them, each with the crispness of a new book, to check out the silk bookmarks, where they were, to see if there was a commonality. The pages marked were different from book to book. The only connection he noticed was the ribbon markers were all in the Old Testament.

"Look at this one, Judge," Owen said.

The Gideons' King James Version, and the only Gideon Bible in here. Something one might run across in a motel room, complete with a "Property of" notation, the space next to the notation blank.

Beatles lyrics drifted into Judge's head, fractured by the Tourette's, all of it staying dormant, a short burst about Gideon's Bible, and:

...Rocky Raccoon, bu-bu-bubba baboon...

A festive book, with colorful depictions of Biblical events, its pages with edges gilded in a reddish gold. In it was a tiny prayer card pressed flat, its edges frayed, with a pious picture of a nun and a printed notation, "In memory of Saint Teresa of Jesus." This saint was a Carmelite, the card said. Correction, per Judge's phone search: she was a sixteenth century "discalced" Carmelite.

'Discalced.' As in barefoot or wearing sandals, per Wikipedia's entry on Carmelite nuns. Plus this saint wasn't just any 'discalced' Carmelite nun. Saint Teresa of Jesus was apparently *the* discalced Carmelite nun. She founded the order.

"Any issue with me taking this Bible?" Judge asked the super.

"Any issue with you giving me twenty bucks?" he said.

Back in the van, Owen repeated the word of the day: "Discalced."

"Yes. It means..."

"I already know. Means barefoot monk-like hardship, some shit like that," Owen said. "Your smartphone search also tell you discalced nuns are cloistered, like in monasteries? 'Cause they are."

"And you know this how?"

"There are some discalced Carmelite monasteries not far from here. In Dallas, and in Fort Worth."

Interesting. Something else, something religious, hit Judge. "She waited."

"Who? Waited for what?"

"Our bounty. The boy at the trailer park, his words while he was burning up, the kid said he and his mom saw her at the morning service. The pastor's time of death was late afternoon. She didn't go into the church after him, instead waited for him to come out. She's a murderer, but she's respectful. Give me some cross streets for one of the monasteries, Owen. We need to talk to some nuns."

"And you plan to convince them to let us inside their monastery how? You got a phony badge or something? It's not like they're gonna want us snooping around their nun hangout."

"My fugitive recovery license. Plus the dogs. They're charmers when it comes to women in uniform."

Owen gave him cross street info that Judge keyed into the van's GPS. ETA twelve minutes to the nearest monastery.

So. T. Larinda Jordan, the pill-popping bounty, was an eccentric who apparently took Bibles from motels. She also assassinated a church pastor, her motive unknown. She quit teaching to become a nun, a monastic nun, and she kept her habit.

And she read the Old Testament, which was heavy on fire and brimstone. A vengeful, disaster-movie God, last time Judge checked.

"Give your police chief buddy a call to let him know what's up, then we'll head over there."

Owen sneered, stroked Maeby behind her ears. She loved it.

"Call Frannie? The hell with that. We'll call him later."

TWELVE

Larinda stopped at a rest area on Interstate 81 just inside Virginia's southwest corner. The rain pelting the car, front, back, sideways, sounded as heavy as hailstones in an Oklahoma tornado. The noise was chaotic, intimidating, but she was oblivious to it. The reason: a brainstorm.

She keyed one more item into her disposable phone, was then able to scroll through all the info she ever wanted to know about Planned Parenthood in Virginia. Locations in Blacksburg, Roanoke, Charlottesville, Richmond, Falls Church, Hampton. Places where babies were killed on a daily basis. Three locations were on her route to D.C. Forget making the Capitol tonight, she needed to make time for this. Two hours to the first address, in Blacksburg. She would arrive by nightfall.

A suitcase, two gym bags and a hanging garment bag occupied the back seat. A carpenter's canvas drop cloth covered the cargo that sat between the back seat and the SUV's tailgate, tucked taut and level with the bottom of the windows. Under the tarp, things she took from her offsite storage locker. What she'd need to eliminate the threat. Deadly-force things, some very good at leaving a large, deadly footprint. One could never be over-prepared or underpowered.

About IEDs: they were easy to build, and materials like Tannerite and Tovex explosives were legal and easy to acquire. Fully functioning flamethrowers, she knew from experience, were even easier.

Naomi and Deputy U.S. Marshal Edward Trenton exited the plane and entered Dulles International's bright, sky-lighted Concourse C, Edward a step in the lead. Naomi's laptop bag looped one shoulder, her purse the other. Her large rolling carry-on trailed her. Edward's carry-on gym bag looked no bigger than a doll-sized backpack on his expansive back. His body language said he felt sheepish about the difference in their respective loads. She'd scolded him once for attempting to wrest her load from her. He'd get his chance at baggage claim.

At the arrival gate, a bronze-skinned man in a dark suit and a flattop haircut held a placard that read TRENTON in a bold black font. Edward reached him first and gave the man's hand a hearty shake. "Deputy Marshal Abelson, good to see you again."

Deputy Abelson's smile widened. "My, my, my, you are still a monster, Toes. Looking good, sir."

"Appreciate that, Hugh. Your Honor, this is Deputy U.S. Marshal Hugh Abelson."

"An honor, Madam Justice," the marshal said, shaking her hand. "Baggage Claim is this way, ma'am." He tucked the placard under his arm and reached in the direction of her wheeled luggage. "Can I help you with your…?"

"Not required, Marshal, but thank you. Excuse me," Naomi said, cutting him off to reach for her ringing phone.

She retrieved it from her purse. Checking the name of the caller, she pulled up short.

POTUS COS.

She veered right, headed into an airport gate empty of customers, and walked as far away as she could from the concourse corridor. Her two bodyguards followed her step for step. They kept their distance when she raised her hand. Tucking herself into a corner, she put the phone to her ear.

"Hello, this is Justice Coolsummer. Yes, I'll hold for the president's chief of staff."

To Naomi, if the color black had a smell, that smell would have been diesel exhaust, probably from this specific truck. Out front of the airport terminal a black Ford F250 Super Duty four-door pickup sat idling curbside as they approached. The throbbing engine made it uncontestable as the baddest-sounding vehicle in line for passenger arrivals. Marshal Abelson shook hands and clapped shoulders with the driver. The driver quick-stepped into another waiting vehicle that soon reentered traffic.

"This truck is Deputy Marshal Abelson's personal ride, Your Honor," Edward explained.

"Oh. Yes. Thank you, Marshal Abelson," she said. "A bit large, isn't it?"

"We need the room, ma'am." Edward eyed her baggage. "And the heavy-duty shocks."

Some sarcasm from Edward. Her trunk was filled with a hefty chunk of her home library, most of which were law books. When stacked, the baggage squared off two large luggage carts that had required help from her bodyguards and a porter to get it this far.

To Naomi, the pickup truck looked indestructible. Macho overkill, but she figured they meant well.

Marshals Trenton and Abelson hefted the luggage into the enclosed truck bed. Edward helped Naomi into the cab extension then settled himself into the front passenger seat. The truck entered traffic.

"Arrival time Georgetown, fifty-five minutes, ma'am," Marshal Abelson said.

"Thank you, Marshal. Edward?"

"Yes, Your Honor?" The traffic absorbed them, Edward remaining attentive to it.

"Are you available tomorrow morning?"

"Yes, ma'am, I'll be assisting you in getting you settled into your home."

"Yes, of course, but that's not what we'll be doing. The call I took was from President Lindsay. She summoned me to the White House for Sunday breakfast. It seems I'll meet her before I meet with the other justices later in the day. I'm making you my plus-one."

THIRTEEN

It was prime afternoon rush hour outbound, east from Fort Worth on interstate I-30, but luckily they were on the other side of the highway, allowing them to cruise at the speed limit.

The hunch was their bounty had at one time been a monastic nun. 'Their,' Judge allowed, meant his canine deputies and him, not necessarily inclusive of one Owen Chigger Wingert. The jury was still out on Owen, asset versus liability. At that moment, asset was a hard sell. He had curled his lumpy little cowboy ass up in the seat and was asleep, not looking much different than Maeby did on the floor between them, close to the dash. Judge's Shepherd stayed in his crate in back and sat solemn as a sphinx, eyes shark-like, black, intense.

Their destination: monastery number three on a short list of cloisters filled with discalced nuns. At the first few stops, two monasteries in Dallas, they hadn't gotten past the gate.

Fort Worth–16 miles, the road sign said.

The nun's habit she'd left behind looked similar to the traditional habits worn by Carmelites in images Judge retrieved online. White wimple plus a white bib as big as an artist's palette, and brown robes. Except for the color, from the neck down the outfit was close enough to the floor-length habit of every nun in active ministry who had ever gotten into Judge's face as a kid, especially after his affliction had revealed itself. Which made Judge nervous because nuns, in general, had that effect on him. Owen, on the other hand, was more than relaxed. With his nose crammed against the door panel, he was snoring.

"Owen."

The snoring sputtered. "What?" came out annoyed. Owen's eyes didn't open.

"What about your Mustang?"

"Stadium's too far out of the way."

"Won't they tow it?"

"Wouldn't be the first time." He crossed his hands on his stomach, smacked his lips. In ten seconds he was snoring again.

Fuck this. Judge was awake, so Owen needed to be awake. He reached into Owen's cowboy vest pocket and helped himself to his phone. He held it up, found the button for his air horn ring tone and pressed.

HAHHNNK! The dogs jumped and Owen bolted upright.

"...the hell?" His hat tilted then fell to the floor. Judge tossed the phone into his lap.

"Cattle crossing," Judge said, straight-faced. "Sorry."

Owen retrieved the hat, snugged it up on his head and straightened himself. "Not funny."

Judge patted a startled Maeby on the head until she lay back down. His Shepherd's whining from the horn blare stopped. "I might as well tell you, seeing as you're awake and all now. The nuns pretty much cut off my balls when I was a kid."

Owen rubbed his sleep-encrusted eyes. "I don't really give a shit."

And Judge didn't really give a shit that Owen didn't give a shit, he was going to hear about it anyway. Judge's nun phobia had made for some nasty memories when dealing with them as authority figures.

"When the Tourette's hit, my language got so bad they treated me like I was a leper. It put a target on my back in the schoolyard. Then it became too many fistfights, too much acting out. Plus I knocked out a priest. That got me expelled. I had to earn a GED."

"Ahhh. The third sex," Owen said, resettling into the seat. "You've got yer males, you've got yer females, you've got yer nuns and priests. The genitalia under those habits, pussy, prick, both, neither, is anybody's guess. And if they're obeying their vows, they're not getting any action. That makes them ornery as hell."

Listening to this guy was like listening to a raunchy comedian, one hundred percent vulgar, nothing sacred. People would laugh at him then scold themselves for it. How Owen kept himself together long enough to write decent news copy escaped Judge.

"That's just sick, Owen. Insightful, but sick."

"Yeah, well, the nuns gave me the creeps same as they did you. First six years of school were my worst, inside and outside the

Catholic diocese. Kids are cruel, but adults, especially people of the cloth, they're supposed to refute those behaviors, push back on it, man, not validate it."

"Fine. No picnic for either of us. I get it."

This was supposed to be Judge's rant not his, narcissist that Judge was. Owen's eyes narrowed, measuring Judge with his stare. Owen broke it off to scan his new friend head-to-toe, and grunted his displeasure. "No offense, but look at you. You've got your seat pushed all the way back and your feet still reach the pedals. I see your childhood as a whole lot different than mine."

"Careful. Grass isn't always greener."

"Really? Let's see. You were huge for your age, broad shouldered, a real physical specimen. No one fucked with you. You always got picked first for games. Every team game, every sport, you were a star. Am I right?"

"Only for as long as I could keep my mouth shut."

Owen sneered. "Fine, there's that. But you at least started out on the plus side of the equation. Then there's me. When I was ten, one kid told me they'd let me on the baseball field only if I could lie still enough in the dirt. They needed something they could use as second base."

He took his hat off, dented the top with a soft karate chop, and paused to admire his work before returning it his head. "That one hurt near as bad as my mom's abortion comment."

Fort Worth – 8 miles. Traffic was building. Still a lot of pickups and semis. Owen wasn't done.

"Craziest thing was, when I was really young, before I knew what it meant to be small, I had a normal childhood, up to age six, age seven maybe, with great kid friends. The best. The difference in size was barely noticeable. Only odd thing was I was black, and all my buddies where either white or Mexican." Owen rolled up his left sleeve to his bicep. "That cost me too. Check this out."

His arm was discolored, a splotchy tan and red that surrounded his elbow. A burn scar that on him looked like a reverse farmer's tan, from his bicep to his wrist. "You'll never guess who did this."

"And I'm not gonna try."

"My friends. I was eight years old. They wanted to surprise me. Blindfolded me then stuck my elbow in a bucket of bleach, figured if it turned cracker white they'd dip my whole body in it.

Thought they were doing me a favor. One of them was Frannie, the police chief."

Judge took another look at Owen's disfigured arm. "Hell, Owen, that's really...horrible."

And it really was, but his story, the innocence of children, their misguided intentions, had ruined it for him, made the whole of the experience almost comical. Judge snickered, waved it off, finally stifled himself. "Sorry, that wasn't very mature of me."

"Damn right," Owen said, but his mock indignation fell way short. "You suck. So give me your story."

Two guys dropping bro stories on each other on a road trip, minus the beer. What the hell. Judge laid it out for him, an abridged version.

"...molested as a kid for years by my uncle. My father, a crooked U.S. senator who was never around, looked the other way...

"I flipped off Nixon, yes, that Nixon, while he was shaking my hand when I was a teenager. The Secret Service broke my arm when I couldn't stop the gesture. Dad got me enlisted in the Marines, Tourette's and all, traded a senate vote to make it happen. To him, there would be only two acceptable outcomes of my enlistment. 'They'll either kill you or cure you,' he told me. When it looked like neither would happen, he kind of sucked on the barrel of a loaded shotgun and ended it."

Two words got Owen's attention: "'Kind of' sucked on the barrel?"

"When my mother found out about the molestation, she lost it. She was in the room with him when the gun went off. It was ruled a suicide, operative word, 'ruled.'"

Owen was reverent enough to clam up and let this sink in. The silence didn't last long. "Flipped off Nixon, huh?"

"Yep."

"Ha. That's really cool."

His father's suicide might have been a murder, and Nixon was what he keyed on. "You're a moron, Owen."

"Don't you know it, brother." Outside Owen's window, the rolling countryside gave way to a few houses. The road was filled less with pickups now, more with minivans and SUVs. The few houses they passed soon became small subdivisions with backyards that abutted the highway. Suburbia. Judge caught Owen watching families on their house lawns, parents pushing kids on swings, kids on gym sets and trampolines, with him looking curious, or maybe sad.

Fort Worth – 2 miles.

"Ever been married?" Owen asked.

Judge's jaw muscles tightened. He gripped the rabbit's foot. "Yes. Long time ago."

"How'd that work out for you?"

A throat-clearing swallow. "My wife was a Philly K9 cop. It was great until she, her K9 partner, and my infant son, were all killed in a mob hit."

"Wow. That's some shit. Sorry, Judge. Anyone caught?"

"Not enough of them."

Owen got quiet, the dead air necessary for them both. Then, "I was married once, too, to an average-heighted woman," Owen said. "We had some good years. Then I lapsed into being what I used to be, a badass drunk midget with a chip on his shoulder. She left me. After that, I slowly started circling the drain."

"Sounds like that should have told you something."

"Yeah." A slug from his flask, then he pointed at a road sign. "But I'm not much for listening. Here's our exit."

They exited the highway, entered a divided four-laner. On the left they passed pre-fab houses, a motel, then a self-storage facility. All the houses and other buildings were one story. On the right, a large, lush property behind tall iron fencing paralleled the road, the property and its fence extending too far ahead to see where it ended. Behind the fence and buffered by twenty yards of lawn was a cement viaduct that was bone dry. Farther back on the property a red brick wall paralleled them, meandering up and down the hills into the distance, like the Great Wall. They coasted by, looking for an entrance to the monastery.

Impressive, well maintained grounds. A property that lent itself to the whole meditation thing, but the expanse of it blew up the austerity aspect associated with monasteries. Still, they weren't there to judge. They were there to get in, ask questions, get out, then hit the next Carmelite location until they found the one Ms. Larinda Jordan had lived in.

They turned into the entrance drive. The brick wall there was taller on both sides of the two brick columns, as tall as the bronze-colored iron front gate. None of the brick and wrought iron mattered as a barrier; the gate was already open. At the top of a long drive, a tan, adobe-like single story house with terracotta roof tiles sat squat in the middle of two wings that sprawled east and west.

Owen unfolded a flyer with Ms. Jordan's mug shot on it; he studied it. "You got a brown or black marker in here somewhere?"

The dogs were leashed for their trek up the sidewalk. Owen was jabbering, closing out a convent joke he just had to tell.

"So the nun at the Irish convent door tells Paddy, 'No, there's no such things as leprechaun nuns.' Paddy turns to his Irish buddy and says, 'It's like I been telling you, Seamus. You been fucking a penguin.'"

To him, the punch line was knee-slap funny, to Judge not so much. "Midget humor, Owen? Really? Show some pride, dude."

"Bite me, Judge."

Now under the overhang, the four of them stepped up to the monastery's front door. Judge pressed the doorbell. The chime was a bell tower version of "Hark, the Herald Angels Sing" but it was off, sounded closer to "Take Me Out To The Ballgame." Owen reached up, pressed the doorbell again just for grins. He reached for it a third time, but Judge's look stopped him cold.

Seconds later a young woman's face appeared on a small color video screen that protruded from the doorframe at eye-level, left of the door. Short espresso-colored hair, dark, owlish eyes, and glasses. Cute. If she was a nun, she wasn't in a habit. Judge's first impression was she was from south of the border, or was maybe Native American. Her coloring, hair, eyes, the whole package, reminded him of Geenie, his main squeeze back in upstate Pennsylvania, with some Spanish ancestry somewhere in Geenie's background. Common in Texas, but not so much in the Poconos, coal-cracker country USA.

The woman's eyes shifted to view past Judge's shoulder, down the incline. She was annoyed. "One moment please," she said. She moved off screen. The iron entrance gate behind them clanged into motion, sliding shut and snapping locked. Her face reappeared. "Yes?"

Judge opened his mouth, but what he heard was Owen's voice instead. "Hello, miss. We're bounty hunters here on business."

She was visibly confused. Someone had spoken but Judge's lips hadn't moved, and Owen wasn't on camera. Judge gripped a dreadlock behind Owen's back and yanked it. Owen grimaced and shut up.

Judge held up his wallet, opened to a photo ID. "Judge Drury, miss. United States Marine Corps, former enlisted, and a fugitive recovery agent. My deputies and I," he did a head dip south, "are tracking a woman bail jumper. She might have lived here at one time as a Carmelite."

The camera motored itself down, scanned quietly left to right. Owen showed a big friendly smile, with J.D. and Maeby sitting stiff as cardboard cutouts on their haunches next to him. The woman's expression stayed guarded, but the door unlocked and swung inward, letting them enter.

Owen sauntered forward, a business card in his outstretched hand. Judge clamped a hand on his shoulder and stopped him in his tracks so the dogs and he could enter first; Owen trailed them in a huff. A runt of a woman greeted them inside a large vestibule, her resemblance to Judge's girlfriend ending just below her chest, which sat above matchstick legs and was too big for a woman her height, yet still a head taller than Owen.

"The sisters are attending vespers," she said. In a tan skirt with a white high-necked blouse, she smelled fresh and clean. She eyed the leashed dogs, adjusted her glasses, did not contest their presence. "Take Your Dog To Work Day?" she asked, a faint, pleasant smile to go with the question.

"Every day, miss. Trained as military working dogs. They're my partners."

"Ahhh. Follow me."

They passed a footstool she most likely used to see into the camera. She guided them across the tile entry to a softly lit parlor the size and ambiance of a hospital bad-news room. They should sit on the sofa, her open palms suggested. Judge complied, and his dogs settled on the floor in front of him. Owen remained standing. He handed her his business card, introduced himself and stared at her boobs. In his defense, for him they were eye-level. Still, Judge wanted to choke him.

Owen's hand felt inside his cowboy vest pocket. If he pulled out that fucking flask...

Judge stared him down until his hand retreated.

"I'm Mary Veronica," she said, seating herself. "I'm not a nun, and not a resident, but I'm here every day to assist the Carmelites. They don't typically receive visitors." She smoothed out her skirt with both hands, a bit on the anxious side. "Actually they never receive visitors. You're on the grounds only because I neglected to close the gate after a delivery this morning. You're inside the monastery itself because...."

Her smile gone, her dark, skeptical eyes now showed a major interest in, or fear of, whatever else they might have planned to tell her about their bounty.

"...because of my concern that this day might come. Do you have any pictures of this woman?"

Judge liberated a flyer from a pouch on his dog's vest. She studied the mug shot, examined the name on the bottom. "Her name's not familiar. Is blonde her real hair color?"

"Probably not."

"Maybe this will help." Owen pulled a flyer from his own vest pocket, unfolded it and handed it to her. It was the same mug shot Judge had given her, but Owen had blackened everything around the bounty's face with a marker. A poor attempt at showing her in a nun's wimple.

She nodded, the nod sober, heavy with resignation. "That's Sister Dolorosa," she said. "She was a novice here. She left the monastery maybe eight months ago." Mary Veronica kneaded a hem. "Sister was also our carpenter. What has happened?"

Owen spoke up. "We think she..."

Judge hadn't missed her body language. He stepped on Owen's cowboy-booted toes, which shut him up. Judge wanted to know what she knew before they told her anything. "She's been charged with possession of illegally prescribed painkillers."

"I see." Their hostess sat up straighter, folded her hands. She eyed Judge, then Owen, then Judge again. "And?"

Judge didn't want to volunteer any 'ands.' "And what?"

Jane's Baby

"Please. People don't skip town because of forged prescription charges, Mister Drury. What else is there?"

Shit. "She's also been linked to the death of a pastor."

Mary Veronica's eyes closed softly in meditation, like she needed a visit to her happy place, like, right now. They stayed closed, one-Mississippi, two-Mississippi. Her pursed lips added to a general impression that at the moment, air intake was unimportant to her.

"How many dead. In total?"

"Like I said, she's been linked to a pastor's..."

"Mister Drury," she said, steely-eyed this time, her tone chiding. For this woman, tiny didn't mean timid, and patience might not have been a virtue. "Spare me the soft-peddling. The order knew she was capable of larger scale aggressive behavior if she acted on her impulses. So. How...many...dead?"

"Three."

"Thank you." She locked into Judge's stare, didn't blink. "I'm sorry to tell you this, but..." Her chin lifted, her jaw muscles clenched. "...there could be more."

Larinda Jordan's monastic conduct, fresh from this church mouse's lips, had become intolerable to the monastery's Mother Superior. As a cloistered nun she'd had major trouble adhering to one evangelical counsel in particular, obedience. "The other counsels, poverty, chastity, they weren't issues. But obedience, reverence, or submission, for her, it was reserved for her interaction with a higher power. It didn't apply to the monastic order's hierarchy. She took her orders from God the Almighty only."

"A direct pipeline to a supreme being?"

"Yes. Or so she fashioned herself as having."

Great, a misguided fucktrumpet, out there knocking off church pastors. Religious fanaticism: very dangerous.

"And God's Old-Testament, militant leanings," she continued, "according to Sister, are about to make a comeback."

Evidenced by the bounty's interest in the Bibles.

"Smiting down the adulterers, the gays, the abortionists. Especially the abortionists. Sister was eager to do her part. When the Mother Superior gave her another attitude adjustment session for not doing her chores, she didn't come back."

"'Attitude adjustment session'?" Judge asked, puzzled.

"She had to leave the monastery for a few days, which for her meant going to a motel." She eyed Judge's Marine camo-green tee shirt. "Like a weekend pass, Mister Drury. Mother Superior wanted her to pray for the strength to recant her militant beliefs. To meditate on adhering to all her vows, obedience included."

"To chill," Owen said.

"Yes, to chill. Exactly."

Owen got all bright-student, look-at-my-bad-self smug hearing her kudo. Judge wanted him to just sit the hell down. Again he went for his flask inside his vest, a reflex, but he stopped himself before he connected.

"This wasn't the first time she'd needed an attitude adjustment," Mary Veronica said. "It was maybe number three or four. This time she didn't come back. Mother Superior never heard from her again."

There was something their hostess wasn't saying, Judge thought. "Mother Superior never heard from her," he repeated.

"That's correct."

He leaned forward and studied her closely. "But you did. You heard from her."

More skirt kneading. "Yes. Nothing for eight months, then, after Easter this year, she texted me."

"What about?"

"She thanked me for being kind to her. She said she found a new calling, with new spiritual guidance. She signed herself off," she paused, sharpened her stare, "as 'The Church Hammer.'"

Judge absorbed this; nicknames didn't get much more nut-job militant than that. Owen, his hand over his mouth, stifled a snicker then couldn't help himself. "That's really good. 'Church Hammer.' Like a superhero, or a pro wrestler."

Judge played through Owen's giddiness, but something didn't work for him. "A vow of poverty, right? So where'd she get the money for the motel? Nuns who leave their orders walk away with nothing. From her parents? Other relatives?"

"She has no family," Mary Veronica said. "The money was my doing."

"Why help her?"

"Because, frankly, while she was here, I thought she was amazing. Cloistered nuns tend to be submissive. They need a voice within the Church. I felt she could be that voice. I thought that if she took a deep breath, and looked more closely at her convictions, she would come back."

And there they had it. Mary Veronica was an enabler, a buyer for whatever Larinda Jordan had been selling. "How much money did you give her?"

"Enough for the motel for a few days, for her to meditate on how best to fit in, how to work within the system. Plus to pay off her overdue storage locker rent."

"Her what?"

"She confessed she kept some belongings in a storage unit. She said she hoped they were still there."

"A storage unit where?"

"I don't know. Somewhere near here."

"All this happened eight months ago?"

"Her leaving, yes. But her text was recent."

"What about the request for the money for the locker? How recent was that?"

"Nothing any more recent than eight months."

"That storage locker shit's gone by now, Judge," Owen said. "Sorry, miss. My bad." He removed his hat as part of the apology, held it in both hands in front of his crotch.

She overlooked his poor manners. "Sister's meditation, it took her in a controversial direction." She blinked a few times in rapid succession. A few tears squeezed out. "I think she's capable of great things, but also of great damage."

J.D. went on alert, his ears raised. He padded a few feet toward the entrance to the room. He arrived at the end of his leash, sat again and faced the hallway. Maeby followed and sat next to him. A nun poked one eye around a corner of the arched entrance to the room, silent as a cat. Maeby and J.D. both snorted at her. Startled, the curious nun disappeared.

Mary Veronica checked her watch. "Goodness, I lost track of the time. The sisters are back from vespers. You'd better leave now."

"One last thing, miss," Judge said, "She texted you. You still have her number?"

She scrolled the number list on her phone, found and read it while Judge keyed it into his own. She escorted them to the front door.

"We'll pray for her safekeeping, Mister Drury. Hers, and the others she'll try to take with her."

FOURTEEN

Larinda, aggravated, sat in her Durango in a Wendy Restaurant's parking lot in Blacksburg, across a four-lane street from Planned Parenthood. At six-fifty-four p.m., she was too late.

Her grip on the steering wheel was prohibitively tight, her crucifixion wound breaking open from the strain. She seethed, some from the physical pain again jabbing at her healing hand, some from craving an oxy mellow, but mostly it was from the inconvenience caused by the severe weather.

"Please, God, give me the strength..."

The clinic closed at six-thirty. At this location the baby killers worked Tuesdays, Fridays and Saturdays, and tomorrow was none of those days. She didn't want to and couldn't wait three days for the next opportunity.

She slipped into a thin Old Navy hoodie and tucked her hair into a baseball cap. The hood went up. She grabbed a pair of sunglasses and exited the SUV.

Sliding casement windows lined the front of the two-story rectangular building, the windows inset in its birch-colored, steeply slanted shingle roof. The building occupied the corner of a city block. She stepped onto the sidewalk and walked the perimeter. Around the first corner a set of stairs led to the second floor, a red door at the top. Video cameras jutted from the roofline at both corners. In the back of the building, no rear exit, and all windows were flush to the wall under three more video cameras and three floodlights. She reached the third corner and another set of stairs, with more cameras. No building lobby, front, back or on either side. Which meant no public elevator, and no interior access to upstairs. Larinda climbed the exterior stairs and tried a fire door at top. Locked.

She returned to the SUV, climbed in, had a decision to make.

The drive had been long, tense, her eyes aching, prickly, jabbing pains shooting into their sockets. The tornado-like weather had followed her into Virginia and strained all her senses, each on high alert through every curve and straightaway of every mile for the last three hours. She'd get some relief with the oxy, but she desperately needed sleep. She dry-swallowed another of the mint-green pills. The relief came to her closed eyes in waves, and what felt before like a plucking at her eyelids by spindly, probing bird claws gave way to a gentle high, and an angelic-fingered eye massage.

She unwrapped the red-tinged gauze that encircled her hand. Crimson droplets dotted the absorbent pad under it, and under the pad, blood trickled through a split in the wound. She centered a new sterile sponge in her palm and rewrapped her hand with more gauze. That would do for now. Back to deciding about the abortion clinic, and how to do what she wanted to do.

There were more clinics in Virginia on her list. One in Roanoke, less than an hour away. The next closest was three-plus hours, in Richmond, but out of the way.

She was already here.

So be it.

The building's first floor housed a martial arts school, a tanning salon and a dry cleaners. The clinic's second floor space spanned four casement windows, above the studio and the tanning salon. Next to the clinic was one additional casement window, for a small law office.

She checked her face in the mirror. Smooth white skin, hazel eyes, and a dose of Irish freckles. "All-American sexy," her long-ago college boyfriend had called her. Her auburn hair, its natural color, blonde now, plus the orange-brown freckles on her nose and cheeks made him want to have sex with her mouth more than any other part of her body. Freckles also dotted her lithe, toned arms. She became sexier, all of her, he'd said, after she spent time in the sun. After him, she'd given up men, had given up sex, but she did agree her fair skin always needed more color, with her preferring the tanned, Oklahoman ranch hand look that her time in the pastures gave her while growing up.

The tanning salon was still open. Opaque storefront windows diffused its interior lighting making it impossible to see inside, giving it a massage parlor look. Above the salon, the clinic.

She decided. She located a tightly packed backpack under the tarp, opened it so she could switch out one full Gatorade bottle for another. She jogged across the street with the bag and entered the tanning salon.

A female attendant sat at the counter, early twenties, her colored red hair in a bun. The attendant quickly finished a text on her phone and greeted Larinda warmly. "Hi. Can I help you?"

"Maybe. Is there an inside entrance to the second floor?"

"Sorry, miss, but no. For security reasons." The attendant leaned in, whispered, "See, upstairs there's an abor…"

The attendant caught herself. She straightened her shoulders, acquiring a judgmental face. Larinda didn't miss her furtive glance at Larinda's stomach. "Planned Parenthood is upstairs," she said. "Some people aren't happy about it and cause trouble."

"I'm more interested in the law office." Larinda slipped off her hood but left her sunglasses in place.

"Oh." The attendant relaxed. "The upstairs doors reopen at eight tomorrow. I think the lawyers don't get in until nine-ish." She gave Larinda's freckled white face the once over. "Can I interest you in a specially priced tanning session tonight? Assuming you're not already a member?"

"I'm not a member, and yes, sure, a session sounds great."

"Awesome. Welcome to SafeTan Tanning. I'm Patricia."

"Barbara Hopkins."

"After your session, Miss Hopkins, if you'd like to become a member…"

"I'll take a brochure when I leave."

"Great. Sorry. I always have to ask."

Patricia had a few more questions for her. No, this was not her first time in a tanning salon. No, she didn't live locally. Yes, she was aware SafeTan had salons throughout the south and the Midwest.

"Where do I go to change?"

"Dressing stalls are in the tanning area. You can put your backpack in one of the lockers," Patricia pointed, "over there."

"Thanks, but I'll keep it with me."

Larinda stripped to bra and panties. With tanning goggles in place she entered the empty tanning room, carried her backpack with her to the bed that the pleasant Patricia had set up for her. Patricia suggested eight minutes maximum. Five would be enough, Larinda told her, else she'd burn.

With the session over, Larinda was still the salon's only customer. She dressed again, jeans, tee shirt, hoodie, and sunglasses. Back at the front counter she thanked young Patricia for her kind service. "Not very busy tonight, I see."

"Yes. I might close early."

"Tell me," Larinda added, "are you a religious person, Patricia?"

Patricia's eyebrows tented. "Why yes, Miss Hopkins. Yes I am. A practicing Presbyterian my whole life. A Peace Corps volunteer when I graduated college. Here, look at this." Her young, tanned face became gosh-golly bubbly. She lifted a silver necklace out from under her blouse and showed off a hanging medallion.

Larinda leaned in, read the inscription aloud, the medallion shaped like a military dog tag. "'I heart the Peace Corps.' Very nice, Patricia."

"Thanks. I still do missionary work," Patricia said. "In Honduras, Haiti, and South America. Whenever our church elders decide someone needs help, I go."

"That's good. That's very good, Patricia." She laid her hand on Patricia's, squeezed it tightly like an elderly aunt might do to her dearest niece. "So glad to hear that. God bless you."

The young woman's face lit up in response, her head tilting. "God bless you too, Miss Hopkins. Thank you. And please don't forget a brochure."

Larinda headed to the glass door exit with the SafeTan literature in hand, raised her hood and clambered outside. She teared up, but she felt a little better about what was going to happen. Patricia, young, wholesome, and Christian, had been genuinely buoyed by her blessing. At least there was that.

Patricia the attendant powered off the computer equipment on the front counter and the SafeTan window neon. The door to the tanning beds room was closed. She needed to open it for the cleaning people. She pushed the door ajar.

"My goodness," she said, her eyes lighting up. Her customer had forgotten her backpack. She turned to catch her.

Jane's Baby

"Miss Hopkins!" Patricia called, but she was too late. She hustled over to the bag, grabbed for it, would need to run it outside to her. The unfastened top flap lifted open, spilling out a strip of gauze stained with blood. She set the bag down, picked up the gauze between thumb and forefinger and examined it. "Yuck." She dropped it into a trashcan.

Beneath the gauze was a Gatorade bottle, its contents the color of urine. She wrinkled her nose from the smell, gasoline, but the orange and black wiring, six white Tovex "Blastrite" gel sausages and four attached AA batteries were what made her step back, away from the bag. Her head shook out a no, no no no, this couldn't be happening. Her thin, tan hands balled up. She pivoted and ran.

Blasting through the tanning area doorway, her arms pumping, she slipped as she rounded a corner. She bounced back up and passed the counter, nearing the door to the exit.

Larinda reached her SUV across the street and removed a detonator from her pocket. Electrical tape masked everything except the display screen and a few buttons. Seven-twenty-three p.m., the display said. She eyed the front entrance of the building she'd just exited. All was quiet.

"Godspeed, Patricia. Heaven awaits all Christian martyrs." Larinda pressed a button.

Patricia saw passing traffic through the front door, another ten feet, less than ten feet and she'd be ou...

The IED ignited and blew out the front windows and their frames, the pressure of the blast ripping through the ceiling, the second floor and the roof, shooting its orange flames into the ink-blue nighttime sky. The sky rained wood and shingle and other building shrapnel onto the street and cars and sidewalks, then a gas line erupted. A second explosion shook the entire city block, then a third, with Larinda jolted by the metallic clang of a tanning bed landing in front of her SUV. Another tanning bed dropped onto the roof of the Wendy's restaurant behind her. Street traffic was light but was now chaotic, with terrified drivers speeding to flee the debris shower or braking hard to avoid entering it, the building still sparking and spitting fire.

Bits of ash and other flaming debris floated onto Larinda's SUV. She turned on the ignition, eyed the burning building again.

She jumped when a tiny metal medallion splatted her windshield and stuck there, forcing her to focus on it and the silver chain attached. Larinda made the sign of the cross.

The salon attendant's necklace slid off the window when Larinda engaged the wipers, smearing the glass red. Wiper fluid and a few frenetic wiper swipes rinsed away the smear. She reached for the floor gearshift and backed the SUV out.

At the rear of the restaurant parking lot, an exit put her onto another street. Back on the road, the blacktop still wet from the earlier storm, she remembered a strip of no-tell motels she'd passed in Christiansburg just off Interstate 81. She hated to backtrack, but she needed some rest, and she needed it now.

Sirens wailed in the distance, strengthening as they converged, one emergency vehicle dopplering past her on the other side of the road as she put distance between her SUV and the fire. First responders would administer to the destruction, would gather up Patricia's body parts for a good Christian burial, and would clean up the heinous discharge from the festering abscess called Planned Parenthood that The Church Hammer had just lanced from their community.

She found no joy in this. It scratched the itch caused by her deplorable sin, and she again would await the answer to the question she'd posed in prayer earlier: how many abortions would she need to prevent to complete the penance for the one abortion she'd had?

The answer, as before, was always "more."

It was Naomi's first evening as a D.C. resident, and she was spending it at the five-star 1789 Restaurant on 36th St. NW in Georgetown, there at the invitation of Texas' U.S. Senator Mildred Folsom.

The politics weren't lost on Naomi. Senator Folsom was the Religious Right's legislative pit bull, had been for decades. Proud of her Texas heritage, even prouder of her Christian conservatism. At one time, the media called her "Senator Super-Christian."

"Now, to get with the times, it's Senator Uber-Christian," the senator said to Naomi, smiling through her Texas drawl. "Liberal media types love the new acronym. 'S-U-C.' Twitter-compatible

Jane's Baby

and more disparaging. And I love 'em right back on Twitter when I have the time." She winked. "You can never eat just one."

Her age and a cigarette habit had coalesced to promote a charcoal-filtered gravelly voice that was still very effective after seventy-two years. She'd had work done, on her face, neck and teeth, and her hair had gone from a sexy platinum blonde to a fluffy, august silver-white. A waiter delivered their after-dinner cocktails.

"I'm still very particular about my beliefs, Madam Justice, regardless of whatever tongue-in-cheek superlative someone assigns to me because of them. As I know you are particular about your beliefs as well."

Naomi picked up her cocktail tumbler, sipped from it. "My personal opinions," Naomi said, "need to remain as personal opinions only, and most of the time unexpressed. You know this, Senator, and I'm sure you can respect this."

"Of course. Please, call me Mildred."

"Let's stay with 'Senator,' Senator."

The senator smiled at Naomi's response, took the first sip of her after-dinner drink. She closed her eyes, savoring it. Balcones Brimstone Texas Scrub Oak Smoked Whiskey. Naomi knew this libation. It had been her husband Reed's favorite. Uniquely Texas. The senator suggested it as a dessert replacement. Naomi had accepted, more so for Reed's benefit, wishing to share some of her new life in D.C. with her memory of him. In its aroma Naomi smelled a Texas campfire at sunset, and maybe even a hint of Reed's cologne.

"To all things birthed in Texas, Madam Justice," the senator intoned, raising her glass.

"To Texas," Naomi said, joining the toast.

Accepting her dinner invitation had been the least Naomi could do. Mildred Folsom had been a political firebrand for over thirty years, thriving in one of the most male-dominated, good-ol'-boy jurisdictions in existence in any of the fifty states. Texas' longest tenured senator of either sex. A true woman warrior. This was to be her last Congress and had been widely publicized as such. She would retire next year. Respect for her was too tame a word. Admiration was better, awe was best. There was all of this, but for Naomi there was also something else. Curiosity. She had one lingering question she wanted the senator to answer. It was about Naomi's Supreme Court confirmation hearing.

"It must have been hard for you, Senator."

"What's that, Your Honor?"

"To not mount a take-no-prisoners assault against my nomination because of my feminist leanings early in my career. I'm grateful you were so reasonable in your line of questioning."

The senator's eyes narrowed but recovered quickly. Still, Naomi saw it. A tell that the senator was uncomfortable with the insinuation. By 'reasonable,' Naomi meant 'soft touch.' Had the senator been too patronizing during the hearing? Parochial? Could the conservatives have accused her of extending an olive branch to the evil liberal dark side?

"Oh, I don't know, Your Honor. I thought I was rather my old ornery, transparent self. But perhaps I have mellowed some with age, getting more in touch with my feminine side. Perhaps I do rely more on what a person's beliefs are now, not on what they once were. I do expect you to protect the Constitution to the extreme, and to rule on every argument absent any preconceived biases. You comported yourself well during the hearing, were charming, and you defended your judicial record admirably. You did Texas proud." She raised her glass and took her whiskey on another spin, her eyes following it as it swirled around the bottom. "Tell me, Madam Justice, are you up to speed on the arguments on the docket for this term?"

"Of course, Senator. The term starts Monday. I'm ready to hear them. Where are you going with this?"

"The one case from Texas…"

"Won by the state, appealed to The Nine. Texas women who want to terminate pregnancies now need to view an ultrasound."

"Yes. I characterize it as helping women to make a more informed decision. I wish it had been in place thirty years ago."

The senator's backstory was well documented: her daughter, an only child, pregnant at age eighteen, a pregnancy she'd kept from her mother; her legal abortion at a Texas clinic; complications during the procedure; the daughter's tragic death from septic shock soon after. Naomi knew it couldn't get much more personal than this. For anybody.

"Are you aware, Madam Justice, who is on the stump for upholding the Texas court decision?"

"Senator," Naomi wearied of the discussion, "yes, I'm aware. Much of the state of Texas is on the stump, which is each Texan's right. But let's be more precise. You're referring to Norma McCorvey." Her emphasis on the name, the inflection, showed Naomi's impatience. "Misses McCorvey is now pro-life, and like this case, she might better be characterized as being on the stump to overturn Roe. An even better characterization, in my opinion, is she may now have no more relevant a political voice than the average citizen. She's good for some media sound bites and stories about overcoming personal demons, but other than that, Misses McCorvey has no standing here."

"Try telling ol' Norma that."

"I needn't tell her anything. Her place in judicial history as Jane Roe is solidified. Her newest incarnation will keep the pot stirred and the flash pan primed. And yet I do wish only good things for her, as valiant as she's been, and as a fellow Native American, and that includes a calm mind, an unburdened heart, and a long life in which to enjoy both."

Naomi raised her tumbler of Balcones and downed the rest of it without a blink. She wiped her mouth with her napkin. "This discussion, Senator, needs to close. Thank you for a wonderful dinner. I really must go."

"As must I, Madam Justice. I am in desperate need of a cigarette. But just one more moment, please. Someone else here would like to congratulate you on your appointment." She beckoned a distant diner with a raised hand and a curling finger.

A man rose from the far side of the dining room, someone Naomi recognized instantly. Wide shoulders, trim waist, tall, with a gray mustache and a bolo tie. Texas televangelist Higby Hunt crossed the room.

The man made Naomi's skin crawl. Be polite, she told herself. She stood to greet him.

"Madam Justice Coolsummer! An honor to meet you." A handshake. "And congratulations on your confirmation." The reverend's dental veneers glistened as he pumped her arm.

"Likewise, and thank you, Reverend. But this is poor timing. I'm leaving. I have an early breakfast tomorrow."

"What, no dessert?" His wide-mouthed smile continued to sparkle but it wasn't quite as impressive in person, without TV studio lighting. He added, "You must have dessert. I hear the chocolate mousse bombe is heavenly."

"Reverend," Senator Folsom interjected. She gestured with her cocktail glass. "Madam Justice was already kind enough to drink her dessert with me. I called you over so you could meet her before she left, maybe make her feel a little more at home. And perhaps have her receive a blessing from you to start the new judicial term."

"Thank you, Senator," Naomi said. "I'm glad to make Reverend Hunt's acquaintance, but the blessing's not necessary."

"Nonsense," the reverend said. "It will be my pleasure." He retrieved a pocket-sized Bible from his dinner jacket, found a marked page, and raised his chin. "This is a reading…"

"Please. That's enough," Naomi said. "No prayers on my behalf. None to start the term, none to end it, either inside the Supreme Court building or out. I really do have to go. So nice to meet you, Reverend Higby."

Senator Folsom got to her feet. "But of course, Your Honor. What was I thinking? I'm glad we had some time together tonight. Wishing you great success. And please say hello to the president for me tomorrow."

Naomi squinted while shaking the senator's hand good-bye, trying to read her. "How is it you know?"

"There aren't many secrets here in D.C., Your Honor," she said, winking at Naomi and the reverend both. "Oh, one last thing. I wonder if you see the significance here, what we all have in common, you, the president and I? The humblest of beginnings for each of us. Three abandoned children who matured into pretty darned good, successful adults."

"I never considered myself abandoned, Senator. My adoptive parents are wonderful. I owe everything to them."

"As do I to my adoptive parents, may they rest in peace, Madam Justice. Go, make yourself and your adoptive parents proud. God knows our natural parents, whoever they were, might well have been proud too, if they knew who we became."

FIFTEEN

The electric gate emerged from behind the monastery's brick wall and rumbled past the idling van's rear, the monastery on the other side. It clicked shut when it met up with more iron. Judge eased the van into a left turn onto Mt. Carmel Drive as soon as traffic allowed. He checked his watch; seven-twenty p.m. They were searching for a particular motel.

Owen was less than enamored about the monastery visit. "You told me nuns scare you."

"Yeah, well, you were monopolizing the whole conversation and were really a pain in the ass in there. Besides, she wasn't a nun."

"Whatever. Short Mexican chick with big tits. She was hot, and you treated me like I was a kid. She coulda been a contender, Judge."

"For what?"

"For my next ex-girlfriend."

"Christ, Owen, back home in Philly if you act like that, someone punches you out for being a porch dick. All mouth, no manhood. Not a chance that was going to happen. It's a monastery."

Owen cursed. Judge told him to go find a penguin to fuck, then informed him their little experiment with Owen as a ride-along was winding down. The discussion turned heated until Maeby bolted upright between them, jolted by something. Judge checked his other deputy in the rear view, a force of habit whenever Maeby went on alert. J.D. was at attention as well, growling and yipping. Maeby shoved her nose into the van carpet like a pig rooting for truffles, pushing at it. The last time something like this had happened, Maeby and he were on duty outside a Kabul hospital. An IED had gone off, distant, on the other side of the city. It blew up a cab, the driver and his passengers, yet Maeby had felt it miles away.

Judge screeched the van to a halt on the shoulder. Both dogs lay down but kept their heads raised, their eyes open, assuming their sphinx poses. Maeby's nostrils constricted. She nosed the tight pile of the carpet repeatedly, checking for a scent under it.

"Out of the van, Chigger, now!"

Judge directed Maeby with his hand, had her sniff each of the van's wheel wells while J.D. sat at attention next to Owen fifty feet off the shoulder, in the weeds. Maeby circled the van's perimeter and made no attempt to crawl underneath the chassis or reenter the interior. She finished her route, calmed, sat next to her master and waited for her Milk-Bone reward, which he gave her. Judge called over to his other dog, motioned and called to Owen. "All clear."

Owen arrived alongside them. "What the hell was that all about?"

"Not sure."

The traffic whizzed by, headlights waxing and waning in their eyes, the inky-blue nighttime sky lost to total darkness. Judge ran a hand over his head and its nonexistent hair. "Maeby sensed, felt, something. Tremors maybe. An explosion somewhere." He wasn't totally baffled. It was a nature thing, like when forest animals sensed severe weather somewhere and retreated. He gazed up the highway at the direction they were headed, the road disappearing in the distance. If there had been an explosion, it could have been anywhere out there.

"Whatever she felt, she's not feeling it now. Let's run down this motel lead then grab a bite and call it a night."

Buckled up, Owen scratched Maeby behind the ear as they reentered traffic, getting chummy with her. "At one with the cosmos, are we, Maeby?" He stroked her ears then took an extended pull from his flask. "A couple more slugs of this and I'll be joining you, sweetie."

"Put it away, Owen. The Palace Motel, on your right."

One misaimed floodlight illuminated the "PAL" part of the motel's roadside sign. They were four miles east of the monastery they'd just left, still on the same highway.

This would be J.D.'s recon this time. His master saddled him up with a full shoulder harness and switched out the ragged black

Jane's Baby

leather leash he lived in for a nylon one. In the back of the van Judge located a plastic bag and removed the tee shirt he'd lifted from Ms. Jordan's apartment. After a whiff, J.D. got plenty eager.

Maeby sat at attention in the passenger seat. She snorted and whined, wanting to be part of the effort. Her master raised his finger, which she licked. "Enough with the whining, young lady. No." Her severe face relaxed when he cupped it. "Love you, sweetie."

They were off, Owen included, so they could speak with the manager. "I've got a leash back in the van with your name on it, Owen. Don't piss me off in here."

"Nope, don't recognize her."

The motel's night manager was a skinny guy with a black mustache and a soul patch, and a bad case of adult acne that reached his red neck. He handed the mug shot back to Judge and stared at the dog, keenly apprehensive. J.D. rested on his haunches, apprehensive at him right back.

"So help me God," the clerk said, "your dog better not take a dump in here."

Like anyone would notice. It stank in there of TidyCats. "He won't. Owen, help me out here."

Owen produced the mug shot he'd colored in, handed it to the clerk.

"That one, I know," the clerk said. "She called herself Sister Dolorosa. Wore her habit while she was here." He chuckled. "She was a thief. Sort of." He keyed some searches into his computer, or what passed for a computer, behind the counter. Small screen, with a thick-as-a-brick keyboard attached at the base, it was an old CPU that reminded Judge of a Radio Shack museum piece.

"A thief? How's that?" Judge asked.

The clerk found what he was looking for. "She stayed in room three. Then," more keying, "room seven, then room six. Three stays. Yes, room six was her last. She stole the Bibles in the rooms, according to my brother. He cleans the rooms and remembers shit like that."

He grabbed for his take-out coffee cup, spat in it and smiled for them, showing licorice-colored teeth. What Judge had thought was a soul patch was tobacco juice dribble. The clerk relocated the juice to his sleeve.

"The last time we had a Bible stolen, my brother's note says 'Gideons called,' so I assume another one is gone. It was the first week of September. Three weeks ago. Room eight. The guest wasn't a nun this time."

"You have a name for that guest, too?" Judge asked.

"Maybe. Who are you anyway?" He looked Owen up and down, then J.D, still sitting next to Owen, the dog shorter than him but only by a forehead. The clerk's interest returned to his interrogator. "You for sure ain't cops."

"I'm a bounty hunter. So's the dog. The cowboy is…"

"I already know him. Chigger Wingert from Chigger Bytes. Great column the other day, dude. Fucking Eagles fans suck."

A beaming Owen bowed. "Thanks, but if you read the whole column, the Eagles fan tried to save that kid." Owen nodded in Judge's direction. "Pulled him out of the fire."

Some goodwill, finally, for Judge agreeing to the ride-along. "So we're all caught up then," Judge said, ignoring the slur. "Great. A name please."

"Fifty bucks." He spat more tobacco juice into the cup. "I hate Philly too much."

Judge wanted to choke this guy. "You want any of this, Owen?"

"Twenty," Owen said, "and I'll autograph the mug shot."

The clerk softened, pocketed the money, and looked up the info. "She was registered as a 'C. Hammer.' No phone number, no address. The room's empty. Wanna see it?"

The four of them checked it out. It was what someone might expect to get for sixty bucks a night. Bed, bureau, small flat-screen TV, toilet, shower-only bath. No mint on the pillow, no shampoo. Judge gave his dog another whiff of the bounty's tee shirt. Three weeks was long for a scent to remain but J.D. was good with it, padding quickly to a patch of gray indoor-outdoor next to the bed. He clawed at a spot, sat by it. His master moved in closer to check it out, found a slight discoloration. Closer examination showed it to be a few crusty brown spots. Judge's guess was they were drops of blood.

"Good boy, J.D." A doggie treat for him. No other hits in the room. One last request for the motel clerk. "Where's the closest self-storage facility?"

"Next door close enough?"

Judge gave the live-in Alamo Mini-Storage proprietor a name. "Larinda Jordan."

The storage facility was Vietnam-vet, army-navy chic. American flags, helmets, bayonets, USMC patches, and framed black and white photographs. The crusty proprietor's residence was on the second floor, above the office. He was now a hundred bucks richer, Judge's money. Owen had pushed him on the price, looking to again trade on his sportswriter celebrity, but the fifty bucks he offered soon turned into a hundred. The guy had no clue who Owen was, and no patience. He thought he was with the circus.

His arthritic pointer finger checked a database list of customers. "No Larinda Jordan."

"How about a Sister Dolorosa?"

"If that's a rock or a rapper group been squattin' on their spurs because they got no gigs, we do have some of them losers storing their stuff here."

"No," Judge said. "It's a nun."

"Lick that calf again?"

Owen translated: "He said, are you kidding me?"

"Not kidding, sir. A Carmelite nun, from a nearby monastery."

He hunted then pecked the keyboard. "No. No 'Sister Dolorosa.'"

"How about someone named Hammer?"

More arthritic keying. "Ah. Well throw your hat over the windmill, son, we have a winner. 'C. Hammer.' Except it seems C. Hammer is about to lose his stuff for non-payment."

"It's a she," Judge said. "What does she owe?"

"Three months." More hunt-and-peck, this time on an adding machine. "That's one-ninety-five."

Owen interceded. "Look, we don't want to own the shit, we just want to see it."

Judge stepped hard on Owen's boot again, enough to make it hurt. "That's a deal, sir." He peeled off two hundreds, told the guy to keep the rest. The crusty proprietor took the money and offered his hand in return.

"We've howdied but we ain't shook. Skippy."

Skippy's hand was bony, misshapen, but the grip he offered was firm. His eyes drilled Judge's while they shook hands; he'd figured Judge out. "Tet Offensive," Skippy added. "Corporal, USMC. You?"

"Judge Drury. Gunnery Sergeant, Iraq and Afghanistan. Nice to meet you, Corporal."

In front of the storage unit, the dogs and Judge and Owen waited while Skippy fumbled with his keys.

"Whatever's in here was scheduled to go on the auction block," Skippy said. He slipped a key into the hanging Master lock. "You best not be letting no yellow jackets in the outhouse on me, me giving you a look-see without no key. I got nowhere else to live."

"Roger that, Skippy," Judge told him. "No one needs to know."

He snapped open the lock, then he checked out Judge's canine partners before he unhooked it. "Some of these units don't get aired out much, so keep your guys from marking territory in here please." He nodded in Owen's direction. "Tom Thumb included."

The metal door slid up, drowning out Owen's protests. Skippy tugged on a hanging chain for an overhead light bulb. "Our eight-by-fifteen unit," he volunteered. Its contents sat mostly against the back half so there was room in front for them to enter. But with the dogs in the mix and the three of them inside, it was tight.

First recognizable smell: "Gasoline," Owen said.

"Dirtier and smellier than gasoline," said Skippy. "When it smells as bad as a homeless person, it's diesel."

Maeby's leash tightened up quick. She strained, pulled Judge forward, stopped in front of some boxes and sat. She nudged one of them and retreated, waiting to be rewarded. Judge untucked its flaps. In it were jars of Tannerite binary rifle targets. Good for when gun owners wanted things they were shooting at to explode. Nearby was a box of Tovex gel sausages, an alternative to dynamite. Sitting loose on the floor were model rocketry igniters, the wiring stripped at both ends, plus two radio-controlled toy monster trucks, their packaging open. The trucks were there, but

Jane's Baby

the hand controllers for them, a poor man's, or woman's, remote detonator, were gone. This did not bode well.

"Gunny," Skippy offered, "it looks like your bounty's a full bubble off plumb."

What else was in there was no less scary. Small jugs of diesel fuel and gasoline. Jug water. Empty Gatorade bottles. Flash 21, a fuel gelling agent. A small CO2 tank. And an empty shipping box labeled "X15" with packing materials discarded in a haphazard pile. Judge began to feel queasy.

"I recognize that. It's packaging for a flamethrower," Skippy said. "Civilian model. Damn."

Judge had seen civilian flamethrowers before. The farmer he rented a cottage from had one. Fifteen hundred bucks by mail order. They delivered a liquid fire propellant, like napalm, all legal. People used them for clearing brush from their property. Unless they wanted to use them for something else. This made Judge more anxious.

Owen worked his way farther back into the storage unit. He cradled a large shoebox. "Judge, these boxes here…look."

They threaded their way back. Of interest, two shoeboxes. Owen popped the top on one. No weaponry or bomb-making materials in it. What it did contain were a University of Oklahoma men's class ring commemorating a 2004 Bachelor of Science degree, an elegant, diamond-encrusted pen, a hairpiece, and jewelry, some men's, some women's.

Owen handed Judge the box, retrieved the second one. "Some nice stuff in there. See if there are any…"

"Inscriptions," Judge said. Names, dates, sentimental words engraved on items that would typically carry them. Mementoes, or in this case more like personal effects. What they were looking at here were a killer's souvenirs.

Inside the graduation ring band, the inscription carried a name: Zachary Enders. Judge did a search on his phone. Tulsa Journal Sentinel headline, 2004, "University of Oklahoma College Student Missing." Zachary's parents would be saddened by the discovery, but they'd be glad for the closure, and the return of a keepsake.

Owen removed a large zip-lock bag from the second shoebox. He held it up to get a better look at the contents. Light from the dim overhead bulb glistened off multiple stainless steel surgical instruments. Judge recognized one item: birthing forceps. They were stained red. On the plastic bag, printed in big black letters: MURDER WEAPONS. His guess was these were also souvenirs, from a surgical procedure his bounty had interrupted.

Fuck. Judge needed air.

He doubled over outside the storage unit, needing to barf but couldn't, his mouth losing out to the disease:

"...dripping nipple cock clamper, puke bandit, leg-humping smurf wiper, asswad, tit-balls overalls..."

Within earshot, Owen talked to Skippy on Judge's behalf: "Give him a minute. He'll be fine."

The nighttime air and sounds outside the storage unit were fresh, refreshing, welcome. Pumpkins and gourds and overturned earth and mooing cattle. Judge's mouth finally cooperated. "Call your police chief buddy Frannie, Owen, right...fucking...now."

"I'm on it, boss."

Skippy leaned down to get into Judge's face, draping his arm around his neck: "You feelin' better, son?"

"Yeah."

Judge straightened up then placed his hand lightly onto Skippy's shoulder and squeezed it. "Thank you. Sorry, Corporal, but it looks like we're gonna need to, ah..."

"I know, Gunny. Some yellow jackets about to swarm the outhouse. As welcome as a screwworm, but we'll do our part."

Frannie's Glenn Heights local cop team plus the Feds plus some bomb guys showed up, and they all got busy. It was nearing ten p.m. Cloudless sky, full moon, stars blazing and a fall chill. Owen and Judge were out of the way, leaning against the van and drinking coffee Skippy had made. Inside the van Maeby and J.D. barked at anything that moved in the moonlight, which right about now was everything that had been inside the storage unit, the teams tagging it and readying it all for transport. Skippy handed the storage unit's lock to one of Frannie's guys, told him they should clean up after themselves and lock up when they were done, and went off to bed.

Jane's Baby

The nail in the coffin that confirmed this as the bounty's little stash of victims' keepsakes was the inscription on the Montblanc Pen, "To D.B.: Let them live, and we will help them thrive."

D.B. Darlington Beckner, the murdered pastor.

"The 'Let them live' slogan," Frannie said, "was part of a regional pro-life campaign that originated here in Texas in the eighties. And about the phone number you wanted me to check out…"

They'd spilled everything to get the police chief up to speed. It was the number their bounty used to text the Carmelites' Mary Veronica. "Yeah?"

"Prepaid. At best, traceable to a convenience store, or maybe a Walmart. But the Feds did trace the signal. Its last triangulated location was tonight, through a phone tower in Blacksburg, Virginia, just before eight o'clock."

Last bit of feedback from Frannie: "No guns in this mess, but they found a receipt from a company called TrackingPoint, for an eight-thousand-dollar rifle. Ever hear of precision-guided firearms?"

Judge had. Also called smart rifles. New to the market. Tag the target with a scope, squeeze the trigger, and the onboard computer releases the shot only when conditions were perfect. Some versions were nearly 100% accurate in hitting moving targets up to a mile away. A novice gun owner could suddenly become Chris Kyle, American Sniper.

"Yep," the chief said. "TrackingPoint is based in Austin. Their guns are available to the public."

A few members on the investigatory team mouthed off because Judge and his deputies had "ruined some of the fucking evidence" by sorting through the storage unit's contents. Fine, Judge got it, they screwed up. But he was a bounty hunter on assignment, not a cop, and they had found shit the law enforcement agencies should have found already. Still, for Judge, Mary Veronica's prediction from their visit to the monastery was the last word: *"There will be more."*

SIXTEEN

A buzzer startled Naomi awake. The sound of the alarm, her surroundings, the windows, the ceiling, the room, everything was off.

She sat up, groggy, her mouth cottony. She reoriented herself.

This was not Austin, but rather her first night in her new Georgetown home, in a quaint new community of twenty-eight townhouses, a cloister surrounded by an urban venue. She planned to keep the Austin condo. It was home to her and her kids, and also the last place her husband Reed had called home, with her, which made it home, period.

Out of the shower, she dressed herself in a smart gray skirt suit and white blouse. She wasn't moved in by a long shot. That would happen later in the week when the rest of her clothing, furniture, and other personal belongings were delivered. The townhome came partially furnished, appointed with a well-equipped kitchen, some geeky electronic gadgetry, and an incredible sound system she'd enjoyed last night while she read briefs in her den.

She grabbed the TV remote, found CNN and put on her earrings. A "BREAKING NEWS" header hijacked the news crawl. She raised the volume as the front doorbell chimed. At six a.m. this would be Edward, punctual to the minute. Except now she was preoccupied by the news story. Her feet stayed planted in front of the TV. "Planned Parenthood bombed last night...Virginia...one confirmed dead."

An overzealous sort might think this barbaric act could somehow have been directed at the Court. Then again, she'd have been naïve to think that given the fall case docket, it could be ruled out as having nothing to do with it. The doorbell chimed again. She heard Edward project a low but determined voice through the door. "Deputy Trenton, ma'am. Please open up."

Naomi quickstepped over, her high heels click-clacking the tiled foyer. Another chime, then came a fist pummel. She opened the door. "Edward, I'm so sorry. Have you seen, oh, I guess you have."

Edward's gun was drawn, his phone to his ear. He re-holstered his weapon, spoke into his phone. "Hugh? Trenton. Never mind. I'm with her now. Thanks."

The phone back in his pocket, he addressed Naomi, his tone serious. "Madam Justice, we need to talk."

Larinda was on her knees in prayer, next to the motel room bed. "Thank you, Lord. I am humbled by your blessing." She'd saved unborn lives last night. Her reward had been a revitalizing overnight rest.

Today she wanted to accomplish three things: change her appearance, acquire new transportation, and since it was Sunday, attend a church service somewhere.

Her newest SUV was history. It could have been easy to eliminate considering its contents, a ready-made munitions dump, but she hadn't gone that way, even though she'd been tempted. She instead carried everything into her motel room and abandoned the vehicle in the dead of night in a parking lot off a wooded section of town called the Huckleberry Trail. By midnight she was back in her room.

Preference by L'Oreal. Her hair color choice, for today and the rest of this job, was Purest Black. She sat on the bed cross-legged in bra and panties in front of the TV, eating a jelly donut and sipping coffee from the lobby. Her hair, piled slick and glistening atop her head, absorbed the dye. She'd go from blonde to crow black in under thirty minutes. Draped around her neck and shoulders was a white towel in case the dye got away from her, which it did. Light black shadows colored the tops of her ears, darkened her wispy girly sideburns, and spread onto the sunburned nape of her neck beneath stray hair strands. She would buff the shadows out with peroxide after the news segment ended and she finished her donut.

Blacksburg VA Planned Parenthood Office Explodes. One confirmed dead.

CNN, MSNBC, plus we-interrupt-this-program thirty-second news updates on other network stations. Anchors, experts, a few eyewitnesses, and a pissed-off lawyer from the firm on the second floor of the building, all appeared in front of the cameras. Foreign terrorism or domestic? A gas line leak? A lightning strike? Yes, no, neither, both, all, maybe, probably, and some I-don't-knows. Larinda sipped more coffee, checked the room's thin local information binder, and found a nearby church with a ten o'clock service.

'Pure Black.' Crow-black hair color with a sheen. Like the Montana tribe she remembered from her American History studies, the Crow Nation; stereotypical Indian squaws in general. So proud of their straight black hair and their thick, copper-brown skin. Such savages. She could duplicate the hair, but for the time being her skin would need to settle for the reddish-tan tint the tanning session had given it. She'd maybe augment it with another session somewhere later, or a spray tan, to hide her freckles. All this to sell it, to sell *her*, better. To buy a few seconds of curiosity or hesitation, or misdirection, which could mean the difference between success or failure.

The screen crawl: *"Authorities are currently analyzing footage from multiple security cameras and taking statements from witnesses."*

Larinda needed to determine her next move.

It was Sunday. Unfortunately this one would not be a day of rest.

Back to the binder, to check for rental car information. Enterprise Rent-A-Car: *We'll pick you up.* She left a message, soon received a return call confirming she'd be good to go shortly.

This work had always made her a chameleon. Fake IDs, stolen credit card info, all of it the courtesy of unwary senior citizen contributors to a certain Texas ministry run by Reverend Higby Hunt, her spiritual advisor and her connection to The Faithful. "Use them for God's work only, and only when we assign it," the reverend had directed her. A self-prescribed mission to D.C.? Once they saw the outcome, they'd be good with it.

Rental car delivery was scheduled for nine a.m. The church service was at nearby Christiansburg Presbyterian. She opened an end table drawer, lifted out the Bible. After she showered she would spend some time with it. After that, she'd toss it into her gym bag.

The anchor on the TV screen cut into her thoughts, *"Blacksburg Planned Parenthood explosion now labeled a terrorist act. Homeland Security, the FBI..."*

She decided there was time for only one more clinic. The unborn babies scheduled to die there, whichever clinic she picked, would live at least one more day. She'd pray that their stay of execution, and the spectacle that provided it, would give their mothers the impetus to change their minds.

Larinda was not a terrorist. She was a crusader.

Roanoke was next up on her list, but it was less than an hour away. Too close to Blacksburg. That left Falls Church. Four hours away per her GPS. The last clinic in Virginia before she entered D.C.

SEVENTEEN

J.D.'s low growl awakened his master, this after a decent night's rest on Owen's surprisingly comfortable couch with Maeby across his ankles and J.D. on the floor. Sunlight blasted through the uncovered sliding glass doors. Out back of the house, with the sun just over the horizon, Owen's appliance and vehicle graveyard looked like a mini city skyline at dawn. Judge's fingers rubbed the sleep out of his eyes. Next to the couch at the opposite end, his German Shepherd focused on the view into the backyard. "Grrr."

In front of the uneven skyline on the other side of the sliding glass door stood Señor Quixote, all eighteen hundred gray pounds of him.

A staring contest. Señor Q's bull tail wagged, Judge's German Shepherd partner's didn't. Separating them from the bull, his massive head and his horns, was a flimsy sliding screen door. The danger jolted the grogginess out of him. He lifted himself onto an elbow. Maeby didn't move.

"Owen," Judge called, weakly. It came out evenly, he thought, like he was about to pour Owen some tea, not soil his pants.

From behind them, Owen answered. "Yeah?" Owen's fingers tapped a keyboard. "I'm finishing a column," he said and continued keying. "Relax. Q does this all the time, gets this close then backs off. Too cluttered for him in here to make a move, and he knows it. He sees you and your dogs. He's curious is all."

Judge didn't buy it. Less than fifteen feet away were some big, pointy horns. All those running-with-the-bulls videos in narrow alleys, with gored bodies, flailing arms and legs, and cluttered streets that didn't seem to slow the bulls down...Owen needed to call his rancher neighbor now, or better yet, the National Guard. Judge's Glock was under a couch pillow. He removed it, slowly, wondering how much damage the gun could do to that big, ugly head. He slowly swung his feet onto the floor, raised himself to a sitting position and rested the gun in his lap. Maeby hopped off the couch and joined J.D. in his growl. "Stay," Judge told them, and they did. Smart dogs, considering this was an animal with a whole lotta I-don't-give-a-shit-about-your-gun-or-your-dogs attitude. They watched the bull, and he watched them. Owen keyed his column.

A black blur that was Bruce the cat sprang from a patio picnic table onto Señor Q's head, pushed off from his nose and bolted toward the rear of the cluttered yard. Q snorted like a cartoon Toro, did an about-face and stormed after him in a cloud of dust.

Fifteen minutes later, Owen ambled toward the bull's breached post and rail fence dressed in his coveralls, the bull gone. Judge and his deputies watched from the family room. Owen tossed aside the splintered rails, found three tapered replacements in a weedy pile of gray ranch lumber on his side of the fence. He lifted each end and shoved them inside the empty post rungs. Except for the snapped electrified wires, the fence was repaired. Back inside, he made the call to his neighbor.

They were finishing their breakfasts at a booth inside the Jack-in-the-Box restaurant near Owen's house, the dogs still catching up on sleep in the van. Judge sipped his coffee and depressed buttons on his phone, calling his Iraqi War bud at his home in Allentown. Owen continued to tap away on his laptop in between taking bites from his jumbo fast-food breakfast platter.

"LeVander. Good morning."

"'Sup, Judge? I'm eating breakfast."

...nigger nigger suck my trigger...

A jumbled thought, the tic-like reflex almost escaping his mouth. Judge unclipped his rabbit's foot from his belt, put it on the table. All better.

The furry foot took Owen away from his column. "That thing is offensive, Judge."

Judge still listened at his phone, ignored him.

"You know how filthy those things are?" Owen added. "And you put it next to your food?"

Judge's facial expression said *Really, dude, I'm hearing this from you? Someone with a toxic waste dump for a backyard?* He covered the 'offensive' thing with his hand, which did his anxiety good. Soft bunny, cute bunny...

He turned his back to Owen, told LeVander why he called. "Larinda Jordan. She's got some issues."

LeVander snorted through a laugh, choked on his coffee. "Ya think? You're killing me, Judge. What bail jumper doesn't?"

"It's more serious than that. You see the news yet? The Planned Parenthood bombing?"

"I was at church. No."

Judge filled him in regarding place, time, impact, and national coverage, then reeled off what they'd found in the Fort Worth storage locker: victim souvenirs, bomb making materials, and fuels for said bombs. He finished with "Plus a few motel Bibles, and something else, something odd. Aside from the Bibles, one other book. On Native American religions."

Owen hocked up a huge hunk of hash brown on overhearing that bit of info. He grabbed for his carton of OJ and gulped through the blockage. Judge ignored his distress.

"That sounds off, Judge," LeVander said. "American Indians don't consider their beliefs religion. They call it spirituality. As in being one with nature."

"Fine, I misspoke, but the bounty is interested in it, whatever it is, and for whatever reason."

Owen butted in. "You didn't tell me about no book, dude. Let me see it."

"Hold on, LeVander, my Cowboy fan buddy here seems to have recovered from his perpetual hangover and is now being rude." Judge lowered the phone. "Owen, there is no book."

"You just said..."

"I don't have it. The cops took it," which was true. "Evidence." This shut him up, but Judge saw the gears spinning in Owen's head.

Back to LeVander. "The Feds are looking to connect our bounty to the bombing. I'm heading back east today. I'll make Blacksburg, Virginia, where that clinic blew up, a stop."

"Fine," LeVander said. "But just so you know, there's no combat pay for this. What's on the books for the drug charge is it, Judge. No other bounty money."

Jane's Baby

True, Judge was sure, and validation that LeVander continued to be one cheap-ass businessman. Which was why he still had most of the money he'd earned. "Well then, having re-thought this, LeVander, I'm deciding this one is above my pay grade. The locals and the Feds are involved now. So, sorry, but I'm bowing out."

"Judge, don't be like this."

"See you when I get home, sport. Adios."

Judge tossed the phone onto the table. A stare outside the restaurant window seemed in order. Typical LeVander. Cheap bastard. Screw him. Judge was finished chasing his bounty. He re-secured the rabbit's foot and was ready to leave. Owen punched keys on his laptop, flipped it around, put the screen in front of Judge on the table. "Is this the book on Native American religion you saw?" he asked.

It wasn't. "How about this one?" No. "This one?" No.

"This?"

By Jove..."That's it." American Hero-Myths. A Study in the Native Religions of the Western Continent.

"The E-book version is free today on Amazon. And now, ladies and gentlemen," he waved his hand over his phone like a magician over a top hat, then he pushed a button. "Presto, it's in my phone reading library."

"Happy for you, Owen," Judge said, still irritated with LeVander.

He decided now was when he should call Geenie. He'd promised to tell her when he started on the trip back. His phone to his ear, he laid things out for Owen, waiting for Geenie to pick up. "This thing's run its course. Where do you want me to drop you off, the bus? A train station?"

"Don't you wanna know about the book?"

"You ordered the same book the bounty had. You've got a hard-on for this as a news story. What else is there? We're done here, partner. I'm heading home." Into the phone: "Geenie. Hi. Judge. Hey yourself. Miss you too."

"Fine," Owen said. "Screw the book then. I didn't really need to buy it to know why our bounty has it."

"Hold on a minute," Judge said to Geenie. He covered the phone with his hand. Owen's smug smile said he'd figured something out. Judge didn't have the patience to pull it out of him. "Tell me, Owen, fucking now, why does she have the book?"

The smile widened showing glistening white teeth in a mouth too big for his face, his face too big for his braided head, his braided head too big for his body. "Naomi Coolsummer, the new associate justice, is why."

"Geenie," Judge said to his girlfriend, "let me call you back."

EIGHTEEN

Naomi peered out her living room window at the gated community's private street. A newly planted small maple lay uprooted next to her transportation. The street was littered with leaves and tree limbs. Severe late night storms had pounded the District into the early morning, and a tornado watch that just ended had pushed back the White House breakfast originally scheduled for seven. Edward waited inside the front door of her condo while she gathered her things.

"Marshal Abelson's truck again, I see," she said, and closed a briefcase.

"Still available for this assignment, Your Honor."

"Slight overkill, wouldn't you say, Edward?"

"Before, maybe, ma'am. In my opinion, now it's necessary."

She had no choice. The truck itself was fine, a kick-ass Texas ranch hand's dream machine that was better than fine, armor-plated and with bulletproof glass and bullet-resistant tires, but the fact it was needed at all was what bothered her. The heightened risk facing all the justices, the security measures the U.S. Marshal's office was taking, it was all very bothersome. Not solely because of last night's abortion clinic bombing. That might have only been a coincidence. It was because of *Babineau v. Turbin*, the case she hadn't wanted to discuss with Senator Folsom. Controversial, regardless of whatever the ruling would be. With Naomi replacing a conservative, the case would be a baptism of fire for her. The target on her back might be larger than the one on the other justices.

"I'd offer you something, Edward, but all I have is coffee or tea."

"I'm fine, Your Honor, thank you."

To her, Edward was unflappable, a bit like a Buckingham Palace guard, until the serious discussion he was having with her now, where he'd become atypically conversant and demanding.

"You will follow my orders, you will stay behind me unless I tell you otherwise, you will move when I tell you to. You will stay alert, and there will be no texting or phone usage while walking, and no glad-handing any well-wishers." After eliciting her agreement, he retreated inside his professional shell.

"Why don't you sit, Edward? We still have a bit of a wait before we go."

"I'm fine, ma'am."

The pickup truck entered the White House grounds and was met at the North Portico entrance, where Edward, as her chauffeur, bodyguard and plus-one, relinquished the keys. The truck received the once-over by Secret Service types and their dogs and other investigative instruments. When they entered the White House, they were escorted to the Family Dining Room on the State Floor.

"Justice Coolsummer, this way please." The White House aide stepped aside, her open hand directing Naomi to proceed to the dining room entrance, the door ajar. "Deputy Marshal Trenton, this way please." The aide pointed to an adjacent room where a place setting for one had been arranged at a small dining room table.

"No," Naomi told her. "He's my plus-one."

"But Madam Justice…"

"If you didn't want me to bring a guest, you shouldn't have offered it. He's not going to eat alone. Edward?" She wiggled her upturned fingers at him.

"Ma'am, I'll be fine." Edward remained expressionless, his hands folded in front of him, waiting for his charge to leave his protection before he followed the aide's directive.

"Nonsense." She reached out, grabbed his elbow. "The president intends to meet with me privately after we eat. No state secrets will be discussed over our pancakes and sausage, I assure you. I know you'd like to meet her, and you will. She's a charming woman."

She pulled him along a few steps but he stopped short, suddenly paralyzed. Inside the dining room, standing at the head of the set table with her family by her side, was President Lindsay. The angle of the president's head and her amused smile said she'd witnessed the exchange. Naomi dropped Edward's elbow and shook off the start the president's presence had given them. She advanced to shake hands. "Madam President. Good morning. I brought as my guest…"

"Yes, Madam Justice. So glad the two of you could make it. Good Sunday morning to you, Deputy Marshal Trenton. We're happy to have you join us. Have a seat, folks."

President Alfreda Lindsay, in the flesh, again. Her collar-length, tousled black hair boasted red highlights that weren't natural, this same soft, attractive look in evidence her entire twenty-year political career. A slim face with a dark cocoa complexion. Bi-racial, her African American father's genes much more prominent. Red blazer and skirt, white blouse, pearl necklace. Radiant and photogenic, with round, caring brown eyes that had bought her a lot of votes from all ethnicities. For Naomi this was, what, the third time she'd met with her? The fourth? For Edward it was his first, and Naomi was keen to his reaction.

The introductions with the First Family finished up, releasing some of the tension. First Husband Wesley Lindsay, a former South Dakota corporate lawyer with prematurely gray sideburns, was in a suit and tie today as most days, a dark church-going one with a three-point madras hanky in his breast pocket. And First Daughter Iris, age five, their coiled spring of an only child, with her mother's ebony hair and her father's Germanic-English blue eyes, wore an orange blouse and a black skirt because, Iris said to Edward, "These are Halloween colors. I'm going pumpkin picking with my daddy today. You look like a bear. You ever wrestle a bear?"

"Er…"

The president excused herself from Naomi.

"Let me rescue Mister Trenton." She stepped in, laid her hands on her daughter's shoulders. "Iris honey, let's leave Mister Trenton alone so he can have some breakfast, shall we? Go help your daddy cut up your waffles, sweetie."

"Okay, Mommy. Right, after, this!" She spun out of her mother's hold, sprinted across the room and face-planted herself into a couch cushion. She popped back up, all smiles, skipped back over to the adults and grabbed her father's hand. "Let's eat, Daddy!"

"Well," the president said to Edward, "that should take a little of the edge off. Shall we eat, Mister Trenton?"

"After you, Madam President."

"No, Mister Trenton, after you. You are my guest."

Edward complied without protest, his work face relaxed enough for a smile to form on the way to his seat. To Naomi, this was wonderful.

Fresh fruit, juices, specialty waffles, eggs, breakfast meats, multi-grain toast and muffins; a standard issue American breakfast. Naomi ate more than she should have, even more than the self-conscious deputy marshal Mr. Trenton. With breakfast over, President Lindsay, Naomi and Edward entered the West Colonnade for the walk to the West Wing. Once inside the Oval Office, the president gave them a quick spin.

"The Resolute Desk, carved from the timbers of British Arctic explorer ship Resolute. A gift from Queen Victoria in 1880.

"Portraits of presidents Washington and Lincoln. This commissioned bust of Reverend Martin Luther King. This next piece is of Lakota holy man and leader Sitting Bull…"

Naomi needed no introduction to it. It was a marvelous sculpture carved from red Verona marble, the tribal chief in his braids. She read the inscription to herself.

I am here by the will of the Great Spirit,
and by his will I am chief.

"This quote. It's one of my favorites, Madam President."

"Mine, too."

They were bonding, but for a fleeting moment Naomi was skeptical she was being manipulated. "Madam President…"

"This isn't staged, Justice Coolsummer, so let me put that thought to rest. I identify with those words, as does my genealogy. One of the great chief's two graves is in South Dakota, where my family relocated when I was young. My constituency."

Sitting Bull's remains had been exhumed, or to some, stolen, they were considered stolen, from Fort Yates by his family in what was now North Dakota, and reburied near where he was born, now South Dakota. North Dakota said the bones taken were those of a horse or a white man, not Sitting Bull. Naomi was aware of the history. All indigenous Americans were.

Jane's Baby

"He died in one state," Naomi said, thinking aloud, "and sixty years later returned to his place of birth. Or so the debate goes."

"Yes," the president said. "Which underscores that we're all nomads, with destinations sometimes thousands of miles and decades apart from our origins. It's fitting," she added, "to assume his wandering continued even after his death. Here, let me show you one more thing before we have a quick business chat and call it a morning."

Edward was a few steps ahead of the president's personal Oval Office tour, and standing on the other side of the Resolute Desk. "Ah. It seems Mister Trenton has already found it."

He was engrossed in the contents of a built-in bookcase but gave the two women a wide berth on their approach. Engraved pewter plates, colorful display dishes, law books, and smaller sculptures, plus one very charming photograph on a stand that impressed Naomi so much she felt herself choking up: Buffy Sainte-Marie, the Canadian-American Cree singer-songwriter-composer.

A Massachusetts family had adopted Ms. Sainte-Marie. Before graduating from college she'd returned to the Cree reserve where she may have been born, and was formally adopted by Emile Piapot, son of the famous Chief Piapot. Buffy to this day remained a Native American icon, especially for young Indian girls. Rejecting any ideas that she come on like "Pocahontas with a guitar," here she was, a very real person, with Big Bird in an autographed still from one of her appearances on Sesame Street. Scrawled across the bottom was her handwritten message in bold, black strokes: "Thank you for your work, now and in the future, Madam President. Continue to make us proud. Your friend, Buffy."

Naomi remembered this image from Buffy's first appearance on the children's program. A hero from her childhood in the seventies captured right here, vivid and breathtaking for her as a child then, and no less an inspiration for her as an adult now. Edward offered her his handkerchief. She dabbed her eyes, surprised at the impact this was having on her.

"It had the same effect on me," President Lindsay said before a pat on Naomi's shoulder. "Still does."

Their trip around the room ended at the door to the president's secretary's office. Edward took his cue and stepped inside. President Lindsay turned to Naomi and gestured that they should sit.

They drifted into superficial Supreme Court talk. How were her law clerks faring, were all four on board yet, did she like her office, any funny stories about meeting each of the justices, etc.? The president, thankfully, was dodging the obvious: the fall term Supreme Court docket.

"Well then. A big day for you tomorrow, Madam Justice." A presidential smile. "I know, that's an understatement. Would you mind if I call you Naomi?"

"As you wish, Madam President."

"I'd offer you the same familiarity, but something tells me you won't avail yourself of it."

"It's better if I'm forced to utter all the syllables, Madam President. It keeps me from drifting into any bad habits."

An acknowledging smile from her hostess. "Yes. No blurred lines. But remember this, Naomi." She leaned forward, laid her elbows onto her skirted knees and folded her hands, closing the distance between them. "You have one of the best young legal minds in the country. You are here because you deserve to be here. So don't let the old farts push you around."

"Not a chance, Madam President."

"I didn't think so. Two final things I must bring up. Occasionally," her tone was apologetic, "the elephants need to be acknowledged."

Naomi wasn't sure what her own face registered but inside, her stomach stirred in anticipation. The Belgian waffle, specialty coffee and spicy Andouille sausage she'd consumed weren't helping.

"Stare Decisis. Do you believe it holds? That legal precedents would require Roe to be reaffirmed?"

"Madam President, I'm not comfortable with the question, but I'll be polite. I'd merely be speculating that the decision, if the Texas ruling is upheld, would impact Roe. Respectfully, ma'am, that's all I'm willing to say about it."

The president shook her head in agreement, assessing Naomi's determination at giving a non-answer. "Fair enough."

Jane's Baby

The presidential secretary entered the Oval Office and tapped her watch. President Lindsay nodded.

"Naomi. There is one more thing. The attack on Planned Parenthood on Friday is being heavily worked by the security agencies. It's unclear at this point, but they're proceeding as if it's related to the Babineau motion. If it's a Court bellwether, or a warning, then the message might be for you more than for anyone else, because of your background, and because you're the most recent appointee. Judiciary tells me that security has been increased for all the justices until they can get their arms around this. Judiciary also tells me the U.S. Marshal's Service has authorized Deputy Marshal Trenton to remain assigned to you until further notice."

"I understand, Madam President."

"Good luck, Naomi."

Larinda followed the instructions that accompanied her online purchase.

You must 'tie up' the amount of ethanol in the flamethrower fuel with the equivalent amount of fresh water. Quick method: To produce a thirty-gallon-diesel, twenty-gallon five-percent-ethanol-unleaded-gasoline mixture, you are going to add one gallon of fresh water to it AFTER adding the Flash 21. Add Flash 21-A to the fuel mix. Allow the mixer to run ten to twenty seconds. Add Flash 21-B to the mixer, run ten to twenty seconds. Add fresh water (tap water is fine, bottled water better). Allow mixer to run until you have a consistent gelled product. Finished product viscosity varies from honey-like to a thicker, jelly-like fluid. The Flash 21 mixed product will retain its consistency even after two weeks of aging. Some separation is normal. Remix if necessary.

Simple enough for Larinda to follow. She worked inside her motel room, the windows cracked open, and she was being careful with the mixing. A tap on her door startled her.

"Who is it?"

"Enterprise Rent-A-Car, for Sabrina Norbert."

"Sure. Gimme a second."

Larinda finished loading up her burgundy Chevy Tahoe, larger than the silver Durango and a more comfortable ride, and with an excellent audio system. She popped in a CD from a set she'd acquired at a nearby Walmart and left for Falls Church.

Abraham begot Isaac, and Isaac begot Jacob, and Jacob begot...

The first lines of the New Testament were delivered in a rich, deep-throated baritone, unmistakable as James Earl Jones.

A wonderful voice, but no, no, no, not now, not this, it's all wrong...

She ejected the CD, tried another. "In the beginning..."

Ahhh. Genesis. On these Old Testament pages were God's words, straight from His mouth, with Mr. Jones' voice most excellently suited for them. Lovely. Four hours, five CDs of inspirational listening ahead.

"God's greatest hits," she said aloud. Events of biblical proportions. Perfect for her frame of mind.

NINETEEN

"You're making me regret this, Owen."

His attitude, his tantrums, his two-fisted assault of the van's glove box. And the beer. Lone Star. Right up there with Schlitz, Pabst and Piels. Texas goat piss. And Owen with an open bottle of it while they coasted out of Little Rock in the van, him raising it for a gulp whenever he wasn't pounding the dash.

"How...can they be losing...to the fucking Titans!"

Beer gulp, fist-pound.

It was Sunday, two-thirty p.m., with the Dallas Cowboys visiting the Tennessee Titans in Nashville, the game in the middle of the second quarter. The van was now headed east, about to leave Arkansas and enter Tennessee. They'd make Blacksburg, Virginia by midnight. Owen had his phone plugged into the van's dash, live-streaming the game from a Dallas affiliate.

Like most Philly guys, Judge's two favorite pro football teams were the Eagles and any other team playing Dallas. Owen's team was down by two touchdowns. For Judge, this was hilarious. For Owen, he was about to swallow his tongue. They were in Shearerville, Arkansas, just off I-40 on State Hwy 70, twenty minutes outside Memphis and the Tennessee border.

Gulp, fist pound. "Fucking fuckers..." A general comment directed at the Cowboys and the Titans both. Frustrated, Owen looked over his shoulder at the van's cargo area again.

"You really need all this shit back here, Judge? I mean, Christ, chains, leashes, vests, flashlights, it makes you look like you're into some really kinky shit. How about we get rid of some of it to reduce the weight? Maybe let this van clock in at something like, oh, I don't know, over forty miles an hour?"

They were cruising a state highway in the south with a black man riding shotgun, and said black man was a midget in Rastafarian dreads drinking beer from an open container. The speed limit plus five mph was the most Judge was going to chance, considering where they were. "You know, you're right, Owen. How about we do this?"

He steered onto the road's shoulder, held a sleeping Maeby in place by her collar and jammed the brakes. The tires screeched and Owen's seat belt nearly choked him. "A coupla things I don't need in here are you and your fucking overnight bag." He pressed the button for the locks and they clicked open. Judge nodded in the direction of the passenger door. "Get the fuck out."

"Okay, okay. Fine, Judge, never mind, you made your point. I'll shut up. Sorry."

"And stop pounding my dashboard. You're pissing off my dogs."

The Cowboys were mounting a comeback. "Damn, Judge, now that's what's for dinner, Slick!" So again Judge asked himself, why let this loose popgun tag along on what was now a case with a larger profile? In Texas, Owen had some juice, but now that they were in another state, his stock had dropped.

An admission on Judge's part: Owen was there for more than one reason. Judge saw him as an unedited version of himself; some of his inner demons personified. Plus maybe his behavior and small stature deflected some of the public focus from Judge's Tourette's. Maybe it was also the five hundred bucks Owen offered him for the ride-along. He didn't take the money, but he let him think he might later.

The Cowboys were on an extended drive deep into Titan territory, getting closer to evening the score when Owen turned from his phone and said, "Judge, I haven't had this much fun since my tryout with Wrestlemania. No, wait, that's a negatory. When I punched you in the balls was a pretty good time, too. Before they tased me." Beer gulp, belch. "I feel another installment for my column coming on"

"I'm thrilled for you."

"For my court blog. 'My Trip To The Supreme Court: Thoughts on *Roe v. Wade*.' Yeah. That's the ticket." He put the beer aside, opened his laptop and started keying.

The hum of the van on the highway, Owen keying, the dogs snoring, and the football play-by-play, all this white noise settled Judge back down, allowing him time to think.

Jane's Baby

Earlier he'd texted LeVander, to let him know he was back on the case, adding that he was bringing a Cowboys fan back with him.

Then another attempt at reaching Geenie. With her, what wasn't said kept things interesting for them. He'd given up finding someone after he lost his wife, then he met Geenie. This attractive, adjusted woman, her focused life, and his life for the past six months with her in it, it had all been amazing.

"About time you called again, mister," she said, answering on the first ring.

"What are you wearing?" Judge's best lecherous smile accompanied the question. Owen choked on his beer.

"Orvis," she said. "A colorful autumn print with twelve-point bucks. Flannel, neck to toes, with footies. It's cold in the Poconos today. Plus my face is broken out and I gained fifteen pounds while you've been away." A chiding tone. "Stop trying to impress your new friend, Judge. I know he's right there."

Geenie. The most striking fifty-plus-year-old woman Judge knew. Spanish in her blood, and naturally beautiful, and even if what she'd said were true, she was still an extraordinary gift to him. Before her interest in him, he'd been a most extraordinarily broken man.

"Fine. Busted. Hey, we're closing in on Memphis. Look, I'm still working this thing. We'll be making a stop at the Planned Parenthood clinic that blew up in Virginia, then we head to D.C. After that, home."

"I haven't been to D.C. in a while. Maybe I'll join you."

In Judge's head he said no, absolutely not, too dangerous. Except Geenie was far from the wallflower type. Judge knew this, and she knew that he knew. Still, the macho-guy protector part of him said no, no, no. He'd lost his deceased wife to their respective violent professions. He wasn't going to chance reliving that.

"You're not speaking, Judge, which means you're thinking. Which means you're looking for a way to say no. Which, my dear, makes me want to make the trip all the more."

"Look, a number of agencies and the local police are working this. So yes, the answer has to be no." Experience told him he needed to add a certain suffix to the ultimatum. "Please."

"You're cute when you get like this, Judge. Give me a call when you get closer, sweetie, and get ready for some seriously hot I-miss-you-so-much cuddling. Plus maybe I can help you with your bounty after you catch her. How's that?"

The problem was it was not a hollow offer, and it terrified him. "Um…"

Owen got loud. He was now Skyping with his Glenn Heights, Texas, police chief buddy on his laptop. He tapped down the volume on the phone carrying the game. "Say that again, Frannie," he said at his laptop screen.

"Hold on a minute, Geenie." Judge eased the van onto the highway shoulder and listened in on the conversation.

"I said," Frannie repeated, "tell your Marine bounty hunter friend that the Feds had hits on some of the other souvenirs from the storage locker. From unsolved cases in Oklahoma and New Mexico."

It was confirmed: the pen belonged to Mr. Beckner, the pastor. No surprise there. And Zachary Enders's parents now had his college ring back, but they still didn't have his body. He'd gone missing the year before Teresa Larinda Jordan graduated from the university.

Plus there were surgical instruments.

"This, gentlemen," Frannie said, Owen's phone developing an echo, "I'm struggling with."

The instruments were from a clinic in Oklahoma near the Texas border, according to Frannie, where there'd been an unsolved triple murder in 2010. One doctor, one nurse, one patient, all executed with point-blank gunshots to the head. Plus, "The blood from the smear on the forceps," he said, "is the same type as the murdered patient and her fetus. We're waiting on DNA test results."

Judge felt queasy all over again, but a few swallows choked it back. Owen and Frannie doubled-down with a goddamn Dallas Cowboys chant when they learned their team had scored a go-ahead touchdown. Judge hadn't forgotten Geenie, who was still on his phone.

"You hear all that?"

"Yes," she said. "Sounds like a nightmare."

"You still want to meet me?"

Jane's Baby

Say no. Please.

"Now more than ever, Judge."

Shit. "Fine then." There would be no talking her out of it, but she needed to hear him out. He turned away from Owen to lower his voice, Owen still whooping it up, still Skyping with his police chief friend. The Cowboys had just pulled off a lame-ass come-from-behind victory to stay undefeated for the season.

"Look, Geenie…"

The twist of a bottle cap. Owen bumped Judge's arm to get his attention with a freshly opened sudsy beer. "C'mon, let's celebrate, pardner. Your Eagles won today, too." He eyed the phone, then leaned over to raise his voice at it. "Hi, Judge's girlfriend Geenie. Owen Wingert here. 'Sup? So Judge here tells me you're a nurse…"

Judge hung up, reached over and pushed him back against the seat, his free hand to his chest, and held him there. "Will you just shut the fuck up, Owen? I need to have a serious conversation with her. No horsing around. Just…relax, okay?"

"Jeez. Okay. Sorry."

He redialed Geenie while keeping an eye in Owen. "No accounting for present company," he said, launching into it when she answered, "there's some serious terrorism shit going on here, and I don't want you getting mixed up in it, so…"

"So?" she said. Judge sensed she was enjoying this. "So then what, Judge?"

"Leave your guns at home, Geenie. Please."

"That's sweet, Judge, really it is, but we both know I won't do that."

TWENTY

She could have had a stretch limo for her first day on the job, a nice celebratory gesture offered by the U.S. Marshal's office. Naomi deferred to Edward and declined it in favor of the safety of the pickup truck he had at his disposal. Still, at seven-thirty a.m. on the first day of the new Supreme Court session, having to be concerned about her safety was something new for her, and a feeling she didn't like.

"You look particularly sharp today, Edward." His suit was dark, smartly tailored, and it tamed his beastly proportions in a manner usually enjoyed only by retired pro football players dressed for TV sports appearances. She let him open her door and help her into the back seat of the truck.

"It's a better fitting suit, Madam Justice. For your special day today."

"Well, it doesn't show much. Like there might be less weaponry under there."

"That's not the case, ma'am."

He shut her door, hustled around, and climbed into the driver's seat. They were off.

Naomi shuffled papers, her nerves getting the better of her. She put her law clerk biographies aside and retrieved a case document from her bag. *Babineau v. Turbin*. A hugely polarized first argument, for today, for the term, and for her as a new associate justice. They neared the Supreme Court building. A long line of people extended off the southwest corner at East Capitol Street, toward Second Street. As the truck circled the building, the line circled with it.

"Have you ever been inside the Supreme Court, Edward?"

"The court chambers themselves, only a few times, ma'am. Elsewhere in the building, many times, on special details."

Jane's Baby

"Good, then you can keep me from walking into walls whenever I'm not in my office. At least for the first few days while I get acclimated."

"Yes, ma'am. Ma'am?"

"Yes?"

"I've never seen so many visitors outside before. If they're here for courtroom seating…"

"I know. Most will be turned away."

She was aware this was a large opening day crowd, was also aware that it was less likely the result of it being the first day for the term, and more likely because of the first case to be heard. A once-in-a-generation thing. Historic. And, as she analyzed the crowd, looking more closely at their faces, she observed one phenomenon she hadn't expected: there were a number of Native Americans in attendance. Clusters of them. She blushed at this, again humbled by the interest.

She chided herself: *my ethnicity is my parents' doing, not mine, people.*

"Undeserved," she murmured.

"Did you say something, ma'am?"

"Nothing worth repeating, Edward. Let's get in so I can have a quick chat with my clerks before we start the day."

Larinda had dressed herself in exercise clothes with a woman's leather bag looped over her head, its strap across her chest. Facing her were three identical tan brick buildings in arrowhead formation, four stories each, comprising a small office park at the intersection of Maple and Gibson streets, Falls Church. She entered the tiny lobby of the middle building, stopped at the glassed-in registry and checked its list of occupants. Medical and legal offices, title searches, county offices, other professionals. Planned Parenthood, Suite 304.

She pressed the up button, exited the elevator on the third floor. Three glassed-in vestibules lined the wall on her right, all floor-to-ceiling panels with closed drapes: a social work agency, a county child services office, and a suite with no tenant. Her full-length reflection got the better of her. She stopped, lifted her sunglasses, and confronted herself.

Cher. Sixties or seventies Cher in sunglasses, but without the heavy mascara and eyeliner behind them. Tall and slim, with straight black hair. She remembered Cher from full-length glitzy glamour posters on the college dorm room walls of one homosexual student's room in her boyfriend's building, before she'd realized this was what this repulsive human defect was. Cher, with her rumored Cherokee ancestry, was all glammed up and on the dorm wall next to Mariah Carey, Lady Gaga, and Madonna. Today's Cher look wasn't planned, it had just happened, and it made her skin crawl.

At the end of the hallway was the entrance to Planned Parenthood, which occupied the three suites on this side of the building. She slipped a baseball cap out of her bag and onto her head, grabbed the door handle and pushed through. It was a little after nine a.m.

The waiting room, all warm earth tones and new age music, empowerment posters and baked cookies. Each of the feminist clinicians at work here deserved a bullet for such obscene, paganistic manipulation, for tricking these vulnerable women into getting in touch with their inner feelings. For soothing their consciences before the women descended deep into the bowels of this office to have their babies scooped out of them like chunky undercooked pudding.

She reminded herself that some of these people were innocent, specifically the pregnant women who hadn't yet made their decisions. She would destroy the clinic only if she could get the people in the waiting room out.

At the counter, a ceiling camera showed a green light. She shielded her face from it with her hand. A nervous, frightened pregnant woman might do this, so her shyness would draw no special attention. She spoke with a receptionist who was dressed in a nurse uniform.

"I, ah, don't have an appointment. Is there a doctor here today who performs the procedure? Would he have a moment to speak with me?"

"Yes there is, miss, but she has no time right now. I can make an appointment for you for this afternoon. She has time at four-fifteen. Can I have a name?"

"Jane Roe."

Jane's Baby

The receptionist/nurse moved her glasses down her nose and peered over them, her look skeptical. Her eyes softened, became compassionate. "Sure," she said. "We'll see you at four-fifteen, Ms. Roe."

Larinda exited the facade of the building, reconned both sides of it, reentered the lobby and left the building through the rear exit. One narrow sidewalk connected the rear exits for all three huddled buildings. Security cameras dotted the rooflines, just like at Blacksburg. It was tapered and tight back here, cool and wind-swept and given to shadows, but the payoff at the end of the sidewalk was worth it. A number of late-model luxury cars occupied the spaces. Reserved parking, with four spaces labeled "Agency Staff" all occupied.

When she flushed them out the clinic's staff would use this building exit, so they could get to their cars.

Something else she'd gleaned from her visit inside, from a slip-up by the receptionist: the doctor was in, and the doctor was a she. Larinda had been smart enough not to ask for a name. Asking could have been a red flag.

Back at her SUV she climbed in, sat, observed. Property Security consisted of one car, an old Hyundai Accent clearly marked "SECURITY" that sat idling in the front parking lot, its driver probably a retired cop. While she waited, the Hyundai took three slow cruises around the lot at fifteen-minute intervals, each time returning to the same parking space.

A half hour of recon was enough. It was time.

Two blocks away, up a nearby residential street, with single homes on deep lots on both sides, Larinda settled her Chevy Tahoe into another parking spot. She shoved a gun into a holster and the holster into the small of her back, under her exercise shirt. She wrapped herself in a hoodie, her long hair inside and down her back, the hood down. She exited the SUV, walked to the rear. Inside the carpeted cargo area was a jumble of equipment. She liberated a guitar carrying case and a motorcycle helmet. She didn't ride bikes, wasn't a musician either. With the guitar case tightly packed and heavy, she fit her head into the helmet and flipped down the tinted visor. Good to go.

Half a block away, the Hyundai rent-a-cop cruised the buildings and settled back in the same parking space. Nearby, on a park bench, Larinda sat with her helmet off, her guitar case next to her. Helmet on. She stood, retrieved the guitar case, and took a walk, ending up alongside the Hyundai. She rested the case on the blacktop. When she straightened up it was with her handgun drawn. She took one shot to the Hyundai driver's head. He slumped onto the passenger's seat. She and her guitar case resumed their walk into the front of the building.

Inside the first-floor lobby, her helmet on, the tinted visor up, she yanked a fire alarm and calmly retreated through the rear exit. At the end of the walkway she opened the guitar case, removed a midnight black propellant tank, two high-pressure hoses wound together in one sleeve, and a metal wand with a plastic grip. She assembled the brass spray tip to the wand and twisted the assembled handle into the high-pressure hose ends, then the two hose ends into the base of the tank. She slipped her arms inside the backstraps and lifted the apparatus onto her back. The wand in her hands, she pointed it in the direction of the sidewalk and waited. The wind picked up, whooshing toward her from between the buildings in waves. Forty-five seconds into the alarm, she got the response she wanted.

Three nurses exited the building and hustled toward her, their heads down as tiny swirls of dust and plastic bags and bits of paper whipped around them in between the buildings and against their faces. A hobbling matronly woman followed them, ushering her associates forward, making sure they remained in front of her. Larinda stood directly in their path, the face shield to her helmet raised.

The nurse in the lead, the clinic's receptionist, made eye contact with her. The woman's expression said *I recognize you.*

Yes, nurse, you do. Larinda internalized. *Jane Roe, today's four-fifteen. I'm a bit early.*

Larinda fired up the flamethrower and closed the face shield. The women had nowhere to go.

She squeezed the wand. The napalm-like liquid streamed forty feet, like a clothesline dripping liquid fire lighting up the sidewalk and its shrubbery, bright as a lightning strike in a California forest, drenching the receptionist, then a second victim. Inside her helmet their screams reached her ears, sounding hollow, like deep echoes from a sea conch. The two victims retreated a few yards until the fire streams overwhelmed them, dropping them into the burning fuel that pooled at their feet, the flesh melting off their legs, their arms, their faces. Larinda advanced, and with a lengthier controlled burst she incinerated the remaining nurse attempting to reenter the building, the stream of fire traveling sixty feet. The glass doors to all three buildings opened onto the walkway, with additional office workers about to exit. Larinda torched the shrubs in front of each, forcing them all back inside.

The last victim, the older silver-haired woman smocked in white as far south as her knees, backed up on wobbly legs. Larinda flipped up her helmet visor so she could look into the eyes of this murderer. The baby-killing doctor, in her sixties, maybe older, remained expressionless, almost resigned. "Please, show some mercy, this is murder."

"You're the murderer, Doctor." Larinda flipped the visor back down and tightened her grip on the wand.

The doctor turned and attempted a gimpy trot back to her office. Larinda stalked her, following her in no real hurry. The doctor trotted as fast as she could, lost her balance and fell palms-first onto the concrete sidewalk. She struggled to lift herself onto an elbow. Her squinty eyes turned into slits behind the shade from her raised arm. Larinda stood over her, her shadow tall. The doctor lowered her arm and opened her terrified eyes their widest.

Larinda's words were cold, joyless. "Here, Doctor, is a taste of hell before your condemned soul gets there."

"Please...no..."

Larinda stepped back and squeezed off another stream of liquid fire, held the wand steady even after the fiery baby-killing heap on the ground had stopped its screaming.

Sirens gathered strength from fire and police equipment still some distance away.

Larinda reentered the building through the rear exit, took the stairwell to the third floor and burst through the fire door. At the end of the empty hall she kicked her way into the Planned Parenthood suite and moved from room to room, torching each one until the smoke and flames got so bad she had to leave.

The office building's front entrance delivered one more person to the street-side parking lot, a tall, attractive woman in exercise clothes, long black hair, and sunglasses that she slid down over her eyes. No helmet or hoodie; Larinda had left them in the burning clinic along with the flamethrower. She hustled up the street toward a few huddled people, curious local residents gathered out front of their homes. Word of the carnage between the buildings had scattered most of the building's evacuees.

"Fire's on the third floor," she said to anyone who would listen. "I almost didn't (cough) make it out…"

The small crowd swallowed her up and gasped as flames shot from two third-floor windows, licking the brick exterior and increasing in intensity. Larinda strode swiftly to her car like any other panicked evacuee might, got in, and drove off.

TWENTY-ONE

Mind farts. Judge's affliction could generate thousands of them. An outburst was queuing up.

"...pig-faced, mung testicles..."

Inside the yellow caution tape, he and his two dogs and Owen stood in what used to be a tanning salon in Blacksburg, but was now a day-old crime scene, unmanned at the moment and picked over by the authorities, maybe even by the locals. He was glad it had been worked already. It reduced the chance of finding uncollected body parts. Otherwise it could become Iraq and Afghanistan for him all over again. This time his anxiety grew from the tangle of wires and wood and broken cinder blocks and exposed plumbing, plus a horrible blood splatter on a surviving section of ceiling and wall near the front entrance to the salon.

"Judge…"

Owen gave him room while swiveling his head to check for witnesses to the TS lapse. "Bro, it isn't cool you losing your shit like this in the middle of, you know, a crime scene."

Like Judge didn't already know. Like he could control it.

The meds, they did work, but sometimes what he saw in this business got the better of him, his inner being, his soul.

Judge launched into it again, a string of spit-laden holy-fucks and shits and things that rhymed with pig testicles then doubled over at the waist like he'd been gut-punched. Maeby pushed into the crook of his neck, to comfort him and to be comforted. The tirade soon petered out. Overhead, next to the bloodied ceiling, a large hole showed through to a clear morning sky where the roof had been blown into pieces, exploding onto surrounding properties.

The reasons for the yellow tape: one, it was a crime scene, and two, what was left of the middle of the store appeared to be unsafe, including the floor. A gas explosion after an IED blast, this was the official ruling by the fire department according to an overnight cable news report. When Judge and team got there after midnight last night they cruised the scene. Well-lit enough then, but seeing it in daylight made a lot more sense, and would be a whole lot safer. They had found a local mom-and-pop motel and crashed until morning.

What they were looking for now was proof that this was Larinda Jordan's doing, and Maeby's nose was getting hits all over the place from different bomb-making materials, some on the floor, some on what was left of the walls, some on a tanning bed. They were pretty much past the bomb discovery phase, so Judge gave her leash to Owen. It made them both happy, and it gave Owen something to do.

"Yo. Judge. She likes this spot over here."
"Good. Thanks. Give her a treat."

Something Judge had learned when they checked into the motel last night: Maeby liked Owen. She stayed with him in his room while J.D. stayed with Judge. There'd been one challenge with the arrangement: Owen said he talked someone at the bar into coming back to his room, and Maeby didn't let her in, forcing him and his "date" to consummate their arrangement in the woman's car.

"Judge. Over here, too," Owen said.
"Great. Give her another treat."

After Maeby's third hit and treat, a wizened Owen said, "Hell, dude, I'm just babysitting her, aren't I?"

"She likes you, Owen, but yeah, pretty much."

Judge concentrated on his big guy, newly rejuvenated with a whiff of Ms. Jordan's tee shirt. J.D. nudged a metal trashcan, upside down in the rubble, small, round, and blast-furnace black with a hint of a pastel green enamel in one section, like it had once been a trendy office cubicle trashcan, or something from a powder room. He pushed at it with his nose until it flipped onto its side. Judge tugged him away from it so he could get a better look. False positive; the can was empty.

They moved through the rubble, not sure how much time they'd have before an authority-type showed up and told them to get the hell out. The Shepherd jerked Judge into an about-face and stuffed his head back inside the same trashcan, pawed at its interior, pulled back out and barked.

Jane's Baby

"All right, you convinced me." Judge looked closely again at the bottom of the can. Not any less empty. "Sorry, J.D., I don't see anything."

He pawed at the inside wall of the can, his nails removing some of the soot to expose green enamel underneath. He licked at his paw. Judge put a hand inside, scratched with a fingernail at more of the blackened metal. Caked against it were threads from a flimsy fabric. He peeled a small patch of it back, its visible side black, but its underside had thin layers of material soiled a crusty brown, like a gauze pad with dried blood on it. In Ms. Jordan's apartment they'd found gauze and gauze pads and blood on her bathroom sink.

His dog wanted to eat the evidence. Judge wrenched him away from the trashcan and sat him down, rewarding him with kibble. "Good boy, J.D."

Two vehicles hopped the curb at the corner, one a cop car, the other an unmarked sedan, no sirens but both were advertising. Screeching tires, slammed doors. As trespassers Judge and Owen hustled back under the yellow tape and tried to nonchalant their way toward their parked van across the street. Judge resisted the urge to whistle while they walked.

"ATF! You two, stop!"

They complied and turned around, with Judge more resigned than nervous, then nervous as hell when he saw the guns. Four drawn firearms, two plainclothes ATF, two uniformed cops. His dog almost left his feet, snapping at the sight of guns and bulletproof vests that weren't his master's.

"Stay. Easy, boy…"

Judge reined J.D. in and had him sit, his deputy growling but otherwise behaved. Maeby, also growling, hadn't left Owen's side.

"Show me some ID," one of the ATF agents said, the only black guy.

Judge's fugitive recovery ID came out first, then his permit to carry, then his driver's license.

"I have a Glock. In my belt, around back. Nothing else on me." One of the cops relieved him of his piece and its holster. He shushed his dogs while the agent patted him down, except he couldn't shush himself.

"...testicle."

A Tourette's aftershock. Not much more than a peep, but still too loud. He coughed, gritted his teeth.

"You say something?" the agent said.

"Just quieting my dog," he said, stroking his deputy's head.

Another car arrived, screeching to a stop. "That's FBI," the ATF agent announced. "This is an ATF crime scene, but they piss off just as easily as we do, gentlemen, so be smart and cooperate."

Two more men climbed out, both in suits. They assembled alongside their gathering. Owen got more questions than Judge did, produced his driver's license and was polite, but Maeby stayed wary. They searched Owen, took his flask, but didn't try to search the dogs. A wise read on their part.

The black agent: "What were you doing in there?"

Judge answered before Owen could say anything. "We're tracking a bail jumper from Texas. This could be her work."

"This your van, Mister..." he looked at the ID, "Drury?"

"Yes."

"We need to look inside."

Owen's beer, far as Judge knew, had been fully consumed, but there were a number of empties in there. "Suit yourself."

His canine deputies needed to relieve themselves. A cop escorted the troupe to a nearby grassy patch while other cops tossed the van. The black agent motioned them back after the search.

"What is in your van scares the shit outta me," the agent said, "but my FBI friends here say you both check out. You, Mister Drury, apparently know someone in the Bureau. Some advice, gentlemen. In the future you need to consider this yellow tape, all crime scene tape, like it's a fucking radioactive pest strip. Don't go near it. Understand?"

"Yes, sir," Judge said. "We were just leaving, sir."

"Here's your gun, Mister Drury."

Owen spoke up. "How about my flask?"

"You're lucky it was empty. You guys are both lucky the beer bottles were empty, too," the agent said. "Quit while you're ahead, Mister Wingert. Go."

Jane's Baby

Judge was feeling benevolent. "You need to check out that office trashcan," he volunteered to the agent, pointing at it in the debris.

"For what?"

"Just look it over. My dog's nose says the fugitive we're tracking left something behind. Something that probably has some DNA on it."

They'd gotten what they came for, proof she was here, which also proved she was more dangerous than at first thought. The agent's thank-you for the evidence lead said they scored some points.

On their way back to the van they gave the unmarked FBI vehicle a wide berth. Owen got chatty again, looking to fill in some new blanks. "You know people in the FBI?"

"Geenie's daughter is an agent. Actually a supervisor. The two of them have this love-hate thing going on between them. Too much alike."

They ignored that the door to the unmarked car was open, and that the agent inside was scratching his balls while he answered a radio call, but they couldn't ignore the exchange. "Go ahead, Dispatch."

A female voice crackled over the FBI radio. "It's confirmed. Another clinic. Falls Church, Virginia. Five dead. Building is on fire. Stay where you are, gentlemen. Homeland Security and ATF are on it. More info when available. Out."

Four more hours to D.C. They'd be there by early afternoon. The clinic was across the Potomac from the Capitol; they would pass it on their way.

Same itinerary as Larinda Jordan, except she apparently decided to make it a stop.

TWENTY-TWO

"Enter from the left and take the left-most chair, Your Honor," the Marshal of the Court reminded her.

As the most junior member of the bench, Naomi followed two of her associate justice peers into the courtroom and sat as directed. She nodded at her newly minted law clerks, the four sitting together as part of the thirty-plus clerks observing the proceedings from the right side of the bench. In this morning's audience Naomi recognized four Native Americans in indigenous clothing from the line outside the building. She too had sat in on sessions before, as observer, guest, and an arguing attorney. This newest trip, to this side of the bar, was giving her goose bumps.

The Marshal of the Court called the Court to order. "The Honorable, the Chief Justice, and the Associate Justices of the Supreme Court of the United States. Oyez! Oyez! Oyez! All persons having business before the Honorable, the Supreme Court of the United States, are admonished to draw near and give their attention, for the Court is now sitting. God save the United States and this Honorable Court!"

The Chief Justice opened the proceedings. "Today's first case will be number fifteen dash nine-seventy-three, *Babineau v. Turbin*. Ms. Island?"

Some paper shuffling in front of the microphone, then began the opening argument from Kristin Island, representing the petitioner.

"Mister Chief Justice, and may it please the Court: The instant case is a direct appeal to strike down a ruling made by the Northern District Federal Court of Texas. The Texas ruling enforces a law that, before a pregnant woman is allowed to terminate her pregnancy, she must view an ultrasound image of her fetus and receive information on hypothetical pain levels the fetus might experience during the procedure. Miss Philomena Babineau, the petitioner, would not comply with the new state law regarding viewing the ultrasound image. With no proof of compliance, she was refused access to a legal procedure at a local clinic. She subsequently engaged a medical paraprofessional to terminate her pregnancy. This procedure successfully aborted the fetus but has left her unable to bear more children. It is the contention of the petitioner that the Northern District Federal Court of Texas ruling is a violation of her right to privacy as originally protected by the *Roe v. Wade* decision and relies on scare tactics disguised as prenatal guidance regarding a fetus' potential pain or discomfort in willful ignorance and disregard of the fetus' attained age."

Out of the pro-choice box with a bang. Ms. Island had thirty minutes to deliver her entire case inclusive of Court members' questioning. Then it would be the respondent's turn to represent the Northern District Federal Court of Texas in defense of its initial ruling, also with thirty minutes. The case would be won or lost in conference among The Nine, where posturing regarding a woman's right to choose would again rely on right to privacy, but this time it had to be tempered with the pain factor and the age at which a fetus felt it.

The Chief Justice and three other associate justices questioned Ms. Island during the course of her argument. Near the end of the petitioner's allotted time, Naomi weighed in.

"Miss Island, did Miss Babineau ever try to harm herself as a result of the Texas ruling, either before or after the abortion?"

"Your Honor, yes, she did, twice. Suicide attempts before and after the procedure. And she struggles daily with depression and anxiety in direct consequence of her inability to have children."

The Marshal of the Court signaled the Chief Justice that Ms. Island's argument time was up. "Thank you, counsel," the Chief Justice said. His hands folded, his gaze shifted. "Mister Turbin?"

The two attorneys and their shuffling papers changed places. Not lost on Naomi and the other judges was the sudden yet discreet appearance of six additional court police officers at the rear of the chamber, behind the audience. Simultaneously, two aides to the Marshal of the Court delivered slips of paper, one for each associate judge. Naomi's heart fluttered as she read hers.

"Falls Church Planned Parenthood arson. Five dead. No specific threats have been made to the Court. The additional court police you see are a precaution."

Mr. Kenneth Turbin, Assistant Attorney General for the State of Texas, began his argument. "Mister Chief Justice, and may it please the Court..."

Senator Folsom lit a cigarette and put a phone to her ear. She closed the glass partition separating her from her driver, her car on the way to the Capitol for a Senate hearing.

"Does anyone know where she is?"

She heard a pencil tapping and some nervous coughing from the other end, both sounding cavernous in her ear, the coughing first by a man then a woman, but the senator got no other response from within the conference room at Reverend Hunt's Christian Charismatic Ministry of Wisdom and Light.

"Higby, I swear to God, I thought your group had convinced her it was in everyone's interest that she disappear. Hello? Goddamn it, I hear you breathing! Answer me!"

"Mildred, calm down please." The reverend's Texas drawl was more of a deep-in-the-heart-of kind, evident even on the phone. "For all we know, she has disappeared like we told her. She would normally contact someone on my staff during an assignment. We have no confirmation that either assault was her doing."

"Assaults? These are terrorist acts! The second was an execution of five people!"

"Fine, Senator. But it seems out of character for her to..."

"Listen to me, Higby. The federal agencies are tracking multiple persons of interest now, domestic and off shore, all with MOs like this, and they're looking to close this out before another tragedy hits. The Capitol police tell me she's on a short-list for this, damn it! How did she get on this list? Why can't you find her?"

The reverend took her off speaker. "Mildred, she's out there, alone, and not contacting us. I get no answer from her phone. If she's involved, I don't know why, and I don't know why now. We're checking credit cards associated with some of the aliases we gave her. We're working our way through them. It might not be her."

Jane's Baby

Mildred rubbed her forehead. This timing had been nothing short of bullbat crazy. The swirling cigarette smoke hung inside the limo; she powered her window down to let it escape. When the Supreme Court building popped into view, she took measure of it.

This arm's length, public view of the Court from the outside, this is the reason.

"She's anti-abortion, but..." Mildred said, thinking out loud.

"Aren't we all, Mildred?"

"...but she has no idea what is about to happen."

Larinda Jordan aka The Church Hammer knew only what the public knew, that a liberal feminist was now on the bench as the potential swing vote that could overturn Texas' *Babineau v. Turbin* at the Supreme Court level. Overturning Babineau meant *Roe v. Wade* would again survive intact. Like the rest of the public, this was Ms. Jordan's worldview.

"Could she get to her?" Mildred asked.

"To whom?"

"Our new Supreme Court justice."

"She's a force to be reckoned with, Mildred. It's possible."

The senator took another drag from her cigarette, held the lit end up and pondered it. Smoke slipped through her lips, rose languidly in front of her eyes.

"Our Church Hammer needs to be found, Higby, or she'll ruin everything. Someone needs to hand her an angel harp. Immediately."

One oral argument was scheduled for the afternoon, with new presenting attorneys and new Court guests. When everyone had settled in, Naomi picked out Deputy Trenton in the Court's guest section, prearranged per her invitation, and here as her guest, not her bodyguard, or at least that was how she viewed it. Edward sat stiffly in his seat with the other invitees, the seat a bit too confining for him. Upon closer inspection, the U.S. Marshal's Office had apparently decided on similar treatment for all the justices. Many of this session's Court guests gave the appearance of bodyguards.

Naomi scanned the audience again, located another small pocket of Native Americans, a copper-skinned man and woman sitting together. A few seats removed from them sat a third, the woman's dark hair straight and long, tucked behind her ear on one side to expose a distinctive southwestern earring with feathers, reminiscent of bygone days on the sunny plains. A younger version of Buffy Sainte-Marie, Naomi told herself, now feeling warm and smiley inside at the thought, until the woman retrieved a pair of sunglasses from her pocket and put them on. A no-no in the courtroom, like cameras, radios, phones, other electronic equipment, and weapons. A court officer arrived at the end of the row and gestured for her to remove the sunglasses. She returned them to her pocket.

TWENTY-THREE

Judge eyed the middle building, one of three arranged in a triangle, and the floor where the Planned Parenthood office was. Or used to be. A hook and ladder engine, some police vehicles and one emergency van still sat helter-skelter in the parking lot, close to one of the entrances. Firemen continued pouring water into the gap that was once a large portion of the building's third floor, damaged as bad as if a small plane had hit it. The brick corner was missing, blown out from the intense fire, all the windows on this side of the floor gone, the tan brick above them discolored by black fingers of smoke that reached up and connected with the floor above. They reconned the perimeter, staying on the blacktop and away from snaked fire hoses, Judge holding his leashed deputies, Owen alongside them. More fire equipment plus an unmarked cop car in the rear parking lot, where crime scene tape surrounded a yellow Hyundai sedan, the body removed. Here they were able to get close enough to see between the buildings, where the carnage had gone down.

Wall-to-wall scorched black earth. Yellow tape sealed off the sidewalk, keeping bystanders from the corridor, in it a tiny paver patio, a charcoal barbecue sitting amid metal picnic benches on more pavers, and the skeletal remains of a Corona umbrella sprouting from a circular stone table. The shrubs and grass and everything at ground level were gone, the black from the fire creeping up one wall. For Judge, a throwback to a crazier place and time, in Iraq, where occasional scorched earth initiatives produced similar results. He coped with it, stayed in control. At the base of the blackened wall, on landscape mulch tamped down by heavy-footed firemen, a pink spray-painted outline stood out. More spray-painted grass and sidewalk were in evidence beyond it amid the char-broiled scenery: three fluorescent pink amoebic outlines that looked vaguely human in shape. The remains of these people had been removed. Judge found a fireman and volunteered his services and those of his deputies.

"They're trained as military working dogs. Explosives detection and fugitive tracking. Need any help?" He did the introduction up right, badging the fireman with IDs.

"Check with the federal agent over there. He's in charge of the criminal investigation."

Judge learned quickly the agent was Homeland Security, and like Judge, a former enlisted Marine. The agent said no, he didn't need their help but yes, he'd share what he knew. He pointed at the third floor, "a flamethrower did that," then at the exit corridor on the ground, where four of the five people had died, "and all this. The guy left the flame-throwing equipment behind, on the third floor."

"It's a woman," Judge offered. "Here." He handed him Ms. Jordan's mug shot. The agent barely looked at it, handed it back, looked Judge over instead.

"We know." The agent sniffed, his way of apologizing for having shaded the truth. He suddenly tired of Judge's questions. "Look, sorry, Gunny. The gender info is part of the person-of-interest qualifier we're holding back. Keep your mouth shut about it. Now go, so I can get back to work."

Owen was doing his own thing near a transit stop, talking to two women who had just gotten off the bus. Judge checked his phone. Multiple texts had queued up.

From Geenie:

—On my way, love. Be there by eight tonight. Where to meet?

From LeVander:

—IEDs and flamethrowers and shit? For real? Cut bait dude. Feds will handle it. Bail gets settled either way, just not by you.

One of the two women Owen was speaking with, a teen, was whimpering. Owen offered her a hanky, seeming genuine about it. The older woman accepted it on the younger one's behalf.

"Gracias," the older one said. The girl continued crying. Owen had them sit on an empty bench inside the bus stop enclosure.

Jane's Baby

Judge and his dogs kept their distance but Owen soon motioned them over. Maeby was a hit with the teen, the girl's tears finally receding. She scratched Maeby's brindle head, was entertained by her wiggling stubby tail. His German Shepherd deputy J.D. stayed out of it.

More Spanish between them. It was a mother-daughter thing, with Owen eventually in the middle of it, holding his own in the conversation. He sounded serious, compassionate. Their bus arrived.

Owen tucked a business card and some cash into the mother's hand, then took down some info in return. Mother and daughter climbed aboard, peered out the window from their seats, the mother throwing a kiss in Owen's direction. He gave her a thumb's up.

"I'm afraid to ask," Judge said. "What was that all about?"

"The daughter's pregnant," Owen said. "They have no money and can't afford to travel to another clinic. I gave her a few bucks and my phone number, told her to call if she needed more help."

"Generous of you, Owen, but it's not like you live around the corner."

"I'll figure it out. Right now, I feel a social media rant coming on. Let's get back to your van."

They started back to the other side of the building. Owen stayed quiet, his silence masking a mounting anger or a resigned hopelessness, Judge not sure which. "Hey. Looks like you could use some fur."

"That sounds so wrong, Judge, but yeah, sure, if you'll let me walk your dog, I'd like that."

He handed him Maeby's leash. Owen pet her tight brindle coat, she gave him a lick on the hand, then tugged him forward.

They hadn't had this conversation, hadn't shared their views, pro-choice vs. pro-life, and Judge didn't plan to. It had to have been conflicting for Owen, with him maybe even buying into his mother's reasoning for not wanting him, knowing how things continued to be a challenge for a person his size. Judge expected the other part of him was just thankful he got to have this discussion with himself at all. It was something this young girl might now get to do, her options maybe kept open because Owen had offered to help.

Judge texted his girlfriend Geenie as they walked:

—Find a restaurant dtown DC. Text me when you can.

He sent the next text to his bondsman buddy LeVander:

—Still out here fishing dude. She's a cold-blooded killer. I'm in it for the duration.

TWENTY-FOUR

Naomi exited the courtroom with the other justices, the court's police officers shadowing them step by step, foot echo by foot echo, the justices peeling off one by one to retire to their respective chambers.

Inside her chambers she settled in with a late afternoon cup of coffee, served in an elegantly hand-painted Johnson Brothers Wild Turkey Native American cup and saucer, part of a set her clerks had presented her in celebration of her first day. As she sipped, she thought about *Babineau v. Turbin*. It had two prongs, the second prickly as a porcupine.

She expected Stare Decisis, the been-there, done-that doctrine of precedent, as in rendered decisions reigned authoritative in future cases, to address the first prong, as long as the facts were essentially the same. Her read, and corroborated by questions and comments voiced by her peer justices, was that the fourteenth amendment's right to privacy provision, rendered as it had been in *Roe v. Wade*, would dictate striking down the lower court decision that had instituted mandatory ultrasound viewing. Ms. Philomena Babineau would prevail, the decision could have written itself, if this were all they'd need to address. But it wasn't.

Called into question, and hanging as a tangent off the Texas ruling, was the pain of the fetus. Ms. Babineau had had the abortion at twenty-two weeks after fertilization, within the legal federal maximum of twenty-three weeks, but past the new legal Texas age max of twenty weeks. Twenty weeks was becoming the new pro-life cry in many states, not just Texas. Beyond that age, per some doctors' opinions but not yet validated by science, it was posited that a fetus felt pain. If true, or if ruled as true, this could be a game-changer. This case was therefore all or nothing for both the petitioner and the prior Roe v Wade decision. To affirm the Texas ruling by accepting the twenty-week premise would change the factors used to originally decide Roe. If one undermined the facts, one undermined the decision. There'd be no recourse if the Texas statute were upheld: a new strain of Roe would rear itself, with the strong likelihood of obsoleting the 1973 decision. Abortions would return to the back alleys.

Advantage, pro-life, disadvantage, pro-choice and feminism. She admitted she disliked this prospect. The admission of this bias, in these chambers inside this hallowed courthouse, with disregard to her oath, and ignoring whether her bias did or did not play well with the Constitution, shamed her. She lowered her coffee cup to its saucer, the contents suddenly bitter and undrinkable.

"Come in," she said, in response to a knock.

"Your Honor," Edward closed the door behind him, "sorry to bother you. Can you tell me when you plan to leave today?"

"I'd like to stay until around eight. No need to wait for me, Edward. I'll get a cab."

"I'll wait, Your Honor."

"Senator." Higby Hunt was on a speakerphone with Senator Folsom.

"Reverend."

Senator Folsom sat in her Capitol Hill office awaiting delivery of a print version of the morning's oral arguments, bootlegged by a sympathetic law clerk. Higby Hunt spoke to her from his office in Texas.

"How did she do?" the reverend asked.

"The new kid on the block. Fairly quiet as I understand it from our Texas district ADA, but that's typical. Once I read the transcript we'll know better."

She watched cable news as they conversed. The names of the dead in the abortion clinic fire had been released early afternoon. No suspects had been identified per the news anchor, but there were "persons of interest. The dead include a long-time resident physician of the clinic and three medical assistants. No patients were involved."

"Mildred, turn off your TV please," Higby's speakerphone voice asked. "I have an interesting development."

She lowered the volume instead. "What is it, Higby?"

"A news item from that local anonymous Texas blogger who fashions himself an expert on state and federal court cases. You need to check it out. I've decided to come back to D.C. tomorrow. I think it's necessary."

Larinda double-parked her Tahoe SUV on a D.C. street a block from the Supreme Court Building. Binoculars raised, she watched a Lincoln Town Car limo leave from an underground garage exit, then another, then another. Two black, one charcoal. She was here to pick out one to tail, but she had no reason to select one over another. This process of elimination could take a few days. A fourth car service limo exited. Four out of nine, all within an hour of the end of today's session.

She decided. She'd tail the last car to leave, except she hadn't a clue how late that would be.

Funny. Some justices reveled in their freedom from needing security, well documented as to how much security was not in place. They traveled the city, the world, unnoticed, like everyday citizens. The two clinic attacks and one of the Court's fall agenda items had changed this. If an interested party were able to uncover these security details, enhanced court police presence, U.S. marshals, car service, the anonymity these judges enjoyed on the outside would be removed. Oh, the irony. A self-fulfilling prophecy, and she liked prophecies. Prophecies were good. The Bible had many.

She lowered her binoculars. In her rearview she caught a Segway as it scooted past the end of the street. It backed up, stopped, circled in place, then changed direction. It now moved swiftly up the street, closing in on her SUV, the operator's features more discernable the closer it got. Dark helmet, grey uniform top, navy uniform pants, fluorescent yellow vest. A black female, no weapon visible; a parking authority employee. The Segway arrived.

"You can't park here, ma'am," the officer said into her open window. "Move your car."

"Yes, officer. Sorry."

Larinda circled the block, a two-minute ride, returned to the same spot, and with the Segway gone she again double-parked, hoping she hadn't missed any of the exiting limos. She raised her binoculars. Ten minutes passed. It was close to four p.m. Another limo exited the garage. She'd now seen five.

The limo rounded the corner just as another parking authority Segway quickly bore down on her. She lowered her binoculars to the floor before it arrived. The operator tapped on her passenger window then showed Larinda his thumb, mouthing "Move."

Larinda again circled the block, taking a little longer this time, returning to the same spot. She was getting annoyed. Limo number six exited. Impatient, she decided to follow this one.

Another Segway arrived, this one gliding into her SUV's path before stopping. Goodness, it was the same Segway operator who'd stopped by thirty or so minutes earlier. The operator glared at her.

"Ma'am, I gave you a chance," she called, loud enough to better the SUV's idle, "now I'm writing you up. Pull in over here."

The operator pointed to a short alley in the middle of the block, with dumpsters and a loading dock and room for maybe three vehicles, the alley surrounded on three sides by multiple stories of brick. Larinda complied, checking her mirrors. The operator dismounted the Segway and recorded her plate number. Suddenly the operator stopped writing, leaning in closer to the rear of the SUV. She squinted into the tinted window.

Larinda saw it too, in the rearview. The tarp covering her cargo had an un-tucked flap. A carton of ammo and the butt end of a rifle were visible.

She had a split second to assess the situation. Short alley lined with commercial waste containers, an empty loading dock, after hours, no witnesses. An easy decision. The second decision was pending: handgun or knife?

Larinda pushed open the driver's door. Ambulance sirens rose and fell, chasing away the white noise of a city at night.

"Ma'am, you need to stay in your vehicle," the meter maid said, raising her voice to better the sirens.

When Larinda reached her she raised her weapon, a handgun with a suppressor. The woman's eyes got big. "No! Wait! Please..."

"You're just doing your job, miss. I understand, and I'm sorry. God bless you."

Jane's Baby

She cut her down with one shot to the face, the pffft overwhelmed by a crescendo of ear-piercing sirens as they dopplered past the alley.

Larinda grunted as she hefted the body over the side of the dumpster. She leveraged the Segway, handle first then the wheels, not as heavy as she'd expected, and she deposited it with the body. The Segway ignition engaged when it hit the metal floor. It banged around inside, its wheels kicking up trays of bread loaves and cheeses and vegetables and other scrapped food, sending some of it airborne before it shut down. She tossed the woman's electronic ticket pad into the passenger seat of her SUV, snugged up the cargo tarp, and quickly backed the SUV out of the alley.

Some luck: an empty space opened up near where she'd been double-parked. She executed a three-point turn and slipped into it. Chances were, not all of the justices had left. She raised her binoculars again and settled in.

TWENTY-FIVE

Another text from Geenie:

—It's 8 pm, hot stuff. Time to make the donuts.

"She's at a Dunkin' Donuts," Judge told Owen. They were still in the van, negotiating D.C. streets near the Supreme Court building.

"I like Starbucks," Owen said.

"Geenie doesn't. Me neither. You lose."

At a red light he texted Geenie back and got the location. Somewhere on 23rd Street, on the George Washington University campus. They'd get something to drink, some light sandwiches, "...and then we're checking into a D.C. bed and breakfast that accepts pets," Judge told Owen.

"A B&B? Sweet. How'd your girlfriend know I'm a B&B kind of guy?"

"She didn't, and I'm guessing you're not. Best behavior tonight, Owen. She traded on her B&B network reputation to make these rooms happen on short notice. That means no whores in your room. We have a deal?"

"What's the alternative?"

"You find another hotel. Or you're on the street."

"Well, not really, there's your van."

"You're funny. That's not gonna happen."

A trendy address for the donut shop, on the first floor of a multi-story brick and stamped concrete university low-rise, not too far from Georgetown. The sunlight was gone and the campus lighting had claimed the tree-lined street, with Maeby and J.D. chilling in the van, the windows open far enough for Maeby to sniff at the foot traffic. J.D. sacked himself out in his crate. Basic Dunkin' Donuts décor inside, with plastic tables and a tiled floor.

Jane's Baby

Holding down a table in the corner of the shop was Judge's girlfriend. Judge made the introduction.

"Owen Wingert, meet Geenie Pinto."

Owen took off his hat. They shook hands and exchanged pleasantries, him devouring her and her dark, porcelain-smooth face and neck, her healthy pecs and toned arms, and her short, espresso hair. Judge surrounded her with a tight hug. After they all sat, Owen couldn't contain himself.

"Damn, Judge," he said, admiring her. "Just…damn."

"Chill, Owen."

Sandwiches and drinks for the three of them. They ate, talked, and Owen stayed cordial, although it was clear he was impressed. His reaction said his bounty-hunting mentor didn't deserve this exquisite creature, and in Judge's estimation he was right. If Judge told Owen she was Judge's senior by a few years, he would have choked on his food.

"I'm not sure what my next move will be," Judge offered.

"Simple," Geenie said. "Be near the person your bounty is after."

"That's what I told him," Owen said then sipped his coffee. His laptop was open and he returned to pounding away at it. "That's why I'm going to Court tomorrow, to get in as a visitor. Did it once before, years ago. It's cool, even when someone isn't trying to kill a justice. Now it's way cray-cray."

"It'll be easier, Geenie, if you act like he isn't here."

"First stop tomorrow," Owen said, ignoring Judge, "will be the Supreme Court building. Early wake up. Seating for oral arguments opens at nine-thirty. If I get in line by seven, seven-thirty at the latest, that should do it."

"Sounds doable," Geenie said. "What do you think, Judge?"

"That's early. What about breakfast?"

Owen keyed while he talked. "Not a problem, Judge. You sleep in, have your crepes and quiche and fresh passion fruit while Geenie and I check out the oral arguments. She'll be fine with me."

Judge would sooner have a lit firecracker up his ass. "Fine. I'll miss breakfast then."

"Tell me about this bounty," Geenie asked.

She heard all of it. Background on Larinda Jordan, the murdered pastor, the murdered mother-and-son parishioners, the stolen Bibles. The storage locker and the description of the damage to the two clinics. One blown-up teen, four torched Planned Parenthood women, and a security guard executed at point blank range.

"I'm not getting the connection," she said. "The clinic attacks, I get. The pastor...what's his name again?"

"Darlington Beckner," Owen said.

"Why him?"

Owen googled him on his laptop. He retrieved an obituary first, read some of it out loud.

"Seventy-four years old. Adoption agency director earlier on, until 1989. His wife predeceased him but, hell, it wasn't by much, only three weeks. He's survived by four adult kids and a slew of grandkids."

No new insights from the obit. "Other Internet crap on him. Personal interest stories and kudos from the press, things like that, for his past adoption agency work with orphaned kids, then with underprivileged Texas families as a preacher."

"Larinda Jordan's either a serial killer," Judge said, "or a militant pro-lifer gone off the deep end."

"Or a hitwoman." Geenie's chiding look said not to struggle with the concept. "They're out there, Judge, in real life, not only in the movies."

"Okay. Maybe. But the clinic damages tell me she's an unhinged pro-lifer."

"Assassins get assignments. This church pastor murder sounds more like a hit to me, Judge. Could be both."

"But why him?"

Owen's phone rang. "Hey, Frannie, how the fu..., ah, how the frig are you, bro?"

Judge dished for Geenie: "Owen's Texas police chief buddy."

"So how'd you like it, Frannie? Wait, stop. Aw c'mon, Frannie, relax. Stop yelling, asshole. Fine. FINE. I'll take it down, goddamn it. Look...hello? Hello? Shit."

Judge squinted at him like, what now?

"It seems a few law enforcement types caught up to the blog entry I posted an hour ago."

"Who'd you piss off this time, Owen? Dallas Cowboy stadium security?"

"The FBI." He went sheepish. "And it's the court beat column, not the sports column."

"You use a pen name for that one," Judge said.

"I do local police blotter stuff, too. Frannie knows the alias."

"Which is?"

"Thurgood Cochran. You know, a combination of Thurgood Marshall and Johnny..."

"I get it, Owen. Let me see the column."

"I have to take it down or they're gonna come after me for obstruction of justice. Might still come after me anyway."

"Christ, Owen, just let me see it."

He pulled it up. Judge and Geenie read it in silence.

Your trusted local court reporter, reporting from the granddaddy of court venues, Washington D.C., on the road with a real-life bounty hunter. Tomorrow I visit the Supreme Court to watch America's federal justice system at work during the first few days of its fall term, with newly confirmed associate justice Naomi Coolsummer from the great state of Texas on the Bench.

No, Judge thought. Fucking no.

After that, it's back on the job, knocking on doors in the District with the bounty hunter, a former enlisted Marine...

Goddamn it, no.

...who's chasing a Planned Parenthood terrorist...

NO.

...with his two dog deputies trained by the military. And here they are, folks. Don't let the small one fool you.

Judge couldn't believe what he was seeing.

Any comments or info or leads, put 'em in the box below. Wish us luck.

Owen might as well have painted a target on their backs. No pictures of any people, but there were phone snapshots of his canine deputies. Add to that, his girlfriend Geenie was with him now.

"How could you possibly think this was a good idea, you...fucking...idiot."

"We need leads, right?" he said. "Publicity gets leads..."

Judge was about to lose his shit all over the little bastard, Tourette's-assisted or not. "It also gets people killed. I don't get you, you self-destructive, alcoholic..."

"Judge," Geenie grabbed his hand, "calm down."

"...goddamn clueless little..."

She repositioned his hand to the rabbit's foot on his belt loop but it wasn't helping him one bit, no siree, didn't stop him, wouldn't stop him from saying it, it was coming out right...the fuck...now.

"...piece of shit SECOND BASE."

The rabbit's foot, plus Geenie's hand in his, plus the most hurtful look Judge had seen on a human being in a long time, finally worked together to calm him down. But his mind was made up.

"That's it. You're gone. Tomorrow morning I'm shipping you back to Cowboy country. Get in the van."

"Bro, look, I'm sorry, we needed leads..."

"Shut the fuck up. Take the blog entry down. We're getting the hell out of here."

The laptop started burping before he touched another key, giving off single ploink and bloink noises that sounded more appropriate for comic strips or cartoons than a computer.

"Judge..."

"WHAT?"

Comments were popping up, the bloinks and ploinks and kerflinkles all passing gas on their way to filling up the bottom section of his blog, and quickly. "Wow," Owen said.

They looked over Owen's shoulder. What Judge saw was horseshit, a page full of crazies come to visit, witnesses to every alien abduction and Kennedy cover-up and gun-grabbing conspiracy ever posited, one after another, misspellings in all of it. "It's all BS, Owen. More trouble than it's worth. Like I said, tomorrow, you are gone."

"Look at this one," he said, pointing, "here."

One entry stuck out because of the name of the person who had posted it.

Email me at the funeral home address with your phone number. I have additional information. Darlington Beckner Jr.

TWENTY-SIX

Larinda, her binoculars up, waited on more limos to exit the Supreme Court's VIP parking garage. The street lighting for this part of the District was overkill, as good as an urban college campus at midnight. She'd seen seven limos leave. She'd prayed on this, hoped, expected, that one more, or maybe both, hadn't yet left.

After she purged the Court of the savage justice who could ruin everything, she'd need a place to go. Mexico, or maybe return to the Philippines. Yes. They loved her in the Philippines. She tossed an occasional look down the alley to keep tabs on a certain trash container. No one had come looking for the missing meter maid. Yet.

Limo number eight, another Town Car, exited the garage. She twisted on her SUV's ignition, ready to follow, except...

A large black pickup chugged out of the underground lot. Oversized tires, four doors, with chrome exhaust pipes that reached upright behind the cab. Distinctive. A workingman's diesel that a Texas girl would be proud to call her own. Like all the cars before, it needed to pass her parked SUV on the one-way street before it could go in any other direction.

It lumbered toward her like a tank. The side and rear windows were tinted, making it too dark inside to know if anyone was sitting in the back seat, but there was no tint on the windshield. She'd gotten a good look at the driver on the truck's approach up the street, a large man with an earring that looked like a...yes, it was a bear claw.

An Indian? A surprise, but then again, not really.

Forget the Town Car. This would be the Texas judge's preferred ride, and the Indian her preferred protection. Larinda eased the SUV away from the curb and entered traffic.

The Indian driver would be super vigilant. Larinda prayed for protection as soon as she started the tail, but prayer only did so much. The Tec-9 on the seat next to her would handle anything that divine intercession would not.

Edward caught the end of the yellow light then floored it up T St. NW, to the middle of the block. A sharp right onto cobblestone brought the truck another fifty feet to an abrupt halt in front of the townhouse community gate, the brakes biting. Naomi recoiled from the stop, bouncing back against her seat.
She caught her breath. "What is it, Edward?"
"One moment, ma'am." He spoke a few crisp, final sentences of marshal-speak into a wrist phone, something he'd been doing for the past few minutes. She understood the implication when his eyes focused on the last intersection they passed through, visible outside the right passenger side window about a half-block away. Her gaze followed his, up this street full of parked cars on both sides and some moving traffic, with the cars from the next block cruising casually through the green traffic light to pass one-by-one behind their idling truck at the gate.
"Burgundy or dark red Chevy Tahoe, copy that," Edward said into the phone. Then, to Naomi, "Let's stay here a moment, ma'am."
He remained seated with his back to her, but he removed his right hand from the steering wheel to reach inside his jacket. When it reemerged it didn't return to the steering wheel, instead was left where she couldn't see it. Two cars from the moving traffic passed behind them at the townhouse entrance. A third car, or rather an SUV, a large one, crept up the street.
The traffic light at the intersection a half-block away stayed red, traffic queuing up behind it. A dark sedan careened onto the street and accelerated quickly, stopping within inches of the creeping SUV, then a second nondescript sedan arrived from the other direction, jamming its brakes short of a head-on collision. A D.C. police car slipped in behind the first sedan, its lights flashing.
A gruff bullhorn voice announced "FBI!" and told the Tahoe's occupants to show their hands out the window. Two seconds passed, three, four...The driver's window opened and a pair of hands reached out.
"ANYONE ELSE?" the bullhorn voice said. "SHOW US YOUR HANDS. NOW!"

The other windows powered down, revealing three more sets of empty hands, all shaking.

Multiple law enforcement types with guns drawn dragged a woman out of the driver's side of the SUV and crammed her face against the blacktop.

The second, third and fourth occupants were pulled from their seats: two Asian women, whose unsteadiness gave away their advanced age and a younger Asian man, all with their hands up as directed.

Edward punched in a security code Naomi read to him from her phone. The truck entered the community and the gate closed behind it. They waited.

Edward spoke into his wrist, answering a call. "Trenton."

The FBI agent laid it out for him. "It's an Uber car service, marshal. Tourists looking for their Airbnb lodging. False alarm, buddy."

"Thanks. Thought it was a tail. You guys did a nice job. My bad. Sorry."

The truck rumbled down the gated community street in less of a hurry and stopped at the end of the block, the engine still running. "My apologies, Edward, for causing you this much excitement on my first day. Would you like a bottle of water or a soft drink for your ride back? Some hot chocolate?"

"No, Your Honor, I'm fine. My apologies to you, too, ma'am, for the false positive. I'll get something to eat shortly."

After a quick visual canvass of the street, Edward opened the truck door for her. She stuffed some papers into her bag and stepped onto the truck's running board. Edward helped her onto the sidewalk.

"Once we get past the inconvenience of these public circumstances," she spoke as they climbed steps, "and we know the last day I'll have you to myself as a marshal, I'd like to cook you a meal before you leave. Does that work?"

They arrived at the top step of her home. "I'd need to clear it with my supervisor, ma'am."

She rested her hand on his arm, squeezed it to show she was serious. "The answer needs to be yes, Edward. You've been most kind to me through all this. Make your supervisor understand. Please."

Jane's Baby

"I'd be honored, ma'am," he said. "I'll do my best." His thick, serious face and his eyes softened, their blinking a bit more rapid.

He regained his composure. "I need to escort you inside, ma'am."

The truck Larinda tailed caught some of the green lights she hadn't, which opened up the distance separating them by almost a city block. She goosed the gas, needing to keep her target in her headlights. They were deep inside Georgetown now.

A vehicle slipped in front of her, another large SUV entering from a side street. The traffic light at the corner turned red, stopping the interloper and Larinda both. Larinda fumed, had to calm herself with an oxy while waiting for the sidewalk LED indicator to count down the time pedestrians had left to enter and leave the crosswalk, the seconds ticking away, seventeen, sixteen, fifteen...she was going to lose her target...

Tick, tick, tick...

The vehicle in front of her looked familiar. Another Chevy Tahoe, in a dark red...no, a burgundy, just like hers.

The light changed, the traffic advanced up the busy two-way street, all vehicles including Larinda's moving slowly, slower than the speed limit, another intersection coming up.

Hustle it up, people, move, move, move...!

The yellow traffic light turned red, the burgundy Tahoe in front of her drifting through the intersection. It crept away from her, moved up the next block, its brake lights tapping on and off. Larinda's jaw tightened, she craned her neck...

Her target, where was it?

She eyed the traffic in both directions.

Run the red light. Do it.

She didn't get the chance. A car careened into her path, roared up the street. A second car followed, this one the D.C. police, the two vehicles screeching to a halt followed by a door-slamming interception and assault halfway up the block. She heard a third speeding vehicle arrive. Three vehicles from two directions, all with law enforcement personnel exiting their doors, all with weapons drawn. They rousted the occupants of the SUV, four bewildered civilians with their hands up, two of them elderly. All were made to lie down on the blacktop.

There...the truck...it was on the right a little farther up and perpendicular, sitting on a side street, hanging there, waiting...no, not on a side street, it was stopped in a driveway...

Her target truck moved a few lengths forward. An iron gate closed tightly behind it, the truck gone from Larinda's view.

Paralyzed, she witnessed the federal agent takedown in progress. Same make, model and color Tahoe as hers, on the same street at the same time, stopped by federal agents, and now in their possession. It could have been her, might well have been her, was maybe supposed to be her...

"Almighty Father," she prayed, teary-eyed, "Your benevolence, it is...overwhelming. Thank you. Thank you, Heavenly Father..."

The traffic light changed. She turned, found curbside parking, breathed deeply, and cleared her head. A brush with capture, and yet her reconnaissance wasn't finished, couldn't be finished, because she needed more info. She grabbed a ball cap from the backseat. Time for a touristy walk. With her SUV locked up she hustled around the corner, onto the block with the police activity.

The lookalike SUV shakedown was wrapping up, with D.C. cops controlling the small crowd Larinda joined across from the gated entrance to a townhouse community. On the sign attached to the community's glossy black iron fence: "A new private enclave. Twenty-eight distinctive residences in prestigious Georgetown. One elegant home left..."

There it was, the black diesel pickup truck, parked at the last of six townhouses on the right, the three-story end house visible. Behind Larinda and a few onlookers, the stoop she sat on led up to an older brownstone. She climbed to the top step, which gave her the view she needed.

The driver stood side-by-side with his charge on the townhouse's front porch, remained vigilant while he checked out the crowd, his glances lingering at the apprehended vehicle outside the community gate, its former occupants still being questioned. The big man dwarfed the truck's female passenger, yet to Larinda the relative height, body shape and hair color of the woman all fit. This was the Indian judge. The justice unlocked her townhouse door and the two entered the unit, its first floor lights switching on.

Jane's Baby

After five minutes the driver exited the residence. Once back inside the truck he fired it up and let it idle a moment, its thrumming interrupting an otherwise quiet, empty community street. The truck left the curb, reversed direction and returned to the front gate. It lingered there facing the police activity, then exited right.

"Show's over, folks," a cop called to the small crowd. "You need to disperse. Go back into your homes or keep moving..."

Larinda now knew the house. A good thing, sure, but at the expense of a bad one: the Feds might still have a bias against burgundy Tahoes. As she walked, she spoke into her phone. "Hello? Enterprise Rent-A-Car?"

She circled the perimeter of the small community on foot, confirmed it was fully enclosed, the iron fencing interspersed with sections of brick wall, all of it too tall to climb. Each townhome style featured a large rear deck off a French-door kitchen with a patio beneath it. The judge's end unit had four entrances, front, side, and two rear. The community's construction appeared finished except for final street paving, the paving equipment already on site. She finished her walk where she'd started, outside the community's front gate, and took a seat on a sidewalk bench amid the nighttime foot and car traffic that continued past her in both directions.

Time for a close-up of the keypads for the entrance gate. Across the street from the entrance, Larinda played with her phone, adjusting the zoom.

One keypad was affixed to the perimeter's iron enclosure, eyelevel for pedestrians, and the other sat atop a pole next to the cobblestone driveway entrance, for residents and guests in vehicles.

Zoom in, zoom out, zoom in, hold, press, save. Now to wait.

Patience. A phone app generated multiple Bible scripture verses on "patience as a virtue," and she used them to pray while she waited, another oxy helping to mellow her. But her phone also gave her something else.

Info on today's Supreme Court session. Broadcast news for the general population that the *Babineau v. Turbin* ultrasound case had been argued, that it was now in the hands of the justices, that the decision could come as early as this week, or it could come at the end of the judicial year, or anytime in between. Such was the independence of the Supreme Court.

Also trending on the Court: new Associate Justice Naomi Coolsummer, the destroyed abortion clinics, and a blog entry by a court beat writer traveling with a bounty-hunting Marine and his military trained dogs. The entry already had a few hundred views since its posting late today. According to the blogger, the Marine was tracking the person(s) responsible for the abortion clinic deaths.

The descriptions, the dogs, the circumstances: it was the same guy who dragged the faggot boy and his dead mother away from the trailer park fire. The blog said the Marine and the blogger were now in D.C.

There was space at the bottom of the blog entry for comments.

Footfalls stopped her keying. A woman jogger legged it up the street on the other side, slowed and stopped at the gate, still running in place. Larinda raised her phone, pressed zoom then began recording. The jogger punched numbers into the keypad and entered the community.

TWENTY-SEVEN

They fit well together, Judge and Geenie. Porters of extraordinary baggage, and sharers of deep, dark secrets. Seekers of agnostic absolution. They forgave each other their faults, transcended their differences. They were superheroes, to themselves and, at times, to others. They were mistress and master of the woebegone, because they were humble enough to count themselves among them, and wise enough to realize that together, along with the other emotional downtrodden, they could be stronger than the perils out there. And when Judge and Geenie made love last night and this morning, it was caring, it was savage, it was tender, and it was glorious, and it was something Judge had believed he'd never find again, until he had.

Five a.m. Geenie's head and arm rested on Judge's bare chest in their room on the second floor of a lavish B&B, a double brownstone in the middle of a chic residential block in Georgetown. Her breathing was soft, warm, and sensual. She was the epitome of contentment and comfort, her cooing so calming that Judge balked at slipping out from under her, but he needed to, to find out if Owen had heard back from the dead pastor's son yet.

There was also a familiar toxic bouquet that originated at floor level, a gift from the room's other occupant. His Shepherd deputy paced next to the bed, his security-blanket leash attached to his collar. The air about the room said he needed a walk.

Maeby had roomed with Owen. It was against Judge's better judgment after Owen's dumbass, unconscionable blog entry, but he let it happen based on Geenie's prodding. Owen's lucky day.

"Grrr." A reminder from his deputy that a bio break was necessary.

"Can it, big mouth, I'm on it. One quick stop first."

He knocked on the door to Owen's room. No rustling inside, no dog bark, no answer. He could well be drunk. As soon as J.D.

did his business and they got back upstairs, Owen would get a wake-up phone call.

Man and dog padded through the well-lit B&B parlor, steering clear of a baby grand and the hurricane lamps and other beautiful heirlooms on antique end tables, musty oriental rugs the only knock on the place. They stepped down onto the back porch, and in the predawn shadows Judge eyed a "Pets go here" sign on the other side of a garden, an arrow pointing to a gated alcove in the rear brick wall. In the middle of the garden was a cobblestone patio. Here he found Owen, sacked out and snoring on a cushioned lounge chair, his laptop open, Maeby asleep at his feet, a blanket across them both. He was in different clothes so he hadn't slept out here, and he didn't reek of alcohol. Maeby's head popped up as J.D. passed. She laid it back down.

Behind the gate was less inviting, a section of alley afflicted by a blue waste container with a stench as overpowering as the Philly fish markets, even at five-thirty in the morning. Judge's partner found a weed-covered grass patch and began his process.

"Hustle it up, big boy."

Something rustled in the blue container behind them, cat noises accompanying it, plus squealing, then thrashing. A brown rat catapulted out of the trash and dropped onto Judge's shoulder, slipped off then landed in the alley and bolted into the B&B backyard. J.D. was in mid-squat. No matter; where the rat was headed, it had no chance. Judge leaned back through the gate to follow it while his dog finished his business.

Maeby, on the patio brick next to Owen's chair, had the rat in her mouth and shook it with a terrier vengeance. When its neck broke it stopped squealing, went limp, and was gone. Maeby, her mouth full of brown and bloodied rat, looked to give someone her trophy. She hesitated, eyeing Judge then Owen.

A scuffle behind them in the alley raised J.D. to the balls of his feet. Up, and now galloping, he spun his master around while drawing his leash taut so he could reenter the yard. A blur had already passed them, a second rat bigger than the first, making a beeline for Maeby on the patio. Maeby faced Owen, oblivious to what was coming at her from behind. J.D. barked. Maeby turned, her mouth still occupied. The rat pounced.

Jane's Baby

Owen dropped the thinner end of his closed laptop with a two-handed vengeance behind the rat's head. Squash-splort-crunch. He got to his feet to put his weight into it against the brick patio, grinding the laptop until there was full separation, rat head from rat body.

"Fuck you, rat."

"Owen. Dude."

"Yeah, bro?"

"You okay?"

He breathed heavily, stared at his disgusting handiwork. "Yeah."

Owen now had his own rat trophy, so Maeby pranced proudly over to Judge to show what she'd caught. The German Shepherd reached the headless rat body, nudged it, did an about face and returned to his master without it, awaiting further instructions.

"No return call from the funeral parlor yet," Owen volunteered, studying the decapitated rat. "You bring any poop bags with you?"

"Yes."

"Help me clean this up then, will ya, pardner?"

Judge decided that for the time being Owen had earned an upgrade, from dismissed to on probation.

Geenie and Judge met Owen a little after seven a.m. in the parlor, ready for their trip to the Supreme Court and a close-up look at the target of their target. Maeby and J.D. would chill in their B&B room for the morning. Owen, on his phone, paced the parlor while winding down a call.

"Flowers, too? No, no, I got it, all off the record. Flowers and a card, but I can't report it. I promise. So sorry for your loss, Mister Beckner. Bye."

Owen flashed a smile that took up two thirds of his face. "Learned some really tight shit, guys. Dope Frannie didn't tell me." He sauntered toward the B&B exit, his index finger pointing forward. "To the Bat-van! I'll tell you on the way."

"Look, Owen, you're still on a short leash."

"Sure thing, boss. Let's go."

Owen sat in the van's fold-down jump seat behind Geenie. "Let's hear it, Owen."

"Darlington Beckner's son is a fan of my Thurgood Cochran blog. When the Secret Service interviewed him he shared some info, with them and with Frannie. They told him not to share it with anyone else."

"So he tells you, a stranger? An Internet blogger with an alias? And he expects that info to go nowhere else? And why the hell is the Secret Service involved?"

"No idea about the Secret Service, but, you know, I wouldn't tell anyone anything..."

Judge grunted, stifling a laugh. "Whatever he told you is BS, Owen. A hoax. Bad as the birthers and the tinfoilers out there. Someone is funnin' you."

"Really? How about this then? He knew about the killer's Montblanc pen trophy. The one that was his father's."

A detail not released to the public. "Fine. Go on."

"So Junior says his father had a reservation for a flight to D.C. scheduled for the day after he was murdered. And..." He lengthened the word, paused for effect, and waited for Judge to give him a drum roll.

"Cut the drama, Owen."

"And they received flowers and a sympathy card from the White House! No clue why, he says, considering they hate the Feds. Especially, and I quote, they hate 'that mongrel president.' Now that's some shit."

By themselves, the airline ticket info and sympathy card weren't much more than well-intentioned surprises for his family, but the Secret Service saying not to tell anyone about them was, well, odd.

"Any other leads, Owen?" Geenie said, trying to be supportive. Judge's eyes narrowed at her, his don't-encourage-him-else-you'll-regret-it look. Her stern face said to back off, hot shot.

"Two hundred seventy-two reader comments on the blog entry. I read 'em all. Some crazy shit, but nothing else worth following up." Owen's meaty brown fingers paged down his phone screen.

Beep. "And here's two-seventy-three," he said.

They entered a line of cars waiting to enter a parking garage. The Court website warned that no weapons were allowed on the grounds, and that inside the Court building there were lockers for hats, overcoats, cameras, radios, phones, books, briefcases, etc., but visitors needed to leave their Second Amendment rights elsewhere. Judge removed his holstered handgun from behind his back after they advanced another car length, opened the glove box and shoved it in. He left the glove box door open for Geenie. Presumptuous on his part.

Geenie's emotional baggage was of Sherpa-guide proportions, and only a little less violent than Judge's. She'd lost her father when she was a kid, in a bank hold up. He took a bullet for her, and she saw him die. It was something Judge had accepted as providing much of her worldview, both deeply ingrained and irreversible, and she trusted few people outside of her hometown Pocono Mountains friends. She stared at the open glove box before retrieving her small Glock and its holster from behind her back. She put the gun on top of his, was casual about it, but discreet enough to pull it off without Owen noticing her doing it. In Judge's mind, maybe she subconsciously hoped she didn't notice herself doing it either.

"Whoa," Owen said. "This last comment. Some hard-core church shit here."

"Let me hear it," Judge said.

Owen read. "'If a man hurts a woman with child, so that her child departs from her, and yet no harm follows to the child, he shall pay as the judges determine. But if there is harm to the child, then thou shalt give eye for eye, tooth for tooth, hand for hand, life for life.' Exodus."

"Your blog entry is a pro-life crazies magnet. I told you this would happen. Delete it like Frannie said. Or the Feds will come after you, us, for not paying attention."

Another phone beep. "What is this shit?" Owen struggled with the new message.

"You gonna share it with us or what?"

"It says, 'A righteous man regardeth the life of his beast. Proverbs.' Both entries are signed Anonymous. 'Sup with that crap?"

Beeeep. One more entry. Owen silently read it; Judge waited. Owen pushed himself out of the jump seat and leaned forward. "It says, 'I'll kill your dogs if I have to.'"

Judge eyed the locked glove box for a pregnant moment. It stayed locked, had to stay locked, because they had no choice if they wanted to gain access to the Court for the reconnaissance they needed. But his affliction cued up a response filled with alliterative pearls about stuffing crocodiles and kumquats and Croatians into his bounty's lady parts, comments best left for the confines of the van. The parking lot ticket machine spit out a ticket. Judge ripped it out, and at unsafe speeds they found a space two levels up.

Seething, Judge warned them both. "Get out."

Geenie opened her door mid-TS tirade, said, "Let's give him a moment, Owen."

TWENTY-EIGHT

Larinda sipped burned black coffee while she keyed search info into a desktop computer in a motel lobby in Arlington, Virginia. She paged through an online Bible, stopping on occasion to read a few passages. She'd give herself five minutes more before she left for the Georgetown Waterfront Park in D.C., where she'd lose her most recent prepaid phone in the Potomac. After that, she planned to do some escape route planning. Her online response to a certain Internet blogger had garnered feedback.

—To Anonymous: Let's meet. You can tell us what is troubling you. Maybe we can help.

She chuckled. A funny man, this Thurgood Cochran.
Larinda typed another response in the comments area:

—You should hope that meeting never happens.

'You can tell us what is troubling you.'
Larinda crossed the Francis Scott Key Bridge into Georgetown with her new SUV, a Toyota. Rush hour traffic, both sides heavy. Alternative routes per the navigation system were no help. Toughing this out was her only choice. On the river below the bridge were a few kayaks, paddleboats and an outboard. It was considerably less crowded. A better place to be than where she was. She made a mental note to that effect.

She punched the radio scan button in search of a good D.C. evangelist for the few minutes she had before Reverend Higby Hunt's morning Power Hour. After a spin through the dial, she found no preacher worthy of her time. Radio off.

'...tell us what is troubling you.'
What troubled her was what would happen after she killed the justice, because her elimination was not a permanent solution. A

new appointment, another confirmation hearing, and a new justice would take a seat. Still, she could only deal with what she could control. And what she could control was killing the judge. It would keep this Court, now suddenly a festering scab of liberal majority, from rendering decisions detrimental to Christians. Decisions that had killed millions. Eliminating the judge counted for *some*thing. She was doing *some*thing.

Which included getting herself all worked up. She needed some scripture, needed to tune in to some soothing, reaffirming scripture. She popped an oxy.

Her phone on, she found KLTY, her go-to online radio station. It was the top of the hour.

"Now, back to the Christian Charismatic Ministry of Wisdom and Light Cathedral based in Dallas, Texas, streaming live to you today as a simulcast from W-M-W-L Christian Radio studios at FM one-oh-five-point-one in..."

A godsend, always, to hear the clarity of a good, God-fearing person deliver God's word.

...the nation's capital...

Here? In D.C.? Why hadn't she known this? Car radio on, phone off.

"Reverend Higby Hunt. Let's give a big virtual clap of the hands for evangelist Higby Hunt!"

...virtual clap of the hands for evangelist Higby Hunt!

"Thank you, dearest friends in Christ, for your hospitality." The *reverend turned full preacher, now punctuating every phrase. "I do not have a prepared sermon. I am here, in this great District, for the next few days, as an observer. To provide unqualified support, to a very important, yet difficult, judicial process. To bear witness, to the birth, of change."*

Jane's Baby

Also in the studio, Senator Mildred Folsom. She faced the reverend, headphones around her neck, there for when it was her turn to speak. She felt the electricity in the room: Christian evangelism royalty was on the air, on their airwaves in particular, in their studio. The reverend would introduce her shortly as a guest on this, his daily show, which had temporarily taken to the road. Right now it was all him. And it was all about today's very special message."

What the senator and Higby both knew: Larinda Jordan would be listening. She did not miss a sermon.

"Yesterday an attorney presented to the Supreme Court an argument regarding a case first decided in my home state of Texas, but the case could have been decided anywhere. Texans know the case's importance, and the reasons the original decision was handed down. To inform women. To let them know that a fetus feels pain earlier than first thought. Not all women, not all Americans, agree it is necessary to teach pregnant women about the life they carry inside them, and that, my friends, is a shame. However," he raised his index finger to make his point, visually scanning the studio, connecting with his small audience, *"there is such a thing as too literal an interpretation of the Bible. And trust me, my friends in Christ, that I do know me some Bible."* He winked at the senator while he dialed up a little down-home vernacular. *"And an eye for an eye only makes everyone blind.*

"We need to let this judicial process play out. I, and the rest of the faithful, implore whoever is responsible for these horrific, violent acts against these clinics to please stop. If the urge to commit this violence rears itself again, call me, or the studio, or another clergyman. The message you are sending is wrong. The justices our representatives have chosen as our nation's interpreters of the law are smart, caring people; each of them, young and old, new and not so new, from wherever they hail. They are sworn to follow America's jurisdictional bible, the United States Constitution. But like us, they are human. Imperfect. And like us, they can be led down a sinful path. God will forgive them if they seek His forgiveness. God will give them the grace they need to make things right, however many times they are called. We, the faithful, pray

that this time, they do. That this time when they rule, they will see the light. That they will correct the sins of the past. But they must be given their space to do so. The space to let the process happen, without interference.

"And now I have the distinct pleasure of introducing a U.S. Senate stalwart for over thirty years, a woman who has done everything humanly possible to help shape the American judicial process in God's image. One of the faithful. A true Christian, a true Texan, and a true American. My friend for over forty years, Senator Mildred Folsom."

The reverend reached over, offered a fist bump to his tag team partner in Christ. The senior senator returned it. The small audience in the studio clapped and hollered.

"Reverend, thank you very much. I won't take up much of your time, 'cause I know some of you out there still got to slop the hogs, dig the well or dress some beef before breakfast. (Laughter.) Aside from reinforcing the reverend's message about non-violence and adding that I too am a good listener should those who are responsible want to reach out, I have one important notion to get across today. There walks among us, assuming she is still alive forty-plus years after her birth, a person most of us would not believe exists. Someone who is the antithesis of all the other someones whose lives were terminated. Those terminated someones, because of a certain Supreme Court decision, now number in the millions. I speak, of course, of Jane Roe's baby. Because nature took its course before Roe v. Wade was decided, she was not aborted. Yes, she is out there, an adoptee, but no, she has never known who she is."

"So we need to ask ourselves this: If you were this person, how would you feel if you suddenly learned your identity? Would you be happy to have lived your life? Happy to have produced your own progeny? Knowing the alternative, yes, of course you'd be happy, and thankful, for all of it. But would you be thankful enough to want to make a difference for future unborn lives? One would hope so. Now take it a step further and indulge me. One of you is this person. The Roe baby. If given the opportunity to

preserve life, as this person you should choose to do so in acknowledgment of the death you were spared. And, again reiterating the reverend, you must have faith in the judicial process. Have faith that we, the faithful, have put the right justices in place to achieve this outcome. What is upon us now is a decision that will stop the marginalization of the unborn. Let the process that is in place for producing that decision produce it. Thank you, and may God bless you."

There had been four distinct references to, or more like messages from, 'The Faithful' on the reverend's program. Larinda counted them. This was code. It meant listen up, Larinda, this broadcast is for you.

The message: no more clinic attacks, no more violence, period, and oh, by the way, you need to call us. Everyone, it seemed, wanted to talk with her. The blogger, the reverend, the senator. Federal agencies. Everyone wanted her to come in.

She tapped on the steering wheel, processing this. Her SUV crossed the bridge, and a beautiful day that had started out with so much promise in Arlington had soured, rain coming down in torrents on the Georgetown side. She killed the radio, listened to the rhythmic swipe of her wipers as the SUV crept forward in the traffic.

For her, the math was obvious. With the new associate justice in place, every Supreme Court decision Larinda might care about from that point forward would be five-to-four or worse, always the wrong way. She didn't get the senator's logic. It was out of character for The Faithful to leave something to chance.

'Let the decision be rendered. Do not interfere. Trust us. It will all work out.'

They were speaking in tongues. The things she had done at their behest over the years, in the name of God, horrific things. Larinda was living proof The Faithful did not risk outcomes to random throws of the dice.

Someone, the liberal left, the feminists, the atheists, maybe all of them, was holding a gun to their heads. No other explanation. Political blackmail. To get to Larinda. To help neutralize her as a threat.

In Georgetown now, she headed to Waterfront Park, but she made a snap decision. A hard left into an entrance road curled her around under the Key Bridge, the blacktop ending at a festively colored boathouse. The thunderheads that shuttled through had dumped their rain and dissipated, revealing a morning sun that blazed against the bridge's concrete arches, steaming away the dull wet gray, and in that process returning the arches to a clean, Caribbean-sand white. She switched off the wipers, parked, and got out. The Potomac lapped against the boathouse docks, was a bit rough, its aggression left over from the downpour. The boathouse hadn't opened yet. Fluorescent-colored kayaks were layered haphazardly on the docks like flopped flounder, and next to them were canoes as bright as the kayaks, stacked neatly. Paddleboats were tied to the docks. She breathed in, today's air crisp but not chilly.

'Let the Court decision be rendered.'

No.

'Trust us.'

No.

'Call someone.'

Maybe. To give them a chance to explain themselves. Plus she needed them to do something.

With the sun out again the river quickly calmed itself, became understated and pleasant. Above her on the bridge beeping horns, accelerating engines and coughing exhaust pipes cluttered the noise scape. Down here, no such congestion, just a quiet river.

She decided. This would be her escape route out of Georgetown. Yes. She'd need to get to the river.

She picked out a few smooth stones from the shore, winged them into the water where they skipped before dropping below the surface. She took her phone from her pocket.

'Call someone.'

She keyed in a text message to Reverend Higby, short and to the point.

—I need meds.

Naomi entered the Supreme Court conference room. Wood paneling, built-in bookcases stuffed with law texts, a centered

Jane's Baby

Oriental rug in reds and blacks and blues covering a hardwood floor, plus nine high-backed, wheeled chairs around a long table inlaid with slate. A black fireplace. The room dripped with profundity.

Babineau v. Turbin. Her straw vote would be to vacate the Texas ruling. She had arrived at this decision easily. On the side of overturning the ruling, in her opinion and that of her clerks, Stare Decisis ruled here. No new worthwhile info was presented for this case, which meant for her there was no reason that a person's right to privacy wouldn't again prevail regarding the legality of terminating a pregnancy. About the speculation regarding when a fetus felt pain: no new scientific evidence had been posited, but on the side of upholding the lower court ruling, the doctors' opinions produced as part of the judicial record provided convincing arguments that for sure had tugged at heartstrings and sentimentality.

The preliminary vote didn't take long: five-to-four in favor of vacating the lower court ruling. Not much more than a temperature check, their straw poll was far from binding, and could be quite changeable the deeper they got into the term. Nevertheless it was a good place to be, the right place to be, as far as Naomi was concerned.

One additional Court housekeeping mention before the Chief Justice dismissed them was that the elevated courtroom security would remain in place until further notice. To blame, the Planned Parenthood clinic hits. What remained unspoken among the justices was that until the case was decided, *Babineau v. Turbin* would keep the justices, as well as the general public, on edge.

Naomi's iPhone beeped while they filed out of the conference room. It was a text from one of her law clerks:

—Your Honor: The mailroom tried to deliver an overnight package you will need to sign for, from a Chester Plunkett in OK.

Oh my. Chester Fights Like A Badger Plunkett. Texas tribal elder and a law professor at her alma mater, the University of Oklahoma, until his retirement at age eighty. A strong Naomi supporter for her entire career. Her Indian confidant and mentor. Fond memories of his attendance at many of her major life events rushed her as she neared her chambers: college graduating ceremonies, her swearing in as a Texas federal judge, her wedding, and birthday parties for her children. When she reached the door to her chambers she was suddenly overcome by…something. A presence. It took her breath away.

A tingling from deep within spread its warmth throughout her body, and for a wondrous moment a peaceful calm overwhelmed her. She steadied herself against the doorjamb. When she recovered, she was keenly aware that something spiritual had passed through her.

"Chester. My dearest Chester…"

Another text cued up, this one from Chester Plunkett's daughter. As she read it, tears welled:

—Madam Justice Coolsummer. My dearest Naomi. The spirit of our great and wonderful Badger has left its host to join our ancestors.

TWENTY-NINE

After making it through the line outside the Supreme Court building, then the line inside the building's concourse, Judge and friends were stuffed into a long pew in the courtroom. Good seats, even if they were tight, second row back from the bar, the bronze rail that separates the Court, comprised of the justices and case lawyers, from visitors. The courtroom held two hundred fifty general public spectators in three sets of pews five-deep. At floor level it was a busy place, but above them were three stories of empty space bordered by carved inlays, the white marble walls covered by red and gold drapes two stories high. Day two of the fall term's oral arguments was about to begin.

Each of the justices noticed them, or rather Owen. Associate Justice Coolsummer, the newest judge on the bench, made direct, prolonged eye contact with him. In Judge's estimation it was an optical illusion kind of thing for them, Owen looking like a disembodied black magic voodoo head from their slightly elevated vantage point. To Judge, Owen could have used a kid's booster seat, but mentioning this would have gotten them both tossed out on their rude asses for loud, abusive language. Besides, Owen appeared to be in his element. So serious. He studied every inch of the courtroom, the attorneys, the law clerks, the railing, and each of the justices, even scrutinized a number of the courtroom visitors. The majesty of it all showed on his solemn, beaming face. What Judge was seeing here, finally, was some maturity. An awe-inspiring moment for him. When the solemnity disappeared, it was replaced with a pleasant, contented smile.

"Judge." Owen's beckoning fingers waved him down to him.

Judge leaned in. "What is it now, Owen?"

"I've got a boner."

A face-palm moment. "All this judicial pomp and you're going with that?"

"Well, yeah. Easy to bust a nut, all nine judges together like this. Exciting shit, dude."

His blog entry had telegraphed their intentions, and the bounty said she'd kill Judge's dogs, and here was Owen thinking he was on a choose-your-own adventure.

"You're an idiot. I swear to God, Owen..."

Geenie put her finger to her lips to shush them. Judge calmed, all of them settling in to listen to the presenting attorney at the lectern.

The second reason for the visit was to see how security was handled, considering the increased threat. Protocol now included a full body scan like at the airport, and the courtroom walls were lined with armed law enforcement. Judge counted twelve cops. The place looked secure enough that if someone tried to commit a crime here this person for sure wasn't getting out. Threatening behavior of any kind could be a death wish on the perpetrator's part.

Owen leaned forward to check out the spectators farther down their row. Geenie's gaze followed his, Judge's followed Geenie's. Across the aisle in the other group of benches, same row as them, two Native Americans in nineteenth century buckskin, beads and feathers sat quietly, a man and a woman, each engrossed in the proceedings. Beyond them were more spectators, all settled in for the Court session, until a woman at the far end of the row leaned forward to face them. Black hair, straight and thick covering both sides of her head. She appeared Native American, just wasn't dressed the part. She studied Judge and his friends, didn't try to hide that that was what she was doing, then sat back in her seat.

Owen reached into his pocket, retrieved the doctored flyer of the bounty and smoothed it out on his small lap for the three of them to see. The doodled nun-habit artwork framed the mug shot same as the straight black hair framed the face of the woman across the aisle.

Whoa. Larinda Jordan. They'd made her.

The woman slipped out of her end seat. She'd had made them too.

She walked casually to the closest exit. Judge popped out of his seat, climbed over other Court visitors while keeping his eyes on her. "'Scuse me, 'scuse me, move, move, MOVE."

Jane's Baby

At the end of his row he scrambled to the rear of the courtroom, turned on the afterburners and sprinted toward the exit. He yelled at the court cops to stop her, fucking stop her, tackle her, do something, except...shit...what was in his head wasn't what was coming out of his mouth:

"Fuck her! C-c-cunt! FUUUCK HERRR!"

The court chambers crowd murmured and stared as the court cops converged on Judge, not his bounty. Taking longer and faster strides, she reached the exit. Judge was a few strides behind, still babbling like an epileptic carnival barker. Once in the concourse it was more open, less confining, better visibility and...

A sumo-sized cop crashed into him, jammed his chin into his chest, lifted him off his feet and body-slammed him. A second cop, then a third, joined in. Judge's Tourette's outburst eased up only because he had little air left in his lungs.

They flipped him onto his stomach. Knees pressed into his shoulders, and a bony third knee punished his temple, grinding his cheek flat against the chilly marble. The handcuffs were out, his wrists soon attached together behind his back, his shoulder blades feeling the strain...

"...Wuhmun," came out almost coherent, but was all he had. "Wuh-munnn...!"

The cold steel of a gun barrel bore into his ear. "U.S. Deputy Marshal Trenton. Do. Not. Resist."

Nearby on his left, Owen leaned into Judge's line of vision, talked to him, yelled at the cops until they tased him and put him onto his stomach, his butt cheeks twitching like electrified jumping beans. The concourse pedestrians stopped to gawk, all except one. Geenie slipped past the commotion, picked up her pace, and kept moving in the direction the target had taken.

The cops...they needed to know who, what, they'd missed. Soon as they sat Judge down and his head cleared, they would, but the lights started dimming, he was fading...

THIRTY

Larinda pushed through the Court Building's west exit and descended the steps quickly on light feet, needing to put distance between her and the guy the court cops had taken out. She hit the second set of steps, took them two at a time. Never again would she go on a mission where weapons weren't permitted. Too exposed, too defenseless. She'd had her fill of the Court, and this incident confirmed that an assassination attempt anywhere inside the Court Building would never work.

Larinda passed a plaza water fountain with a circular pool under it, one of two bookending the front of the building, then she broke into a jog on the plaza's flat, sculpted concrete. The last set of steps brought her to street level, the entrance to D.C.'s public transit Metro trains a few blocks away. Good weather for a stroll, sunny, with the late morning air crisp and invigorating.

Slapping footfalls behind her. She heard them too late, was tackled and sent shoulder first onto a patch of lawn before sprawling spread-eagle onto her stomach. In her mouth now was a meal of grass and dirt.

Her assailant barked at her. A woman's voice. "STAY. DOWN!" Knees jabbed the back of her shoulders, immobilizing them, with pressure against her temple coming from a fisted hand, not a gun. She couldn't see her chatty attacker busy shouting at a nearby pedestrian witness. "Dial 911! This woman is a fugitive. Citizen's arrest."

If anyone dialed, Larinda had no idea. She rocked her shoulders then rolled, got off a roundhouse punch against her assailant's jaw, knuckle to bone. The woman's jaw snapped out of place, and Larinda pushed out from under her. Her attacker struggled to stand, groaned, but was still able to reach and connect with Larinda's hand, pressing it backward toward her wrist. She was strong, stronger than Larinda who dropped to her knees from the pain of the hold and the threat of more pain to come. Larinda's other fist delivered an uppercut to the woman's dislocated jaw, her assailant reeling from the punch then dropping to her knees, blood streaming from her mouth, the woman still calling to passersby, "...ine-un-un..."

Enraged and energized, Larinda hovered. She could do more damage to her attacker, older than she'd realized, a surprise, forties-fifties maybe, but buff. One more punch to the jaw knocked the woman out. Larinda sprinted around a treed corner then jogged along the street long enough for a cab to materialize.

Inside the cab her wrist dangled in pain, was maybe broken, the same arm as the one with the poorly healed palm, its cut open again. "Key Bridge Boathouse parking lot," she said, out of breath. "Big tip if you're quick about it."

The driver was a pagan swami, turbaned. Pagan or not, she needed his help. "You have a first aid kit in here?"

A knock on Naomi's courthouse chambers door. The Marshal of the Court entered and delivered an update on the incident. The courtroom had been cleared and the justices were in lockdown, separately, in their respective chambers.

"It's impossible to screen for what just happened," the court officer told her. "We have the man in custody, plus an accomplice. We're interviewing them now. That's all I have to report at the moment, Madam Justice." He made eye contact with Marshal Trenton, at her side and standing at attention. "Nicely done, Deputy Marshal Trenton."

Edward nodded.

Court adjourned early for lunch, maybe longer, to give Court Security a chance to analyze surveillance video plus assess the likelihood of an additional threat. The Chief Justice asked them all to stay loose pending a decision regarding holding the afternoon session. She dismissed her law clerks to their offices while she waited for lunch to be delivered. Edward had already seen the footage.

"Are you all right, Edward?"

"I'm fine, ma'am. The man's name is Drury. He's a Marine. We're going to owe him an apology, Your Honor. We blew it."

Physically, Edward did appear fine. Emotionally, Naomi wasn't so sure. "I'm sure it's not that bad, Edward."

"The Marine's explanation, ma'am, is that a certain woman who was in the courtroom is the threat, not him." Edward swallowed hard. "I had to react like I did. But from the footage I've seen, Mister Drury was right. The woman who left the courtroom before him didn't react to the takedown, didn't miss a step or even turn around, just kept walking." The more he talked, the tighter his jaw got. "I'm afraid, ma'am, we've made a terrible mistake."

"Please, Edward, I'm sure your superiors will understand. I'll speak with them. And I'll also speak with Mister Drury."

"Your Honor, ma'am, respectfully, you don't understand what just happened. See..."

A hard knock at her door; the Marshal of the Court entered without waiting for an answer. "Madam Justice, security footage outside on the plaza shows an altercation between two women. We believe one of them was the woman who fled the courtroom in front of the men we apprehended. It appears the other woman was also in the chambers at the same time. I've just told the Chief Justice. You should remain here until further notice. Mister Trenton, stay sharp."

With the Marshal of the Court gone, Edward finished his thought, his voice serious. "Madam Justice, after analyzing the footage from the cameras at the two Planned Parenthood buildings, the U.S. Marshal's office, the court police, and the FBI all think the woman Mister Drury was pursuing is the Planned Parenthood terrorist."

Edward didn't do exasperation well. His upper torso inflated, his stare piercing. He was looking for something to hit. "She was in the courtroom, ma'am, less than fifty feet from you, and I let her walk."

"Edward. Please. I am fine. All the justices are fine. Those fifty feet will now be the safest fifty feet in America, other than the perimeter the Secret Service keeps for the president." She searched his weather-beaten face, for what, she didn't know, but it pained her to see this brave warrior question himself. "Please know, Edward, that I do feel safe with you."

"Yes, ma'am. Thank you, ma'am. But the consensus among the agencies is this person is less interested in the other justices and more interested in you."

Jane's Baby

Her office phone rang; she picked up. "I understand. Fine. Thank you," she said into the receiver. "Edward, a mailroom employee is on the way up to deliver an overnight package."

"Your Honor, has it been..."

"They're taking the proper precautions, Edward."

"Your Honor, if I may..."

"Yes, you can answer the door and examine it."

The mailroom supervisor arrived, prepared with powder-free sterile latex gloves. He slipped them on and commenced removing pages from the pouch, all handwritten, plus a sealed business envelope. He unsealed the envelope, slipped out a number of folded photocopies. Nothing in the pouch and the business envelope but paper. Edward escorted the supervisor out of Naomi's chambers.

At a small table, Naomi sat unwrapping the lunch the café prepared for them. She would address the letter after she and Edward ate. "Please have a seat and join me, Edward."

"Ma'am, no thank you, they're about to release Mister Drury. I want to be there when they do. A court cop is posted outside your office. I'll be back shortly. Madam Justice, I, ah..."

His face showed his conflict, the concern that he was abandoning her.

"I'll be fine, Edward. Thank you. Go."

The door closed behind him. She worked on her pasta salad, each forkful punctuated by a glance at Chester Plunkett's letter on her desk. To peruse the pages now, while she ate, she'd need to enjoy teardrops in her food, but she couldn't hold out any longer. She unfolded the letter.

The message was on his personal stationery, from the OU School of Law, the words in a shaky longhand.

My Dearest Madam Justice Naomi,

I hope you are having a wonderful day in our nation's great capitol. You receive this note on the occasion of my pending transition to the spirit world. My passing will be joyous, so do not dwell on it, please. The Great Spirit guides me, has granted me a clear, healthy mind, and with it a loving heart, but a heart that gets heavier the sicker it gets. I am so proud of you, Naomi, like your family is, and like our people and the people of Texas and Oklahoma are, but I must make you aware of something I'm sure you never knew. I'm sorry I can't say this to you in person.

Flashbacks queued up inside and played for her, of the Badger moving seamlessly between citing tribal court and national legal decisions, chapter and verse, in the classroom, to performing at Native American ceremonies in Cherokee dress, to practicing the traditions at powwows. A legal pioneer, and a preservationist who had embraced his heritage as a full-blooded Cherokee. She loved this man as much as she loved her father, and she'd known him almost as long. Tears slipped onto her cheeks, down them, into her salad.

I made an inquiry via the Texas Public Information Act regarding the Texas Native American Scholarship Program, this after a number of years of steering students to the same scholarship that provided you with your college funding. For them, their applications met with zero success. Every one. What I learned was the scholarship program had considered only one application during its existence, yours, and the fund was active only for the years in which you were a student. Its support came from a small circle of religious and business leaders and one federal politician. The sole reason for this scholarship program was for your benefit, Naomi. What remains a mystery to me is the why.

Benevolence as welcome as this, so inviting financially for a family of limited means like yours, and awarded as it was to a high achiever, would rarely be questioned. Until your career success outstripped my wildest expectations for you, I thought better than to ever bring this up. What good does it serve to alert you to this now? Forewarned is forearmed, Naomi. Beware people looking to trade on, and assign your complicity with, this curious benevolence. Their names appear in the Freedom of Information response copies enclosed here.

I will visit you before I go, Naomi. Somehow, some way, I will visit you. Elohino dohiyi gesesti. (Peace upon this land.)

With love, your most humble law professor,
Chester Fights Like A Badger Plunkett, Esq."

Naomi was stunned, and now felt physically ill. She reread the letter: "…one federal politician…a small circle of religious and business leaders…"

What the hell was going on?

THIRTY-ONE

"Mister Drury, apologies from the Court. And thank you for the information. We'll take things from here. You're dismissed."

This agent wasn't the one who took him down. Regardless, Judge flew out of the rubber-hose seat in their basement office, took the steps two at a time and headed in the direction of the public locker area, where his phone was. He didn't get far. Overtaking him in a hefty jog was the guy who had actually body-slammed him. His big-ass girth stopped in front of Judge; he put his hand on Judge's chest. It was abrupt, but it was also gentle, as gentle as a refrigerator with arms could manage for itself.

"Mister Drury, apologies from the U.S. Marshal's office also. Madam Justice Coolsummer would like a word with you please, to thank you for what you did."

The guy was sincere, but Judge didn't give a shit right about now. "Look, my girlfriend's missing. I need to get to the lockers so I can get my phone back and check for messages." At six-three, Judge still had to raise his head to face him. "We're not gonna have another episode right here, are we, Shrek, 'cause you didn't get to see the real me earlier. You need to move."

"Fair enough," the marshal said and surprised Judge by backing off. "Follow me."

At this point Judge became an NFL running back following a pulling guard. Early afternoon in the Supreme Court's concourse had returned to business-as-usual busy after the morning's excitement, but with a U.S. marshal as large as this man in front of him, it was like a parting of the Red Sea. As an afterthought Judge remembered Owen had left the court police office with him, so somewhere behind them he was no doubt hoofing it as fast as he could.

They reached the lockers. Judge found theirs and opened it. He stuffed everything from the locker into the backpack they'd left there, except for his phone.

Jane's Baby

Shrek got chatty. He was brownish, so maybe Shrek didn't work as a name. He identified himself. "I'm U.S. Deputy Marshal Trenton, Mister Drury. If I can be of any help..."

"Un-bruise my ribs for me, will you, Mister Trenton? You think you can you do that for me?" Judge didn't smile while he scanned his messages. Two from Geenie. He listened, shadowed by his escort. She left the phone number for the emergency room of a hospital, and she sounded out of it.

"On meds," her message said, "dislocated jaw," and "I had her, Judge," although what left her lips sounded more like "piss-located chaw" and "I sam her, Hutch." Owen arrived alongside them, exhausted. Judge punched in some numbers looking for the name of the hospital and its address. Mr. Trenton put his big mitt over Judge's hand and his phone together.

"I can't undo the damage to your ribs, Mister Drury, but I can get you a ride to the hospital. Except you're going to see Justice Coolsummer first. Now, please."

His gentle demeanor gone, Judge sensed a man who was extremely dedicated to his assigned duties, and who wouldn't be nice to them if Judge didn't let him perform them.

Tough shit.

"Get me that ride now and I promise I'll come back after I check on my girlfriend. Or we go through the same shit we went through earlier, which does neither of us any good." The marshal looked past Judge's shoulder, in ponder mode. "And when we visit with Justice Coolsummer, Mister Wingert here gets included, too."

The marshal hesitated, then, "Fine."

Judge decided that maybe he should stop being such an arrogant asshole. "Look, Mister Trenton, I accept your apology." He offered his hand. "Call me Judge. Judge Drury, USMC Former Enlisted Marine. And a fugitive recovery agent."

They shook. "Your first name is Judge?"

"My whole life."

"A name like that around here, get ready to hear it a lot. I'm Edward." The stuffed Sasquatch smiled. He retrieved his phone and made a few calls. "Transportation will be here in a minute. For you and Mister Wingert both."

This newest marshal's name was Abelson. They climbed into a government minivan with Mr. Abelson driving and they headed up to Howard University Hospital. A ten-minute ride, their driver said.

"They sure do grow the brothers big at the U.S. Marshal's office," Owen said to the back of Deputy Marshal Abelson's black flattop head. With Owen it was always how best to piss off the hand that fed him in ten words or less. Their host ignored him. A quick park job, then they hoofed it with Abelson to the hospital entrance.

"Yo, give a brother a break, bro," Owen pleaded, trying to keep up. "Yo! Slow up!"

The hospital sliding doors slid open. Abelson glanced at Judge. "He always like this?"

"If you mean short, yeah, it's a genetic thing," Judge said.

"I heard that, Judge, you prick."

They moved from room to room, Abelson badging the hell out of everybody. Deep in the emergency beds section, they found her. Judge's heart sank.

"Geenie honey…"

Her bed was raised at one end and she was resting, bandaged around the head and under her chin with gauze and adhesive tape. From the nose down, what was visible of her face was puffy and purple, with some red from bloodstains. Six weeks at a minimum like this, the ER doc said. Painkillers, antibiotics, liquid diet. Six agonizing weeks. Her espresso eyes opened, then her arms beckoned. Judge leaned in, hugged her, kissed her on the forehead, squeezed her shoulder. "Sorry, baby. So sorry."

The doc explained. "No breaks. Only a dislocation and a concussion. Aside from the meds, she's thinking clearly. She can open her mouth enough to talk, but not much more than a sliver."

She winked, acting playful. "A sliver's room enough, for you, lover," she said to him. Her speech was slow, garbled. "Just joking, you big boy you," she said, but without the b's. She squeezed Judge's hand.

"She's still a little looped, Mister Drury."

"But looking great," he said and meant it. No long-term physical effects or disfigurement, the doctor added; her jaw just needed time to heal. And Judge so needed to hurt someone because of this. He went for the rabbit's foot to calm himself, able to choke back a douche-waffle and a puke-slapping rumble-cunt queued up with a prick-bastard chaser. A Tourette's episode there could have landed him in the Psych Ward.

"I had her, Judge," she said, her tongue thick, "then after...she threw...that punch from her heels...I didn't." Her lips moved only slightly when she spoke, like a drunken mummy ventriloquist. Judge was loving her lots here.

"She's right." This was Abelson, interrupting. "I saw the footage. Your friend was awesome on the takedown, just got tagged with a roundhouse right. If she hadn't gone after her, there'd be no additional video. Plus now the perp is hurt. We're checking the hospitals."

Geenie's eyes pleaded with Judge. "Get me out of here."

She wasn't attached to anything, no fluids, no heart monitor, and even though she looked every bit like a shell-shocked battlefield vet, her limbs were all intact, so she was mobile. "Doc, not sure if she told you this, but she's a nurse. If she thinks she can leave, she's good to go. We're due at the Supreme Court Building for a debriefing on what happened today. There's a terrorist on the loose. Let her sign herself out."

"I'd rather not," the doc said.

Mr. Abelson stepped up, flashed his U.S. Marshal's five-pointed star at the doctor. The discussion ended.

A wheelchair ride brought Geenie to Abelson's minivan. Inside the van she asked if she could have her gun back. Judge told her no, no guns, they were still all locked in his van's glove box.

"Dogs?" she asked.

Judge sighed; they had to be tired of the B&B room by now. "We've got an audience with Justice Coolsummer, Geenie, like it or not. They'll get a long walk when we get back."

THIRTY-TWO

The ligaments in Larinda's ballooning left wrist were a mess but she could still move it, so maybe it wasn't broken.

"Stop here," she told the cabbie. He pulled the cab to the curb. She handed him three twenties, told him to wait.

Inside the pharmacy she grabbed a cloth bandage, more gauze pads and some snacks. Back in the cab, she opened a Slim Jim and bit off a generous hunk. She slipped a package of beef jerky into the front seat through the hole in the partition, just to be nice to the swami.

He checked her out in the rearview, ignored the gift, shook his head. In disgust, disbelief, she didn't know which, but it was not favorable.

Then she remembered. Beef was cow. Not a favorite Hindi foodstuff.

No matter. The cabbie needed to read the Bible, not the Bhagavad Gita.

She bandaged her crucified palm then wrapped the wrist and hand, which left her fingers free. The cab left the street, drove down a short, paved incline to the Key Bridge Boathouse dock shack.

"Leave me off there," she said, pointing at the entrance to the shack. She'd rather he didn't see her vehicle. Taking his generous tip, the cabbie hustled off. Around her, people waited for their rental kayaks and canoes. On the dock, and on a small stretch of sand next to it, returned boating equipment awaited check-in by the busy attendants.

The parking lot was where she crashed, more battered, more exhausted than she'd realized, on a patch of grass under an elm at the far end from the rental station, next to a park bench with worn, dark green enameled slats. With minimal effort she tuned out the tourists unloading and reloading themselves in the canoes and kayaks and paddleboats. A short rest here was what she needed,

Jane's Baby

in the shade of a tree holding on to its leaves, the tree enjoying some Indian summer weather.

The questions rattled around inside Naomi's head. When had they planned on exploiting this scholarship sham? Why go to all this trouble? Why her?

At her office window, she parted the sheers for an unobstructed view of an autumn afternoon in this corner of D.C. An unusually warm day for the season. Small whirlwinds churned up stray brown and green leaves around hedges needing a late summer trim, blowing them past smooth stone benches on the tree-lined plaza outlined by marble columns. From her window there was a partial view of the Capitol, which further grounded her in the seriousness of these surroundings, and yet, emotionally, she was a million miles away, this view lost in the gravity of what she'd just learned. Her shoes were off, her stockinged toes free to find comfort in the thick oriental carpets.

The pinnacle of her legal career. She'd either soar to the heights expected of this appointment, or she'd crash and burn before she rendered her first decision as a sitting associate justice. She would address this landmine when the people who had unearthed it arrived.

She removed a framed wall hanging, admired at arm's length the off-white parchment under glass while she carried it back to her desk. A letter opener helped her remove the frame's thin, pressed wood backing. She liberated the document, pondered it a moment more, then tucked it into a desk drawer. Her toes located her high heels inside the desk kneehole; she slipped them back on.

A knock on her chambers door. Naomi expected two separate sets of visitors, in no particular order, and she was quite sure she wouldn't be happy seeing either set.

"Come in."

Senator Folsom barged past her administrative clerk and the court cop. She marched up to Naomi's desk, irate. What Naomi had expected.

"Why are you canceling on my Saturday breakfast meeting?" the senator bellowed.

"Senator. So glad you could fit this visit in with me today. Have a seat." Trailing the senator but entering on a more reserved note was evangelist Higby Hunt.

More senatorial bluster. "I have the District's National Museum of the American Indian booked for the entire morning on Saturday! A number of constituents and their families will be there to hear you speak. Your story is inspiring, Your Honor. You committed to this!"

"Senator, have you ever heard of a Chester Plunkett?"

"Who?"

"Chester 'Fights Like A Badger' Plunkett. Full-blooded Cherokee. Law professor emeritus, University of Oklahoma Law School. A close friend of mine. The Oklahoma Law School and Indian community lost him today. He was eighty years old."

"Yes," Reverend Hunt interjected. "I know of him. I'm sorry for your loss, Your Honor."

"Yes, you do know him, Reverend. You and the senator both." Naomi produced a copy of the document she'd received today from the Badger, may he rest in peace. She slid it across her desk, under Senator Folsom's nose.

"Chester Plunkett discovered this by way of the Texas Public Information Act. It was there for the asking, except no one, least of all me or my family, would have ever thought there'd be a need to ask. One open-ended, phantom scholarship, set up for one person only, worth in excess of two hundred thousand publicly funded dollars. Some people might even view this as money laundering, Senator. It seems," Naomi's jaw muscles tightened, "that in one underhanded, shameless, politically-influenced maneuver expected to yield some preferred treatment to be named later you, Senator, are now in a position to tarnish my credentials and limit whatever effectiveness I might have hoped to achieve on the Supreme Court. You can have that copy. Oh, you can have this, too."

Naomi opened her desk drawer and removed what she'd taken down from her wall. The grandiose document commemorated the occasion of her college scholarship award, done up splendidly with calligraphic letters, gold seals and a few Native American markings, and signed by the senator, a retired Texas governor, and other Texas dignitaries.

Jane's Baby

"My academic scholarship was a pretense. For what, I don't know. You are going to tell me the significance of this sham. Now."

Unflinching stares on both their parts, until another knock on the door broke the tension. Her admin clerk leaned in. "Your next appointment is here, Madam Justice."

"Make them comfortable, please," she told him. "We're not through in here."

Naomi sat up straighter at her desk, folded her hands in front of her. "I need information from you on this, Senator."

Reverend Hunt shifted in his seat, but it was clear he was waiting for the senator to respond. Naomi remained patient, didn't flinch. Senator Folsom was in full assessment mode, evaluating what she'd heard. She tilted her silver-white head, produced an intense, furrowed-brow stare at her accuser. She leaned in.

"Perhaps the state budget wouldn't allow for funding after that first scholarship, Your Honor. Law school is expensive, remember? Don't forget, if it weren't for that scholarship, you might still be paying it off."

A test salvo. A miss. "I would have been like every other law student with loans. But regardless, the state had a budget surplus for more than a decade. The money was there to keep that scholarship going. Don't impugn my intelligence, Senator. This is influence peddling. How you intended to use it, considering at that point I was simply a mouthy student feminist, is what I want to know."

"The committee could not have known, Your Honor," Senator Folsom said.

"What does that mean? Could not have known what?"

"We wanted to make sure you were equipped to do well. To excel. We never dreamed..."

"Look, Senator, stop speaking in generalities. Who is this 'we'? And why me?"

"I'll speak however I want to, damn it. There was no intention of using this 'phantom scholarship' against you, Madam Justice. None. The 'we' was, and is, a small group of conservative Christian faithful who set about to prove a point. That an unborn baby's life matters."

"You're not making any sense, Senator! You funneled money to some random Native American kid...me...to validate that Christians are pro-life?"

"Listen carefully, Naomi Coolsummer. There was nothing random about it." The gravel in her voice intensified. "In nineteen eighty-five, when you were in high school..."

"Mildred, is this the time and the place for this?" Reverend Hunt said. "I thought Saturday..."

"Shut up, Higby. You heard her. There is no Saturday. It has to be now."

She was referring to Naomi at age fifteen. A normally awkward high school experience for her until then, raised by a middle-income, two wage-earner family. But from sixteen forward, a world of difference for her. People suddenly knew who she was, paid more attention to her upbringing, her family.

Naomi's interest piqued ten-fold. "Go on."

"When you were a teenager we learned something about you. Something your adoptive parents never knew. How we learned it, you needn't worry about, but it was information obtained with the best of intentions."

"I'll cut to the chase. Certain closed adoption records were made available to us. We learned who your birth mother is."

The senator was keen to Naomi's facial expression, waiting for feedback. Naomi was angrier about the senator's arrogance than shocked at the revelation itself.

"You pompous, self-righteous windbag. I'm supposed to be thankful you ferreted out this information on me? You had no right to it, and having learned it, no right to withhold it. How dare you!"

"Naomi..."

"Madam Justice to you. You need to leave, Senator."

"Do not mistake my civility with you," the senator's eyes narrowed, "or my willingness to accept your misguided derision, Madam Justice, as a sign of weakness. Few adoptees from back then can say they know the names of their birth mothers. Even I can't say that about myself. This information, once it was in our hands, turned a life that was already special, because all life is, into a life that over time became much more significant. Yours."

Naomi's face tightened. "Again with the generalities. A group of people not including my adoptive parents knows who my birth

Jane's Baby

mother is. Thirty years you've kept this information to yourself. And you rigged public scholarship money for me because of it? I'm supposed to be happy learning this now? This is sick, Senator. What's more, it's probably criminal. Get out."

The reverend stood, ready to leave. The senator didn't budge. Naomi punched a button on her chambers phone. "Send in Deputy Marshal Trenton please," she said into the phone's speaker, "there's a situation in here."

Senator Folsom tented her fingers, leaned farther back in the chair.

"I'm having you forcibly removed, Senator."

The senator drilled a challenging, unblinking stare into Naomi's enraged eyes.

"I'll get to the point. Jane. Roe. Your mother is Norma McCorvey. Jane. Fucking. Roe." She shrugged her shoulders, feigning apology. "It seemed like you weren't going to ask."

The heavy wooden door to her office burst open, Edward shouldering his way into the chambers. His gun drawn, he strode quickly in front of Naomi's desk, inserting himself between her and her guests. In his wake was a court policeman.

"What's the problem, Your Honor?" Edward faced down the reverend, seemed less interested in the elderly senator, who remained seated. In the hallway, heads poked into view through the open door, all three of them, Naomi was sure, intrigued by the excitement.

The pendulum, Naomi now realized, had swung in a different direction, and it could well decapitate her.

"You have proof of this, Senator?"

"Of course. Birth certificate, hospital, month, day, year. Parents' names and ethnicities. I will gather it up."

"Edward, thank you, but I've changed my mind. Leave us alone please."

THIRTY-THREE

The door to the justice's chambers closed again. Deputy Marshal Trenton and the court cop were back on this side of it, with them.

"'Sup with the Wild West show?" Owen asked the marshal.

"Nothing. Court business. You need to wait."

This, after they'd already spent time being interviewed by the FBI, the U.S. Marshal's office, NSA, court police, and the one organization Judge was surprised to see there, the Secret Service. If each of them hadn't badged them, he wouldn't have been able to tell them apart. Geenie had spilled all of what she could remember, some of her info handwritten, some of it verbal with only minor mouth action. Larinda Jordan remained a fugitive, but because of Geenie's information they had more on her now than before.

They waited a little longer for Justice Coolsummer. After another ten minutes, Geenie started to fade. Judge pulled the marshal aside.

"Look, Mister Trenton, Edward, we need to forgo the thank-yous here. Geenie's out of it. Pay our respects to the judge for us, please. We could use that ride back to my van now."

Owen whined. "C'mon, dude, this is a big deal, meeting a U.S. Supreme Court justice. It's on my bucket list."

He ignored Owen and waited for Edward to get on board with his decision. Before he could respond the door to the judge's chambers opened.

The first one to exit was the longest tenured U.S. senator still in office, Mildred Folsom from Texas, flashing her photogenic, cap-toothed smile surrounded by a shoe-leather-tan face. Following her was, no shit, that Texas televangelist asshole Higby Hunt, Judge mused. Edward ushered the new set of visitors inside Justice Coolsummer's chambers.

Jane's Baby

The judge stood at an office window, her back to the room. The marshal waited for her to acknowledge that someone had entered before announcing them. When she didn't he shooed them forward. It was then Judge realized she wasn't looking out the window but rather at something framed on the wall. A law school diploma. She lifted it off its hanger.

"Madam Justice," Edward said. "Mister Drury, Miss Pinto and Mister Wingert are here to see you."

The judge admired her diploma close up, her response distant. "Who?"

"They flushed out the Planned Parenthood assailant, Your Honor. You said you wanted to meet Mister Drury."

"Ah, that Mister Drury. I did say that, didn't I?" She rested the framed diploma on an armchair, finally devoting her attention to her guests. "And with him Miss Pinto, the woman who nearly captured the terrorist. And, of course, Chigger Wingert, beloved Dallas sports writer. That brings us up to speed on the introductions. Have a seat, everyone. This needs to be quick. I have some movers delivering furniture this afternoon. Mister Trenton, you're dismissed."

"Ma'am, I'm sorry, but I can't do that. I'm not leaving you..."

Her face soured. "Wait outside, Mister Trenton. I want a word with them, alone, please. I trust them."

Mr. Trenton frowned at her sharp tone. "But Madam..."

"Edward, stop arguing. You need to get out. Now."

The door closed behind him. Geenie and Judge sat, Justice Coolsummer sat. Owen did not. Things were now a little tense. To their right on a conference table were what looked like a half-eaten lunch with an untouched second lunch next to it. Right about now, she had their undivided attention.

"Fairly exciting day today," she said, "wasn't it?"

They murmured things that went along with agreeing headshakes.

"Yes," she said, "a one-of-a-kind kind of day. Yes, indeed. Well, it seems your government owes you great thanks for your vigilance this morning. I asked you back so I could provide that. Thank you all. Mister Drury, we owe you an apology for what I understand was a nasty bruising by Deputy Marshal Trenton, so let's include that apology here as well, shall we? Oh, and let's be thankful your pain and suffering seems to have been limited to the bruised ribs you are holding as you sit. Is this correct?"

"I won't be suing anyone, Your Honor."

"Excellent. If I'm sounding a bit cynical, yes, maybe I am. Sorry. We all have crosses to bear. Today's crosses…well, today has been especially eye-opening for me, and I can't say I'm all that thrilled with having to socialize much more right now. So, have we covered everything?"

Rude, and not how Judge had pictured her at all. Owen seemed immune to it, smiling like he was about to get laid. "Madam Justice. This is such an honor, ma'am. I also do a court blog through an alias…"

"'Thurgood Cochran.' Yes. Cute, irreverent name. You like pissing off the white majority, don't you? I'm aware of the blog and your interest in the Court, and in me in particular. But, sad to say, Mister Wingert, it seems you've been chasing fool's gold when it comes to me. So, again," she clapped her hands once, signaling finality, "we need to wrap this up, which means whatever else you have to say, Thurgood, you will need to leave for your blog. Thanks for stopping by."

She summoned Mr. Trenton. The big man collected them, ushered them out the door and closed it behind him.

"I'm sorry," he said, staying composed. "I've got no explanation for that. I'm chalking it up to a good person having a bad day. Deputy Abelson will bring the van arou…"

A loud crash on the other side of the door had the marshal whirling, his gun drawn as he shoved his way into her chambers. Judge entered behind him.

Judge Coolsummer stood next to the conference table, her feet apart for balance, her hands holding the split bottom half of a picture frame. Broken wood from the frame's top half and jagged glass chunks were settling on the table and the floor. A law school diploma parchment teetered from the table's edge, a large tear in it. It fluttered, then settled onto the rug. She absentmindedly released the rest of the fractured frame, letting it fall on top of the other debris.

"Ah, Mister Trenton, you're back. Be careful. There's some broken glass in here."

THIRTY-FOUR

Larinda jolted awake, needing to orient herself. It was five after three in the p.m.; she'd slept longer than she wanted. A tree overhead, grass against her arms, a slight wind on her bare shoulders, water lapping against a dock. Her wrapped wrist throbbed. One more reason her oxy stash needed to be replenished ASAP. That, plus the abdominal pains, the body sweats and the nausea. Withdrawal.

She climbed into her SUV. The dead parking attendant's electronic meter was where she'd left it, on the floor in front of the front passenger seat. A glance in her rearview confirmed her cargo remained covered. She surveyed the Key Bridge Boathouse dock, where the kayaks and canoes were piling up, more people returning from their time on the river than leaving. Across the river, which now showed some chop, was a stretch of wooded Virginia coastline. After the near disaster on the Supreme Court plaza, things were coming back together. As long as the reverend came through with her meds.

His response to her text had been yes, he'd meet with her, and he'd bring what she needed. She texted him with a meeting place:

—Foundry Branch Valley Park

The park was five minutes from the Key Bridge, close to the Potomac, according to Google, and full of overgrown green space plus walking and hiking trails.

—Yes. But Larinda, you must agree to stop what you're doing.

The phone beeps kept coming, one after another, when she didn't respond. She'd retrieved a few of the texts, all pleas from him. Her final text to him:

—Just bring the meds. We'll talk then.

But before they met she needed to recon something first, across the Key Bridge, plus she had to get rid of the parking attendant's meter.

She exited the lot in her vehicle and crossed the bridge. On the other side, she offered up another quick prayer, asking for options for later tonight. Her prayer was answered: public transportation. The 38B bus, with a stop along the street paralleling the river. It connected with the Metro per her phone search, and the Metro connected to all roads out of D.C.

Good. Now to pick up her prescription.

Naomi was in a fog in the back seat of the diesel pickup, on her way to her Georgetown townhouse. She blinked at her folded hands, her expression blank, stunned, still, by today's revelations. Also a bother, Edward's sudden aloofness.

Finally she broke the silence. "I'm sorry, Edward."

No response from the front seat. Fine, she got it. After her behavior in her chambers, she deserved this and more. The news she'd received today was significant, sure, but she was a U.S. Supreme Court associate justice. She was above these things, or so she'd thought.

'Significant' news? More like life-changing. Or, dare she to think, world-changing.

You're the same person you were yesterday. Stop the self-pity.

But she wasn't the same person.

She hadn't earned her scholarships. The fix had been in by way of a partisan political sleight of hand. She hadn't been wanted by her birth mother, was alive only because her mother couldn't get access to an abortion. When her identity was discovered, they groomed her to be a nail in the pro-choice coffin. She was to grow up, become a plain, law-abiding, productive citizen, with little need for her to achieve much else. Except she showed the potential of being a lot more, and an initial brainstorm promoting a simple pro-life message became a full-blown conspiracy. A tormented Manchurian Candidate in the Supreme Court. A slam-dunk, that's-what-I'm-talkin'-'bout exclamation point with the potential to blow the lid off Roe v. Wade.

Jane's Baby

All this from a smug Senator Mildred Folsom, today, in Naomi's chambers. The plan, although the senator hadn't had to spell it out, had been to give her juicy legal assignments, build up her resume, play up her Native American ethnicity, and prop up the Supreme Court candidate as being a reformed feminist. Then Folsom, a vocal senator who wore her religious conservatism on her sleeve, would put on a good show at the confirmation hearings but eventually roll over. After this, and only after this, would the senator drop the bomb. Then she could watch Naomi squirm in her liberal juices while deciding how to vote on this and other crucial pro-life cases. Regardless of the irony, Naomi was now poised to be a poster child for the anti-abortion movement, if anyone were to find out.

She analyzed her choices.

Recuse herself. She couldn't; she would need to explain why. Revelation of her true identity could destroy her Supreme Court career before it started.

Vote to vacate Babineau, which would have kept Roe in place. A headline, if she were outed: "Living Hypocrisy: Roe Baby Upholds Landmark Pro-Choice Case."

Vote to confirm Babineau, which could destroy Roe, sending women back to coat hangers and alleys.

"Your Honor?"

Edward called to her, it was twice now, from the front seat. He spoke in an even, professional tone. "No apology is needed, ma'am. It's the way things are expected to work. Marshals protect their charges, end of story. No more, no less."

"Edward..."

"I've put in to be reassigned, Your Honor."

"Goodness, Edward."

"It's best, Your Honor. My investment in this detail..." he paused, calmed himself. "There need to be boundaries. My mistake, not yours, ma'am. Starting tonight, for the near future you and your condo community will have twenty-four hour surveillance. A new deputy marshal will handle this assignment starting tomorrow. After I help you with your movers this afternoon, my assignment to you ends."

This was the first fallout from today's unwelcome news, not that she'd shared the news with him, nor did she intend to.

Regardless, it was an arm's-length message that severed a friendship, from a person whom she admired. And someone who, until this moment, she thought had admired her.

Someone she more than admired, she admitted to herself. Her eyes welled.

"Are you sure, Edward?"

"Yes, Your Honor."

She dabbed at a tear; spilled milk. She rallied. "Fine. You will, however, allow me to cook you a thank-you dinner after the movers leave. Tonight. Before a new assignment takes you to another city."

"Ma'am, that's not a good idea. I can't..."

"And you will offer an invitation to the people I was rude to today to join us, so I can make it up to them also. What they did in the name of protecting the bench was heroic. It will be low key, Edward. I'll make barbecue. Please accept, and please see what you can do about having those nice folks attend as well."

Senator Folsom lit a cigarette in the car, opened the deep-tinted rear window and blew the smoke in its general vicinity, away from Higby. After she dropped Higby off, she'd retrieve the documents kept in her office safe for over three decades. Justice Coolsummer needed to see them. After that, if the judge didn't play along, the information would be released, done so in ways that wouldn't directly involve the senator.

"My opinion, Mildred," Higby said, "is that Justice Coolsummer is now sufficiently motivated, but the Court's decision on Babineau could take months." He tucked a pair of sunglasses inside a windbreaker pocket and zipped it up.

Mildred checked out the rest of his outfit: gym pants, tennis shoes, and a navy watch cap folded in his lap. "So it's to be a walk in the park to meet out little Church Hammer, Higby? Nervous?"

"She's out of her painkillers," he said. "I'll have someone with me." He unfolded and refolded the hat in his lap. Their limo cruised the District's bustling city streets at a leisurely pace. "If we handle it this way, with no federal agency involvement, it will be better for everyone."

They crossed Rock Creek and Potomac Parkway and entered Georgetown, with Higby doing some handwringing while the

Jane's Baby

limo passed D.C. scenery he paid no attention to. "The reality is this needs to happen, Mildred. God will understand."

The Naomi Coolsummer cards had been played. A thirty-year odyssey, with a whip-smart adoptee who carved out an exceptional legal career, one that had been successful beyond their wildest imaginations. A home-team homerun, all for the sake of unborn children, of course. Mildred was still basking in her exchange with her. A part of her felt sorry about how they'd played the associate justice, and for how long. But the dominance, the power the senator now wielded, it was all so invigorating. Like the old days. Still no slack in her rope, even at her age. It was enough to make her rethink her decision to retire. Hell, maybe she'd even run for president.

One angle Mildred wondered about. "Any chance she's suicidal over this...obsession of hers?"

"Our Church Hammer? She's a Catholic who had an abortion. With the guilt she's carrying, what we're seeing is her attempt at penance. She's desperate. She'll die trying to make this happen."

"Good."

"But her mindset will no longer matter, Mildred. Not after today."

Inside Foundry Branch Valley Park, Larinda trotted along a marked hiking trail until knee-high stone walls that rose and fell with the footpath bookended it. Past the walls, the trail intersected with a hardened clay path that curled around and led into a short tunnel running beneath the hiking trail itself. This was where the reverend said he'd be. The tunnel was as wide as the trail above it and was old, carved out of gray and brown limestone, its ceiling arched. So old it looked Biblical to Larinda, its face and walls overgrown with ivy. Her first impression was the Bible's depiction of Christ's sepulcher, but without the boulder.

A hooded jogger passed her, reached the tunnel's mouth before she did, and exited the tunnel's other end. Reverend Hunt waited for her midway through, his exercise outfit loose, and atop his silver-blond head, a dark watch cap. He looked every bit a nondescript fifty-year-old in sunglasses out for an afternoon run.

She slowed, absorbing her surroundings. She stopped just inside the tunnel, in the shade. Here the mildew was pervasive, woodsy smelling and damp, with wind-jostled brown leaves caught in the green ivy, and the late afternoon sunlight slanted near the entrance. The jogger who passed her was already gone. Behind and in front of her, the trail was empty. In here, just her and the reverend. She lowered her hood, shook her black hair loose.

"My goodness, that's quite a different look for you, Larinda. Or should I call you Hiawatha?"

"You shouldn't call me anything. You bring the meds?"

Reverend Hunt raised his arm chest high, dangling a white pharmacy bag from his hand.

"Yes, per our agreement. For you, but only after you hear me out."

Fifteen feet away was the relief she needed, except the scene didn't feel right to her. Too empty a meeting place out here, too perfect. Quick glances front and behind told her the trail was still empty, but...

She slipped her hand under her hooded shirt, removed a handgun from her waistband, and rested it next to her thigh.

"Whoa." The reverend showed his hands. "That's...not really necessary, now is it, child? You agreed to listen, I agreed to bring you some relief. Just...relax. I'm unarmed."

"Go ahead then, Reverend," she said, but the gun stayed out. "I'm listening."

"You are on a suicide mission, young lady, and you don't need to be. Things here are under control. Justice Coolsummer is under control."

"How is that?"

"She's being adequately incented, but it's a little...complicated. You'll need to trust me. She'll vote the way we need her to. Here, take your bag of meds. It's a ninety-day supply. Take them, pack yourself up, get back on the road, and go home."

She wanted to believe him, wanted so much to think this baby-killing odyssey would end the way he said it would, the way it should, the way God wanted it to. She flinched from a jolt to her abdomen, intestinal pain that reminded her she needed some oxy relief soon. "Throw the bag to me."

"So you'll end this now?"

Jane's Baby

Her eyes narrowed. "Yes. The meds."

"I'm not sure I believe you, Larinda."

"You have no choice."

"Fine. But put your gun on the ground, please."

"I can't do that, Reverend."

Larinda, her eyes drilling into his, thumbed the safety lock off. With neither of them moving, the reverend finally got the message.

"Okay then," he said. "Keep the gun. Here."

His underhand toss was off the mark, the bag landing just outside the tunnel, in the sun.

"Sorry. No harm done, Larinda, the bottles are plastic."

She checked each end of the tunnel again, the trail still clear in both directions, then she refocused on the reverend. Backing into the sunlight, her eyes not leaving him, she bent at her waist to reach for the small plastic bag. A shadow crept across the bag from the trail above the tunnel and stopped, became a stationary silhouette, it was directly above her...

She spun, dropped onto her back, both hands steadying her gun, her finger on the trigger releasing a short pffft of a bullet burst skyward. A shotgun blast from above the tunnel blew a hole through the layer of fallen leaves next to her, kicking up dirt and twigs that rained on her as the gun loosened from the shooter's hands and dropped into the grave the blast had dug for it. She rolled out of the way, the shooter's body dropping fifteen feet and thudding next to her, atop the shotgun. Bouncing to her feet, she trained her gun on the dead man. It was the jogger. She raised her weapon and faced the reverend. If he had a gun, it would have been out by now. He was instead frozen in place.

"Truth be told, Reverend," she said, panting, "this is the way I thought it would go. With you, the senator, and the rest of The Faithful. Although I did think you'd also be armed. One question, and please be truthful. Are these meds the real thing?"

"OxyContin!" he said, desperate now, a plea. "Yes! They're what you need, Larinda. Please, child." He backed away, moving toward the other end of the tunnel, his hands raised in self-defense, retreating. "I'm telling the truth!"

"Good, Reverend. Thanks. And I'm sorry."

"Larinda! You don't need to..."

Three quick shots. "Yes, Reverend, I do."

THIRTY-FIVE

Deputy Marshal Abelson dropped them off at Judge's van in the parking garage. Maybe it was the boost he got from retrieving his gun from the glove box, but now that Judge and Geenie both had their guns back, his bruised ribs hurt a lot less. He made Geenie comfortable back at the B&B, walked his canine deputies, fed them, and sat them down for some big ol' Daddy-loves-you hugs. Now to figure out what the hell to do differently about Larinda Jordan than a half-dozen federal agencies weren't already doing. His phone rang.

"Edward. Back at you, sir." Owen's ears perked up. Geenie was in her seat, dozing. "Yeah, well, you're welcome again, Edward. What do you need?...I see. Thanks for the invite, but we can't make it. My German Shepherd's been cooped up all day and needs some attention."

"Bring the dogs," Edward said. "I'll have someone watch them."

It didn't work like that, Judge told him; not part of their training. "Thanks but no thanks," he said and ended the call.

They hadn't moved yet when Edward called again. "Justice Coolsummer won't take no for an answer. Your deputies can stay attached to you at the hip if necessary, assuming they're house-trained."

Judge caved. The dinner invite was for seven p.m. Barbecue. For Owen it was a no-brainer, like he'd been invited to a debutante's ball. And maybe a little more insight from Edward and Justice Coolsummer wouldn't hurt the manhunt effort, Judge mused. The madam justice had invited both dogs. Judge decided Maeby needed to take a rain check so she could stay at the B&B with Geenie, who was running on empty.

At the B&B Judge tucked Geenie into bed then leaned down, his lips soft against hers and her swollen jaw. "If kisses could heal," he told her, "I'd be all over you."

"They're helping," she managed. She cupped his cheek in her hand. "You need to be careful, Judge."

"Justice Coolsummer's residence might be one of the more secure places on the planet right about now," he said. "Rest and feel better."

Seeing Owen in the B&B parlor, Judge regretted his decision already. Judge was in jeans and a navy blue long-sleeved pullover with brown loafers. Owen was dressed like a cattle baron: bolo tie, custom fitted western-cut shirt, jeans, and cowboy boots, all underneath that black, sequined ten-gallon hat. Except...

His clownish behavior, his bawdy attitude and his drinking, the latter not in evidence at the moment, plus his genetics, cleaned up like this, and in his element, Judge saw him better. This was an attractive man who was proud of what he had to offer, and who at this point in his life didn't care about anyone else's perception of him, save for one U.S. Supreme Court associate justice.

"Owen."

"Yeah, boss?"

"You look good, bro. I mean it. Really good. She'll be impressed."

"Thanks, boss."

"Just keep the hat off your lap."

"Got it, boss."

His wink said maybe he would, maybe he wouldn't. Judge decided he was good with that.

THIRTY-SIX

Larinda punched the security code into the keypad and the iron gate at the condo community entrance separated. She drove her Toyota SUV through like she belonged here, had to slow down and fall in behind a chugging six-wheeled dump truck carrying hot road tar that she could smell, giving the truck the room it deserved. Both vehicles moved timidly past a United Van Lines moving van that took up three parking spaces in front of the target's townhouse, the front door to the townhouse closed. Boxes from the moving van were on the street, the grass, and the front steps. She cruised past the house, losing the tar truck when she eased her vehicle around a corner. She now viewed the end unit from its side, then cruised a little more, to where she could view the house from its rear. Four exits confirmed, front, side, and two out back, one to a ground level patio, the other to a deck above it. She braked the SUV, put it into park.

Binoculars up. She scanned for other rooftops visible from where she sat. Binoculars down. Binoculars up then down again several times. What she was after: sightlines and vantage points from outside the gated community that converged on the justice's townhouse.

It was forty minutes past her popping some oxy from the new prescription. Half a pill only, her hedge against the reverend's veracity. The abdominal pain was under control and she wasn't dead, two good reasons for her to pop open the top to the bottle again and chew her way through a few more doses.

Feeling much, much better now.

She finished circling the block, returned to the front of the target's condo, and double-parked next to the moving van, her flashers on. Standard four p.m. residential activity: people exercising their dogs, small children on tricycles and scooters, watchful parents. The movers continued unloading the truck, stopping to read markings on boxes then strapping the larger ones and the few furniture pieces to their backs and shoulders and hand trucks, then depositing them on the sidewalk, the steps and the porch, as near to the front door as possible. All indications were the judge wasn't home and the house wasn't being watched from inside or out, but this would all change soon, otherwise the movers wouldn't have started to unload.

Her black Indian-squaw hair tucked inside a ball cap, Larinda stuffed a few sticks of chewing gum in her mouth and grabbed her sunglasses. She was good to go.

With the SUV's lift gate open, Larinda wrote on a cardboard box then lifted it aside in favor of hefting a dwarf evergreen in a clay pot from the SUV to the curb, setting it there, next to the small city of cardboard boxes accumulating on the sidewalk. She did the same with three other potted shrubs, all eventually curbside.

One of the movers looked at her funny while she unloaded the shrubs. More than a look, a leer.

"From the community's homeowners group," she said to him, her chewing gum cracking. "Gifts for the new resident."

He smiled at her, his beaming white teeth contrasted by his pleasant, cocoa Caribbean face, but he said nothing. "To welcome her," she added. More smiling but still no acknowledgment, only the vacuous look of someone who didn't understand a word of what she'd said. As a last resort, she'd try her Spanish.

"Gift. Un regalo. Welcome. Bienvenida."

More leering. When she showed him a twenty-dollar bill, a miracle happened. "Si," he said.

She pointed and spoke, making hand gestures to direct the potted trees to where they should go. "El portico, el lado, puerta trasero..." Her directions delivered, she handed him the money.

He hefted one of the pots up the steps. His back to her now, she added a box from her SUV to the city of stacked cardboard already strewn about the sidewalk.

The movers' unloading continued, Larinda watching from inside her car, the long front porch filling up, the truck nearly empty. She flipped off her flashers and u-turned through the front gate.

In her rearview at a traffic light, for the second time in two days she watched two unmarked Ford sedans and a cop car proceed down the street toward the community's gated entrance, this time at the speed limit. A man exited the first sedan, read from his phone as he punched numbers into the keypad. All three vehicles entered the community.

Some pieces had fit in place just like she'd wanted, she mused. Others could have only been left to chance. If she'd spent two minutes more out front of the judge's residence she might well have been in a gunfight, and all could have been lost. A reminder that this life and everything in it would always be on God's terms. God's plan, not man's, always.

Ecclesiastes 3:1. To everything there is a season, a time for every purpose under heaven.

She needed to make it happen tonight. She wouldn't get one more day to kill her.

THIRTY-SEVEN

Deputy Marshal Hugh Abelson stood outside the gate to the community, one of two marshals wanding vehicles before they entered, a large security floodlight over his shoulder. He wanded the undercarriage of Judge's van with his mirror-on-a-stick, then he returned to the open driver's side window, a pair of binoculars hanging from his neck. It was dusk.

"Gotta look inside too, Mister Drury."

"Be my guest, Mister Abelson. But be careful of the bomb-sniffing dog back there."

Judge opened the back door for him to peek inside the cargo area. His German Shepherd growled from inside his crate, snapped once, then relaxed.

"You've got more shit in here than I have access to," he said. He crawled inside, did an investigative pirouette, then climbed back out. "This looks great. For an assault vehicle. I can't let this thing inside the gate. Park it up the street. And if either you or Mister Wingert are carrying a weapon, you'll need to keep it locked up in the van."

They parked around a corner. Judge's Glock went into the glove box again.

Marshal Abelson wanded them both, then the dog, then entered the code to let them into the community. They walked back on freshly paved blacktop, the asphalt crew one block over working the night shift. They reached the justice's place and climbed the steps to a long porch with white rockers. It was seven thirty-ish by the time another agent completed yet another pat down. The agent raised his binoculars when he was done, to continue surveilling the surrounding rooftops.

Judge's dog deputy stopped short on the porch, skittish about entering the house. Not the case with Owen, who possessed a Texas-sized swagger fresh from the compliment Judge had given him. A hard tug on J.D.'s leash and they were all inside.

Jane's Baby

Edward, U.S. marshal number three, greeted them. His tightened jaw said he was still smarting from this afternoon's excitement.

"You okay, Marshall?"

"Tonight's my last night for this assignment, Mister Drury. A new marshal reports for duty tomorrow morning. Madam Justice Coolsummer respects my decision."

"Wow. Okay. How many other marshals here tonight?"

"Six, if you include Mister Abelson at the front gate, who'll be joining us shortly. Two more downstairs, one at the rear patio door and the other at the side door. Come in. Madam Justice is on the deck, working on her barbecue."

Inside was a large living room, a den/entertainment center, dining room, and a luxurious eat-in kitchen, all with the furniture haphazardly placed but looking like it had at least made it to the right rooms. Cardboard everywhere, some boxes open, some closed, some already flattened, ready for the trash. Justice Coolsummer had a lot of unpacking ahead of her, not much of which she'd get to tonight.

Judge stopped to absorb this gathering of packed cardboard, assessing the possibilities. His look was telling.

"It's all been either scanned or opened by the techs," Edward said, sensing the concern.

French doors led to the deck at the rear of the home, off the kitchen. Outside, Justice Coolsummer, in tapered jeans, a light-colored zippered workout jacket and an Oklahoma Sooners barbecue apron in cream and red, stood in front of her barbecue, smoking her meats. Not how Judge had pictured his probably one and only social event with an associate justice on the Supreme Court.

"It's not how I see her either," Edward said on the sly, reading his mind. "She gave her clerks an extensive urgent shopping list and had help unpacking the necessary tools. It seems she takes pride in her barbecue."

In her one hand she held a long pewter barbecue fork, in the other a pewter spatula, the two tools rotating Texas red-hots, baby back ribs and burgers on the grill.

"Don't be afraid of the apron, Edward," she said, speaking above the sizzle. "Being schooled in Oklahoma doesn't make me any less a native Texan. Not every Sooner is a mortal enemy of the Longhorns. Beer and wine in the cooler, gentlemen. Kibble over there, Mister Drury," she said, pointing to the far corner of the immense deck. "Please make yourselves comfortable out here. Let me know how you like the deck furniture. Damn it, where are the tongs?"

Judge offered Geenie's regrets. He got to hear how the madam justice had no deck at her Austin condo, and how she was intimidated by the size of this one. These furnishings, even the barbecue, which the movers had set up for her, were all new. "But I'm not a novice. I had a beautiful brick barbecue when my husband Reed was alive, many years ago, before I decided to downsize. Y'all will need to taste my barbecue sauce. From scratch. A Native American recipe. No road kill, but that's the only thing not in there."

They ate, they drank, they talked, they heard "I'm sorry" and "Please forgive me" and multiple thank yous, the four of them on the deck swapping Texas and Oklahoma and Philly and D.C. tall tales and humor, Judge's canine partner there as well. Owen behaved, refrained from any boner references, even had a civil discussion with her regarding minority rights. And one shocker: he refused alcohol. "I need to cut down," he said when the madam justice asked what he was drinking. "This is as good a place to start as any."

Judge gave the associate justice a pass on her earlier behavior. This was a strong woman, someone who had suffered through a stressful patch, and who deserved a second chance. Something, maybe Edward's request for reassignment, had shocked the bitch out of her.

It was nearing nine o'clock, the light from the kitchen doing a poor job of illuminating the deck. Edward stepped inside the French doors long enough to accept a package from Mr. Abelson, a flat but colorfully gift-wrapped present in the shape of a picture frame. He returned to the deck with it.

"They scanned it, Your Honor, so it's clean," he said, and handed it to her.

She opened it. Her eyes welled at seeing its contents: her Oklahoma School of Law diploma, reframed under glass, this

Jane's Baby

afternoon's massive gash repaired. She stood to give Edward a hug where he sat, which he begrudgingly accepted.

"A rush repair job, Your Honor. You would have regretted not having it later, ma'am."

She kissed him on his cheek. "Thank you, Edward." Even in the poor light Edward's eyes betrayed that he'd been moved by her response, much the same she was by his. This surprise show of affection sealed it; time for Judge and Owen to make their exit. They said their goodbyes.

Judge crouched to check on his dog deputy. J.D. was where he'd been all night, loose but with his leash still attached and sitting under the window, close enough to the grill to enjoy the lingering smells, and able to snap up any stray barbecue.

"Is he good with strangers?" Justice Coolsummer asked, hovering. "I mean, can I..."

"Not especially good, ma'am, but after this much time seeing you and I together, off the clock and relaxed, and after all the grilled meat you dropped for him, I'd say you bought your way into some face time. Just no quick moves."

She crouched down and let him sniff her, scratched behind his ears some. She stopped.

"Edward."

"Ma'am?" Edward arrived alongside them.

"That box..."

An unopened cardboard box the size of a milk crate had her attention, left of the French doors, against a railing; the only box out here. She stood over it, read aloud what was written on the top flap.

"It says 'Back deck.' That's not my handwriting."

"Ma'am," Judge asked, "maybe one of the packers?"

"I didn't decide on this place until after they packed me. I didn't know I'd have a deck." She leaned down, reached for a box flap.

"Ma'am, no," Edward said. "Mr. Drury?"

Judge pulled J.D. the few feet from the barbecue to the box. "Check it out, boy." The command put the dog back on the job. He sniffed at each corner but gave no indications. He returned to his master's side.

"Ma'am," Edward looked at her expectantly, "if I may?"

"Yes, Edward, please open it."

Edward split the top and lifted out a handful of pamphlets, handing some to Justice Coolsummer. He read aloud from one of them. "'The American Life Allegiance exists to protect innocent human beings from pre-birth to death.'"

Justice Coolsummer shook her head. "Literature with an agenda. I get it all the time, from both sides of the debate."

Judge turned, looking for his dog, found him sidled up next to a small, potted evergreen near the French doors that led back inside. The dog lifted his leg. "No, boy. J.D., no!"

Edward again read aloud, this time from a handwritten post-it note stuck to the back of the pamphlet. "'This pro-life protection does not include you, Justice Coolsummer. BANG.'"

The dog didn't pee on the shrub, instead sniffed then grunted then sat on his hindquarters next to the clay pot in his I-just-discovered-something mode, waiting to be rewarded.

"Bomb...!" Judge said.

THIRTY-EIGHT

Larinda, on the roof of a low-rise Georgetown apartment building: black hair, a dark ball cap, black pants and athletic shoes, and a black Kevlar vest, all of it adding to the camouflage of nightfall. Seven seconds to the rooftop exit from this vantage point near the ledge, four seconds if she ran.

She lifted the 5.56 smart rifle and leaned its tripod on the ledge chest-high, snugged up the precision-guided tracking optic. She had no business owning this weapon. Too cost-prohibitive for an itinerant carpenter, and affordable only with funding from a hugely popular religious non-profit. Thank you, Christian Charismatic Ministry of Wisdom and Light. Praise the Lord and pass the ammunition.

Something she hadn't counted on, but it would work in her favor: her target was entertaining on the townhouse's raised deck, fully visible. Hanging with the target were the bodyguard, the bounty hunter, his dog, and his midget. Very tempting alternative targets. They were all complicit; she had no compunction about making them all pay.

She positioned herself behind the rifle and found her target with the optics.

The large bodyguard moved into the line of fire.

"No!" she said, gritting her teeth, "move!"

Larinda couldn't tell if the Supreme Court justice was still behind him or had reentered the house. Seconds passed, Justice Coolsummer still not visible. A helicopter made a wide turn, its searchlight scanning distant rooftops south of the community. She had maybe forty seconds before it would make a return sweep in this direction.

"Okay, original plan," she thought aloud, which was explosions and fire at each of the home's exits, with bombs in each of the potted evergreens to be detonated by rifle. They would flush her target outside, where Larinda could cut her down. She re-sighted the tracking optic to the edge of the front porch, to where a shrubbery pot peeked out from a corner.

Tovex sausages surrounded by jars of Tannerite exploding binary rifle targets, bundled together at the bottom of each clay pot, delivered to the side door, the corners of the back deck, the basement patio, and the front porch. All four exits of the townhouse.

Time was a-wastin'.

She pressed a button on the gun. The scope tagged the front porch shrubbery pot, aligning the gun's reticle with the tag; she squeezed and held the trigger. The tracking system delayed the release, waiting for the optimum conditions, its can't-miss technology good for up to five hundred yards. From here it was much less than that.

One second, two seconds...*pffft...BOOM*. The front corner of the porch exploded in a ball of fire, and one flaming, suited body tumbled down the slate steps to the curb. She re-sighted the gun, aimed at the box on the slab next to the side door of the home. One second, two seconds...*pffft...BA-BOOM*. The front and the side of the house were now in flames.

Larinda re-sighted the gun to the rear patio, under the deck. The helicopter did a compact turn from half a mile away and sprinted toward her rooftop. One second, two seconds...*pffft...BOOM*, the patio area underneath the deck was now orange and red, another agent in flames. She raised the barrel of the rifle slightly, re-sighted it.

"There you are, Madam Justice."

The bodyguard enveloped her target, his gun drawn but with nowhere to point it. He hustled her toward the back door, toward cover inside the house, but they needed to first pass the last potted evergreen.

One second, two seconds...*pffft...BOOM*.

THIRTY-NINE

A chunk of the deck next to the French doors was blown away, the deck floor flaming up and advancing. Judge yelled at Owen to drop himself onto the grass a full story below them. Judge lobbed his dog over the railing; J.D. hit the ground okay and backed away from the blaze, then barked up at his master. Behind Judge on the deck Edward was on fire, lying atop a screaming Naomi Coolsummer. He rolled off her, pleaded with Judge... "Lower her down!"...then rolled back and forth against the deck flooring, his chest and back flaming up. The rear of the townhouse was ablaze, the flames nearing the second floor windows. Judge ripped Justice Coolsummer's burning apron off her, lifted her into his arms and wheeled, his Tourette's now kicking in, sapping his breathing...

"...Motherfucker cocknobbin' MOTHERFUCKER!..."

A metallic *pffft* grazed Judge's neck from another shot. He jumped off the deck with Judge Coolsummer in his arms. Owen was down there looking up, his arms open, wanting to break their fall. His eyes got big as they came slamming down, nearly crushing him. Above them a weaving Edward leaned over the deck rail, stripped off his burning jacket revealing body armor also on fire. He ripped the armor off and prepared to jump. Another sniper shot. Edward's shoulder jerked forward, freezing him in a silhouette against the fire. He groaned then was airborne, landing awkwardly on the grass.

"Edward!" Justice Coolsummer tried to stand, her ankle buckling. Repeating shots rained down, chipping away at the burning deck, now in the way of the sniper's line of fire, the angle shielding them, the deck still standing but not for long. The floorboards started snapping from the advancing flames.

"We gotta move!" Judge yelled, sirens gathering in the distance. Neighbors poked their heads out of their townhomes, some exiting their back doors, moving in their direction.

The wounded marshal hauled himself up from the grass, lifting Justice Coolsummer over his shoulder. "My truck," he shouted, panting, "bulletproof..."

The black diesel monster was visible between two townhouses the next street over, thirty yards away on the other side of the common space. Edward lumbered toward it, Justice Coolsummer bouncing against his shoulder as he ran. Judge scanned the rooftops. No gunpowder flash, but a reflection as good as one caught his eye, on a not-too-distant rooftop, city lights mirroring off something metal or glass, the object moving along a ledge. Simultaneous to the reflection Edward's other shoulder jerked forward; he dropped to his knees. The advancing neighbors backed off, returning to the protection of their homes. Both Edward and Justice Coolsummer groaned. Edward struggled, got up, and kept moving.

The gunshot was a tell as bad as a mirror in a desert: a rooftop two blocks away, an apartment house six stories high. Another marshal, Abelson, saw it too. He was now outside on the ground-level patio and talking into a mouthpiece. A helicopter swooped in closer, hovering above the community, its searchlight scanning nearby rooftops. Abelson assumed the position and fired repeatedly, emptied his gun, slid in a new clip, took aim again. A burst of semi-automatic rifle fire took out the copter's searchlight then hacked out chunks of Abelson's thigh like red cabbage cleaved by an axe. Judge's TS kicked in full throttle.

"...motherless motherfucking motherfucker...!"

Judge and his dog and Owen reached the street, huddling together behind concrete step risers; they could see the pickup. Its idling engine roared once from a heavy foot while still in neutral, its interior lights on, Edward draped heavily against the steering wheel, Naomi Coolsummer in the front seat next to him. The truck peeled out, drove erratically, banging off parked cars, semi-automatic rifle fire from the roof tracking it, punching divots into the covered cargo bed before finding the rear tires. The bulletproof tires smoked from the hits but didn't deflate, the truck careening forward, headed into a live road paving scene illuminated by two-story work spotlights. There the pickup fishtailed, slamming sideways into the rear of a tar truck, trapping the driver's side against it. The tar truck bucked. Judge and Owen saw the horror materializing, helpless at this distance.

"No, NO, motherfucker, NO!"

The truck's payload released, the hot tar cascading slowly onto the roof of the diesel four-door like fresh hot fudge onto a brownie, with Edward and the judge inside. The road crew tugged frantically at the pickup's passenger side door, the tar sliding off the roof, about to swallow the truck whole. Judge trotted his dog toward the scene then stopped short when gunfire pinged off the chromed door handles. The roof of the pickup buckled under the weight of the tar, compromised by the heat. Bullets sizzled into the oozing black tar muck, bore their way through it then punched a hole in the buckled window, stopping moments before ordnance from the helicopter sent repeating gunfire at its unseen target. High-powered work lights were unforgiving in their display, even at this distance, until someone got wise and shut them off. Owen hustled in Judge's wake. He caught up, doubled over and heaved up his barbecue.

Judge knew he'd be of little help here now. His rage kicked in, and with it his adrenaline pitched him into overdrive. He grabbed his dog's leash, trotted him toward the community's front gate to find his van, leaving Owen behind to finish emptying his stomach and his bladder. The assassin was two blocks away. He was going after her.

FORTY

Tar covered the truck, oozed off the roof, the hood, the door panels, dripped in huge globs into thickening black pools on the ground. The rifle's optics tagged the truck door handle. Larinda depressed the trigger, waited for the delayed burst of bullets to scatter the road workers. The tall spotlights switched off, the scene of the massacre going dark.

She lowered the rifle, stared, sniffed, showed no emotion. She was satisfied. A bullet shower then a hot tar bath. No one could survive that.

She dropped the smart rifle on the rooftop, retrieved her Tec-9 handgun from her backpack. Cars with flashing lights and sirens bore down on the block that contained this apartment building. Four seconds to get to the rooftop exit, thirty seconds to get down six sets of stairs. Automatic gunfire pinged off the roof ledge from an approaching helicopter as she closed the door behind her.

At ground floor she threw open a fire door and exited the building, the handgun behind her back. People on the street were preoccupied, spectators busy scattering in the direction of the nearby townhome community. She tucked her gun into her backpack, charged around a corner, and approached her vehicle. It had garnered interest, was now blocked by two police cars.

If they wanted it, they could have it.

She made no eye contact with the uniformed cops, strode past her car, the cops shining flashlights into it, about to break the rear window. Screeching vehicles stopped in front of the building. Plainclothes agents exited them, some entering the lobby, others looking for the fire exits, all with their weapons drawn.

She'd chance no bridge checkpoints out of D.C., no D.C. Metrorail searches, no carjacking that could go wrong. It was six blocks to the Key Bridge Boathouse. A ten-minute walk or three-minute jog or two-minute run. Then it would be, needed to be, no more than fifteen minutes max in a canoe, paddling away from

D.C. She expected to make it across the Potomac under the radar because, she knew, God loved her and would protect her.

Naomi was semi-conscious, bloodied, in shock, her shoulder immobilized, pinned by buckled hot metal burning into her skin next to a gunshot wound. Her chest and face were singed, her ankle throbbing. Intense heat and tar fumes made it difficult to breathe. The passenger window exploded, letting in a whoosh of cooler, nighttime air.

A creaking door hinge cut through the fog. "Got you," the little man said, tugging at her forearm. Inside the truck the massive, protective arm that had been around her shoulder, drawing her close, was now limp.

"Edward..." she managed before losing consciousness.

FORTY-ONE

"C'mon, c'mon, move your ass..."

Traffic let up as Judge circled the apartment building. He knew who he was looking for. The Feds might notice her if she were attached to an assault weapon, otherwise, they might not. The low-rise was being evacuated and agents hovered in the lobby, at the bottom of the fire escape and at other exits. This would be a room-by-room search. An SUV on the street was overrun by a bomb squad, the agents dressed for the part.

Judge's assertion was she'd already left, was out here somewhere on foot.

"J.D., you're up, dude," he told his dog, whose ears perked to attention. Judge found space for the van, parked and opened the back door. His dog was in his face. "Easy, boy, hold on."

Kevlar for them both, a longer leash, high-intensity LED flashlight, extra clips, and handcuffs. An ankle holster and handgun. He retrieved the bounty's tee shirt from a plastic grocery bag to reacquaint J.D. with it, his partner now super-stoked. They followed the perimeter of the building. J.D. picked up a scent at a side door.

"Hold it, Cowboy," was directed at Judge. Another agent in a suit. "Don't. Move."

His partner sniffed and continued straining hard on his leash. "Fugitive recovery agent," Judge announced. The agent let him badge him, the agent's associate too busy shaking down exiting apartment residents.

Judge got chatty. "Look, you guys might be wasting your time. My dog is a tracker. His nose says the sniper was here, is gone, and is headed..." he let his partner pull him forward, "this way."

Judge and dog now had company. Two agents were freed up to walk with them, which meant trot some when J.D.'s Shepherd legs got frisky, and run some as well. They put two blocks

Jane's Baby

between them and the apartment building and were headed southeast. He still had a scent, still tracked the sidewalk, with occasional detours into alleys that dead-ended, returning to the street each time, always moving.

Four blocks into their trek an agent spoke up, his hand to his ear, stopping the entourage. J.D. whined, pulled at his master to step it up. "The supervisor says we're two blocks from the Key Bridge Boathouse. He thinks that's where she went. They're setting up on the bridge so they can get a look at the river."

Back on the scent his Shepherd took them around an electric gate and underneath one of the arches for the Francis Scott Key Bridge. At the bottom of an incline were stacked kayaks and canoes on a dock, with paddleboats tied together and bobbing in the water next to a few outboards. His dog paced the length of the dock, soon sat panting and out of breath on the canoe end. He waited for a reward.

"She's in a canoe or a kayak?" an agent asked.

"That's what my deputy says."

"Good job. Pay the man," one of the agents said, and Judge tossed his partner a treat.

Judge retrieved his flashlight, switched it on, the other agents doing likewise with theirs. Their lights swept the area near the shoreline and the dock, showed nothing, so they shined the lights farther out into the river, where distance made them less effective. The agent called his supervisor and seconds later two spotlights on the Key Bridge above them flipped on. A third sparked up, the three of them spaced out along the bridge's pedestrian walkway. Behind them on the bridge, pulsing red and blue bursts of light sprayed the nighttime sky from the cop cars belonging to the handhelds, the spotlights as bright as searchlights at a Hollywood premiere. The cops aimed them down at the river, close to the bridge, the water murky but calm. Suddenly all lights converged.

A canoe. In it someone with long dark hair was paddling like a champ. A woman. She glided through at a silent clip, the spots lighting her up like a figure skater in a darkened stadium. She put the paddle down, stayed seated, motionless. The canoe drifted a little, the lights blinding her; she raised her arm to shield them. A bullhorn delivered a tinny, garbled voice that might have been a cop, might not have been, sounding more like it came from the river. A deafening foghorn followed the bullhorn.

Christ, Judge thought, a fucking boat, it's gonna ram her...

A short burst of semi-auto gunfire from the canoe interrupted the foghorn, chipping the face of the bridge beneath the closest spotlight. A second burst, longer and raised higher, found the spotlight the first burst missed. The agents around him on the dock un-holstered their weapons and fired on the canoe, a distance of maybe seventy yards. An uninterrupted burst from the canoe moved from light to light, wild, erratic, the canoe bucking from the recoil but the burst still aimed well enough to neutralize two lights out of three. Judge's canine pulled hard, wanted to give chase in the water, his master needing two hands to restrain him. The one spotlight on the bridge stayed functional, crammed into barbed wire fencing.

Another blast of the foghorn, and the cop repositioned the last shaft of light to illuminate a cabin cruiser bearing down on the canoe. The cruiser slowed, but not enough. The canoe flipped, was churned underneath, resurfacing in its wake in pieces as the cruiser continued under the bridge. Flashing lights strobed the sky from additional cop cars on the bridge and across the river on the Virginia shoreline, with vehicles advertising in red and blue arriving in large numbers.

A Coast Guard cutter drew alongside the cabin cruiser, both vessels anchoring near the Virginia side after passing under the bridge. A frantic half-hour search found canoe parts and a paddle but no shooter. The effort remained search and rescue for now.

After an hour it became a recovery mission. Divers entered the river to find the body.

On the phone with Geenie, Judge related what he knew, Geenie grunting her responses. After that he read texts from Owen, who'd been trying for the past few hours to get his attention. The texts were frantic, disturbing. Judge and J.D. hitched a ride back to his van then headed to the hospital ER where Owen held vigil.

FORTY-TWO

Naomi awakened, plenty groggy, feeling like she was floating. Her scalp tingled, her head wrapped in gauze. Her left shoulder was packed and bandaged, protecting a bullet wound with a front entrance and a back exit, a nurse told her, but this hadn't fully registered. Her ankle, immobilized by a tight cloth bandage, sat atop the bed sheet, visible but fuzzy to her. She must have said something about medication because someone volunteered an answer. "Some really good stuff, ma'am."

This was Mr. Wingert speaking, the blogger, seated in the right corner of the hospital room. No, he was standing; he was the super-short one. Naomi was now remembering, it was coming back, all the horror was coming back. She held back her tears.

"Edward..."

An authoritative voice bettered Naomi's fog: "This is Nurse Dawson, Madam Justice. You're on a narcotic drip."

To Mr. Wingert the nurse said, "She's awake. The vigil's now officially over. You need to wait outside."

"No," Naomi said, her words wet and sloppy. "He stays. For a moment, please." She turned to Owen and asked, "Where is he?"

The little guy's eyes fluttered then misted up. Beseech was the word her fuzzy mind gave her, his eyes beseeched her, blinked at her beseechingly. His hands moved near his waist, his fingers in search of his absent cowboy hat. She remembered the one.

"Ma'am," he said, "he's gone. I'm sorry."

She gagged, just now noticed there were two other men in the room, in suits, plus another man in a suit posted outside the door. One of the suited men in the room stepped forward.

"Madam Justice. Director Egan of the U.S. Marshals Service. We lost Deputy Trenton tonight, in the line of duty. Him and two others, ma'am. Deputy Abelson was also a casualty, but he'll recover."

Tears built but stayed at bay. She spoke again, but it felt like she was chewing her saliva. "That doesn't...answer...my question. Where is he?"

The director glanced at the nurse. The nurse answered for him. "He's here, ma'am. Downstairs."

"I want to see him."

The nurse said, "Ma'am, no, that's not going to happen."

Naomi strengthened her resolve, "Nurse, yes it is going to happen. Now. Director Egan, do something."

Director Egan had interceded, duly acknowledging the protest of Naomi's doctor. The patient elevator opened at the basement level. A marshal exited first then waved the entourage out, Naomi's hospital bed slightly raised and pushed by an orderly, her doctor striding alongside her, Nurse Dawson keeping up while wheeling her IV poles. Director Egan and another marshal followed them.

At the end of the wide corridor a pair of windowless doors greeted them, MORGUE stenciled in black across each one. On the other side of the doors, a tile floor, stainless steel walls and sinks, scales, microscopes, hoses, high-intensity overhead lamps, and instruments hanging like wands and brushes at a self-service car wash. The group surprised a female morgue attendant about to slide a body back into the wall.

Three bodies on gurneys, all tagged, lay flat in various stages of preparation for temporary storage, all covered in sheets, cadaver style. It smelled of blood and bodily fluids and antiseptic, the floor a mess underfoot. The attendant made quick business of the body she'd been working with and grabbed a spray hose to wet down the floor, the water and body effluence finding a drain.

"Careful, it's slippery," she said. The agents were in shoe leather and Naomi was on wheels, but everyone else had rubber-soled shoes. The orderly pushing Naomi stopped, waiting for orders from someone. No one moved. The doctor called the attendant over. "Mister Edward Trenton. Which one?"

Before the attendant answered, Naomi spoke. "I see him."

Long body, massive chest, one leg partially exposed, the knee black as if it had been dipped in licorice, some exposed bone, the skin below it copper-red, and the giveaway: five discolored toes on his right foot, all milky white, a yellow toe tag on the big one. The orderly guided Naomi alongside.

"Edward," she managed after composing herself, her hand moving from her distraught face to the sheet that covered him. "You were so very, very brave, Edward."

Her emotional pain obliterated the meds. Naomi felt the agony, a gouge driven deep into her chest, her heart sinking, a loss so reminiscent of her earlier one, so…déjà vu. The entourage gave her room. She rested her hand on the sheet again, squeezed his arm, and whispered prayers in Cherokee for the safe journey of one Edward White Paw Trenton to his rightful place in the spirit world.

The trailing marshal spoke a response into a wrist piece. "Roger that. Director Egan, sir, a V.I.P. just arrived at the hospital to see Justice Coolsummer."

"We're giving Madam Justice a few minutes, Marshal."

"Sir…" He leaned over, whispered into Director Egan's ear.

The director turned toward Naomi. "Justice Coolsummer, we need to get back upstairs ASAP."

FORTY-THREE

They sat on stiff plastic chairs with unforgiving seats three doors down from Justice Coolsummer's hospital room. Nearby was yet another U.S. marshal, who cleared Judge and Owen once again before they'd allow them near the justice when she returned upstairs. Judge's Glock was again locked up in the van, the only way they'd let him anywhere inside the hospital. How soon they forgot who the friendlies were.

Judge and his bomb-sniffing dog in training had screwed up. So had the marshals. They'd all missed the explosives hidden in the shrubbery. Judge felt all kinds of inadequate, but the reality of it was, this happened on occasion. Dogs took cues from their handlers. When handlers tensed up, there were more false alerts. Bombs that weren't there. But the reverse happened, too. When handlers were off the clock, or maybe less focused, so too were their partners. Today was one of those days. One he'd have to live with, because it had cost lives.

The U.S. Marshal's office was complicit. And in that business, a mistake like this would mean heads not already part of the body count would roll.

According to Owen, someone other than Justice Coolsummer was in her room. Owen leaned back, deep in thought. Stoic. Not a word Judge ever expected to use to describe him. The door to the justice's room stayed closed, two suits next to it, one on either side, their hands clasped in front of themselves, their heads swiveling like gun turrets. Another suit stood in front of the room's observation window.

"Owen," Judge said. "Dude. You did good. You were a hero helping to pull her out of there."

He looked lost. "It's all here, Judge, in my head, all this bizarre, deadly shit." Judge could see in his eyes he was reliving it as he spoke.

"The blood. Justice Coolsummer. The marshal, fucking Marshal Trenton, pinned in there under the collapsed roof, the tar, the hot tar, him trapped, terrible, the smell…"

Owen had lost some of his hair in the fire, a handful of dreads missing all the way back to his scalp, a small gauze patch covering the burned area. He'd also lost his hat. "My hair…it was like a fuse, it ignited my Stetson…"

Listening to him, Judge knew he was witnessing the birth of a new case of PTSD. He'd been there, was himself still victimized by it. Sitting next to Owen like this, he put his arm around his shoulder, could do nothing else for him right now other than listen.

An elevator door opened; Justice Coolsummer exited on a gurney. They wheeled her to her room, her door remaining closed. All eyes excluding the patient's found Owen and Judge. Conspicuously absent, Judge now noticed, were other voices on the floor, noises, or any activity or movement anywhere near them. No patients, no doctors, no nurses, no orderlies. A guy in plainclothes…casual pants, zippered windbreaker, bulk underneath, and a big, friendly smile…moved to within six inches of Judge's face. A second, larger guy forced Owen to take a seat.

"Guys," the smaller of the two spoke in a friendly tone, "you need to vacate this area for a bit. Go grab yourselves some coffee or something downstairs. We'll call you back up here when we can."

"Sure," Judge said, "but what's going on?" He tried to look past the agent.

"Justice Coolsummer needs some time alone."

That wasn't gonna work, Judge was thinking, considering someone was already in her room, but he stayed quiet, the guy being friendly and all. Except Judge suddenly felt the absence of his piece, the emptiness calling to him from the crook of his back. Intuition said these guys were friendlies, but it was getting a little tense. The door to her room stayed closed, one agent's hand on the knob, everyone waiting for Judge and Owen to leave.

"Badge me first," Judge said.

"Mister Drury. Friend." The agent got deadpan serious, then his smile returned, a verbal version of him patting Judge on the head. "Stay calm, don't tense up, and keep your hands at your sides. We're told this is a good thing going down here. Just go with it. Go downstairs, get some coffee."

"I guess that means you won't be badging me."

"You guessed right. A marshal will escort you. You have to go. Now."

In the cafeteria Owen got a hot chocolate, Judge grabbed a coffee. A U.S. marshal with tea who swore he knew nothing about what was going on upstairs was babysitting them. Right about now all Judge wanted to do was pay his respects to Justice Coolsummer and get the hell back with Geenie, who'd been such a champ through all this. He called her, then he called LeVander, to let them each know the outcome of the chase. The bounty had been neutralized. Her body was in the process of being located. A U.S. Supreme Court associate justice had, at last update, survived an assassination attempt. Things were looking up.

Judge sipped his coffee. They waited for that call from upstairs.

FORTY-FOUR

The door to her hospital room opened and they wheeled Naomi in. Three people waited for her inside. The two who faced her bookended a third who did not, all three dressed casually in workout clothing, the person facing the window in hooded sweats, the window's curtains closed. The nurse reattached Naomi to her monitors. Her meds were fine, she told the doctor and nurse. They both left the room because one of her three visitors suggested they needed to.

She knew who this was, even through the calm of the medication, just wasn't sure the reason for the visit.

The black cotton hood slid back to rest atop squared shoulders that presented good posture, revealing tight cornrows of black hair tinted slightly red. The visitor appeared every bit a professional boxer or mixed martial arts fighter in training, her sweats bulky, not flattering. She wore no makeup yet was still photogenic, her dark skin thick, smooth, almost perfectly so, benefiting from the coupling of two ethnicities, African American and Native American, whose ancestors on both sides had spent a millennium in the sun.

"Madam President."

"Hello, Madam Justice." POTUS Lindsey reached for Naomi's hand, gripped it. "I'm so incredibly happy to see you've survived this mess. I have something you need to hear, in private."

The two Secret Service agents exited. The president dragged a vinyl armchair over to the bed and sat, man-spreading her legs. "We call these 'incognito sweats.' I have many. Pardon my familiarity, but they're too bulky for me to sit any other way."

She began. "Cards on the table. A few influential people have in their possession some interesting documentation regarding your birth parents. I know these people came to you about it, for political leverage. You'll know how I know this in a minute."

Naomi's meds, hearing this, they didn't stand a chance at keeping her fully calm. Sleepy a moment ago, she was now hyper-aware.

"Sealed by the courts," POTUS continued, "like all closed adoptions were back then, this documentation could become a showstopper for a Supreme Court justice's career, regardless of how strong her character is. For her, it might mean a whole new perspective regarding certain issues. Pro-choice versus pro-life comes to mind."

Naomi cleared her throat. "That Supreme Court justice," she said thickly, "would be lying if she said it hasn't affected her. But you should also know that one case in particular is still to be decided."

The president shook her head. "Good."

"These people with the documentation, Madam President...I assume you know who they are."

"Yes. As a matter of fact, they're on their way over here right now with it, but they won't make it in to see you."

"Please say you're not planning to..."

"No, no, of course not. We intend to simply relieve them of their trump card. Not because the documentation speaks the truth. We need it as evidence.

"The records are forgeries, Naomi. A kind but desperate man falsified them to satisfy their blackmail demands thirty years ago. When you were confirmed as the newest Supreme Court justice, he realized the potential enormity of the fallout, the...power his sleight of hand had given them. He provided the Executive Branch with proof of his forgeries, the real birth documentation, to make us aware of the prospective power play. The perpetrators don't know they're not the real thing.

"We intended to tell you, Naomi, but not until after Senator Folsom played you."

"And the man who did the forgeries is...?"

"Dead. An elderly Texas pastor whom the guilty parties felt knew too much. Murdered last week, by the same woman who came after you tonight. The pastor planned to contact you after he alerted us. He just didn't live long enough." The president leaned in. "Naomi..."

She took Naomi's hand in hers and squeezed it.

"Last year, an extensive vetting process uncovered the Jane Roe baby's identity, to prove that, as an adoptee, she was still an American citizen. Before she could assume her newest duties...very visible duties...as a public servant. This was never publicized, for a number of reasons."

The president's stare waited for Naomi's groggy mind to catch up, to let this revelation sink in, with the president acting every bit like a sister sharing a secret about herself, a secret that must never be shared again.

"I can assure you, Naomi," President Lindsay said, "this person is not you."

FORTY-FIVE

Judge had a second coffee in the cafeteria while Owen ate a pastry. The marshal was getting antsy, checking and rechecking his earpiece. It was almost eleven p.m., and they were tired. Judge wanted to get back to the B&B, see Geenie, hold her, comfort her, have her comfort him.

The marshal cupped his ear to answer a call. "Yessir, I'm here." He scanned the cafeteria. "A few nurses, a doctor and a cashier, sir. And us. No one else...Roger that." To Owen and Judge he said, "We're getting some company. After that, we're good to go."

Some noise swelled the hallway outside the cafeteria's swinging doors. A blob of new customers entered.

No. Shit.

It was the senior white-haired senator from Texas plus a guy in a suit, a New York lawyer type, talking into her ear. They had escorts, all law enforcement, six of them. The two men trailing them swung the cafeteria doors shut, remaining outside. The cafeteria was now temporarily closed.

"I am here," the senator said to the marshal in charge, her Texas-sized senatorial indignation on display, "to see Associate Justice Coolsummer. I understand someone tried to kill her. I want to offer my help. Why did you redirect me to the cafeteria, Marshal...?"

"Director Egan."

"Egan. Right. Is Madam Justice all right?"

"Senator Folsom, the judge is in stable condition and is resting. There have been other casualties. You won't get in to see her tonight." Director Egan paused, pursed his lips. "Or tomorrow, or maybe ever."

"What? Why is that?" Senator Folsom's chin was up, with her doing her best to stare down her nose at him. He towered over her by at least eight inches.

Jane's Baby

"Because, Madam Senator, we have a warrant for your arrest."

"You have what?"

"A warrant for conspiracy to commit murder, for conspiracy to commit blackmail, for terrorism, coercion, illegal wiretapping, and misappropriation of public funds. There's more you'll hear later. I won't cuff you, Senator, but only if you follow me in an orderly fashion after I read you your rights. Senator Folsom, you have the right to remain silent..."

Judge was piecing this together and coming up short. Conspiracy, murder, blackmail, terrorism. The target, Justice Coolsummer. There was also a warrant for the blowhard televangelist Higby Hunt, to be served when they located him. Two alleged perpetrators, maybe more. Few other details were discernible.

Voices rose, the senator not going anywhere without her say, which forced the director to be true to his word. A marshal relieved her of her handbag and slapped the cuffs on her. Another marshal relieved her protesting lawyer friend of his briefcase. "Hey! You need a warr..."

"Not tonight, counselor. Patriot Act. Might be a weapon of mass destruction in there."

Director Egan's nod to their marshal babysitter was the call they'd been waiting for. The marshal extended his arm toward the doors. "After you, gentlemen."

Once back upstairs, they were allowed in Justice Coolsummer's room, sentries still posted outside her door. They were there to grieve, and to help her grieve also. To offer their condolences, and to say their goodbyes. Madam Justice Coolsummer was cried out, exhausted, and in her condition was no source of additional information. But she was adamant about having them stay, so the hospital staff kept its distance. Her two children were on their way from Austin to see her. Like a two year old fighting a nap, she finally began nodding. Unable to dissuade the nurses, Judge and Owen stood to leave.

Justice Coolsummer had energy enough, barely, for one more exchange. "Mister Wingert. Get yourself...another hat...and send me the bill. I insist."

"I knew you liked it, ma'am. All the ladies do. Will do, Madam Justice."

Judge was going to miss Owen.

FORTY-SIX
Three months later
NFL Football Wild Card Saturday

Philadelphia Eagles quarterback Vai Ramsay would be named NFL Offensive Rookie of the Year. "That's my prediction," Judge's girlfriend Geenie told him.

They rented an RV for their trek south, the two of them making a vacation of it. Judge's dog deputies had the week off, were staying with his farmer landlord. Repeated runs at Geenie's FBI daughter Eve provided zilch in the way of new info on Justice Coolsummer's fall term adventure. "National security," Eve had said. "Above my pay grade." Her response validated the media blackout concerning the attack on the Court. All participants and litigants in the government's case against Senator Folsom remained gagged, subject to additional charges if they didn't stay that way.

Also found dead were televangelist Higby Hunt and one of his church ministry's employees, in a park near D.C. That case's findings, according to Geenie's daughter, were also "classified." As far as the public knew, their murders remained unsolved. A small subset of the public, an acceptable percentage from the government's perspective, screamed "conspiracy" and "cover up," and for once they were right.

They entered Oak Leaf, Texas, the road sign said, passed the town's welcome sign, and made a right at the first intersection. "He's got five acres a little farther in," Judge told Geenie.

He was about to say you can't miss it, remembering how his ranch home and property looked the last time he was there two months ago, in October. A town eyesore back then but hell, not anymore. The front of the house surprised him. No truck buried in the mud ten feet from the porch, no tire ruts, and new gravel. His mailbox had been replaced. The shutters needed some paint but at least they were all up, and the roof's missing shingles had been replaced. His Boss 302 Ford Mustang gleamed in the driveway, a buffed-up Cowboy navy blue and silver. If this scene was any indication, Owen "Chigger" Wingert had cleaned up really well.

So the deal was, Owen had invited them to see the playoff football game in Dallas. It had been a miraculous second half of the season for Judge's Eagles. They rode the arm of their rookie quarterback phenom, with mucho touchdowns and fewer passes in the dirt. Conversely, the Cowboys had tanked the rest of the way after starting out nine-and-oh, their collapse almost as gratifying for a Philly boy like Judge as the Eagles' turnaround had been.

The game was in Dallas because of playoff tiebreaker math. Owen had luxury skybox tickets, courtesy of the Cowboys team owner. Judge gave the man credit for honoring Owen like he had, a class move. Owen was Texas' newest favorite son, all because of his role when the Justice Coolsummer attack went down.

It's all good, Owen. You deserve it, buddy.

Owen's front door opened. "Mi casa, su casa," he said, beaming at their arrival. He kissed Geenie's hand, winked at Judge while he did it. He and Judge fist bumped then Owen shooed them inside. His missing dreads were back. How come so soon, Judge asked him.

"Extensions," he said, whispering. "It's incredible the shit you can get at Goodwill." Judge smiled but tried not to think about it.

Three hours to game time. Some hors d'oeuvres awaited them on his center island in the kitchen. A nice spread. But the biggest shocker was the interior of his place was spotless. "Turned over a new leaf in here, Owen?" Judge asked.

"Nah. I'm just banging the housekeeper."

There it was, the Owen that Judge remembered.

"That give you a rise, Judge? Ha. I do have a housekeeper, and I do have a girlfriend now, but they're not one and the same."

They trailed Owen into the family room. Geenie took a seat on the couch. In no way could she have appreciated the hoarding spectacle she'd missed, today versus two months prior. An overwhelming difference because of what wasn't here: his Madame Alexander doll collection. With the dolls gone, the family room walls and floor were visible. Not just visible, but surprisingly clean.

Jane's Baby

"So what happened to the dolls?" Geenie asked. Judge had primed her about them.

"Sold 'em all on eBay. All except two. Made me a small fortune."

The two remaining dolls, Pocahontas and Judge Judy, were on the mantel. Owen was still smitten with their friend on the Supreme Court. Truth be told, Madam Justice Coolsummer had become a favorite of Judge's, too. A tough road back for her, but she'd made it. This coming Monday, according to a Thurgood Cochran blog exclusive, the scoop from an extremely reliable source, the *Babineau v. Turbin* Supreme Court decision would be read. Huge. But the "unnamed authority," ahem, would not divulge to Owen what the Court's ruling would be.

Judge's eyes wandered. They checked out the hallway, then checked the family room's sliding glass doors, which were behind tall drapes.

"Judge, relax. The guest room's in good shape, and the guest bathroom's been redone," he said. "You guys can freshen up whenever. And I know you want to go out back for a look, so go ahead."

He slid back the drapes, unlocked the sliding glass door. The three of them stepped outside onto the patio. Seeing the back yard restored Judge's faith in Owen as the anti-Christ of homeowners. It was still an appliance graveyard, the only change being there was more of it. Bruce, his junkyard cat, welcomed them, getting all purry and cozy with Geenie's leg. Judge shaded his eyes to scan his neighbor's cattle ranch, the property backing up to Owen's. "Where's Señor Quixote?"

Owen shaded his eyes as well. "Right...there," he said, pointing. "See that dark speck on the horizon a few hundred or so yards out? That's him."

A distant blip, something Judge thought was a railroad boxcar, the bull appearing wider than he remembered. Señor Quixote raised his head, trotted a few steps in their direction and stopped.

"Shit, he sees me," Owen said. "C'mon, let's get inside. He can close this distance faster than you'd expect. Dude's been acting a little odd, like he wants in the family room now that it's cleaned out and there's room enough for him." Owen slid the doors shut behind them and drew the drapes. "There. Out of sight for him, out of mind. Look, my girlfriend will be here any minute. I still gotta change. My phone's in the family room somewhere; just let it ring. Oh, and I've got a surprise for you, too. I'll tell you after I shower."

Owen disappeared down the hallway. Geenie and Judge got cozy on the couch and shared some hors d'oeuvres.

Tires kicked up gravel in the driveway; Owen called from his bathroom. "Judge, let her in. She's here."

Judge opened the front door, but no one was on the porch. On light feet he checked out the driveway. A small, empty sedan was now parked behind their RV. "Hello?" he said to anyone within earshot. No answer. He went on alert.

Back inside he closed the door and engaged the deadbolt. He called to Owen. "How many doors to your house?"

Owen was out of his room now, was dressed, cowboy chaps, vest, Western shirt, bolo tie, silver and blue sequined boots, his hat in hand. Another ten-gallon number. About what Judge expected.

"Front door, a side door off the kitchen, a door to the garage, a basement Bilco, and the family room slider. 'Sup? Where's Mary Veronica?"

That name...it sounded familiar. "Who?"

"You know, from back when you were here. From the Carmelite monastery. My girlfriend. She's the surprise."

The tiny admin type they'd interviewed, with the big chest.

"She had my business card, called me, was all excited for me for having saved Justice Coolsummer. I invited her out for coffee, she accepted, found me charming. The rest is history."

Now Judge remembered: the Larinda Jordan sympathizer.

Ms. Jordan's body had never been found. Owen's surprise was suddenly more troubling.

"Lock all the doors, Owen."

"What the hell? C'mon, Judge, she's my girlfriend..."

"Do it. Lock 'em and stay away from them. Now."

Judge quick-stepped around the side door in the kitchen, twisted the lock, did the same with the door to the garage, both of them steel, like the front door. Owen griped but followed his lead, latching the door to the basement.

"Family room?" Judge asked.

Jane's Baby

"I think I locked the sliders," he said. "Look, dude, relax, that's Mary Veronica's car. She's probably on her way around back."

They entered the family room. Geenie was still on the couch enjoying her finger food. She stopped mid-bite when she saw her boyfriend with a finger to his lips. Judge worked his way over to the sliding glass door, checked to make sure it was locked. He reached behind his back, drew his Glock and hugged the wall with it raised, stood there listening, an ear beside the closed drapes, Owen behind him. Quiet, on both sides of the sliders, inside and out. He opened the drapes a little with his gun barrel, and there was Mary Veronica in a Cowboys jersey, still short, still top-heavy, her dark eyes staring back at him. They brightened when she recognized him then got serious when she noticed the gun. Owen reached past him, jerked the drapes back to expose the glass door in full.

"See, Judge, it's my girlfriend. Put that thing away, you're scaring her…"

Owen pushed past, unlocked the door and slid it open. "M-V sweetie! Come on in, we're…"

A hard shoulder-shove knocked M-V off balance, her space now occupied by a woman in camo pants and a sleeveless jacket holding a Tec-9 in one hand. She poked inside the door with it, jerked the barrel up quickly against Judge's Adam's apple. They were close enough to swap spit.

"If you raise your gun one millimeter," she said, "your gray matter ends up on the ceiling."

She backed him up, giving her and M-V room enough to step inside the family room. He was now face to face with a person who looked a lot less like the mug shot of Larinda Jordan, less like a woman at all, and now more like what had to be her assassin persona. Harsh, lean and angular, her face was scarred, her hair military, and some fingers on her left hand were missing, like a survivalist after the Big One hit, or a meth head, or a sixty-year-old diabetic on the streets, or all of the above, but with freckled cheeks.

"Toss your gun outside," she said, "then put your hands behind your head. Do it, now."

The gun skittered across the patio, into the dirt. Judge put his hands where she said. She shoved him an arms length away, continued to walk him backward, the arm doing the shoving in a ragged cast ending with a gangrenous-looking left hand on his shirt. They ran out of room when she'd backed him against the wall, his hands still folded behind his head. Behind her, Mary Veronica closed the screen door. The glass slider and drapes remained open.

"Don't move," Larinda Jordan said, spraying spit at him, then, to Geenie, "Fold your hands behind your head just like your friend, stand up, and join him." Geenie complied. "Now you," she said, nodding at Owen. "You little degenerate. You 'hero.' Hands the same way, then stand next to her."

The three of them stood as directed next to each other, lined up in firing squad fashion against the family room wall, their hands behind their heads. "Now slide down the wall with your hands still folded and sit on the floor, your backs still against it."

When his ass hit bottom Judge found himself next to a wall shelf two feet off the floor, the shelf eye level from his seat, the right height for Owen's everyday use. On the shelf were four urns in a row, Owen's mother in one of them, if memory served. Closest to Judge at the end of the shelf was Owen's phone.

Owen's upturned face pleaded. "M-V honey, talk some sense into her..."

M-V's sneer was smug and exaggerated given their respective vantage points. "I'm not your honey, you disgusting little man."

"But M-V honey..."

"Shut up!" Larinda said. Her chest heaved, her lean face scowling. She was not calm.

"I'll be brief. Abortion...is a sin. Judges do not get to decide differently, and neither do women, and yet, even with our efforts, that murderous law could still remain in place, in defiance of God's will. I tried to influence the outcome, was a good Christian soldier. That pagan judge should be dead! In the ground. In Hell! But I'm too much of a mess now to make that happen."

A smug smile creeped across her tortured face. "But, as you can see, it's fairly easy to get to the people who enabled her."

She aimed the Tec-9 at Judge's forehead, stayed just out of his reach. "You can start your prayers now, Mister Bounty Hunter, but I might not wait for you to finish them."

Jane's Baby

Judge could have closed his eyes or could have focused on the barrel or could have focused on what was behind it, and behind her, where a distant sirocco of airborne trail dust and dirt gathered in size on the horizon. The dust cloud advanced toward the house. So did Judge's Tourette's, moving up his throat...

"Let's work this...suck balls...out, Larinda, I'm sure we can get..."

"NO! You ask God for His forgiveness! Pray! Now!"

Holding back what was in his head, Our Farter, who fart in heaven...cunt!...he started praying. "Our Father, Who art in heaven...hallowed be Thy...cunt-balls!...name. Thy kingdom cunt..."

At the back of the property a fence rail jettisoned sideways, dropping silently in the sagebrush. Some electrical wire snapped, coiling itself up.

"...Thy cunt be done..."

"Stop, you vile man, that is the Lord's Prayer! Stop! You are blaspheming!"

More dust collected in the near distance and kicked up a cottony mist that reached the rear of the property, floating dreamily forward and filling the backyard beyond the patio with an expanding cloud of tan, sooty camouflage. It drifted farther, advancing toward the screen door.

Her gun barrel pushed into Judge's mouth, shutting his Tourette's down, Larinda oblivious to the activity converging on the patio.

Señor Q emerged from the tan dust as it settled, didn't snort, loomed quietly, his eighteen-hundred-pound gray girth overwhelming the view outside, the girth more heavily distributed on his front hooves. He stepped closer to the screen door, his hooves clip-clopping once against the pavers, a single, cautious, light step, but not light enough that it didn't catch Mary Veronica's attention and Larinda's ear.

"Larinda!" M-V choked the name out, terror in her voice as she stared at the bull. Larinda stood her ground, acknowledged nothing other than the Tec-9 she still had down Judge's throat.

"Quiet!" she said with the slightest of gestures, a flinch, in M-V's direction. "Him first!" She returned her attention to Judge. "To Hell with you, now!"

The flinch was all he'd needed. On the shelf, Owen's phone. *The most dangerous eight seconds in sports...*

Judge ripped the Tec-9 barrel out of his mouth, pinned her gun hand against the wall, and snatched Owen's phone from the shelf. He pressed the button for his ring tone. The rodeo air horn did not disappoint...

...HAHHNNK...

The spray of bullets from Larinda's gun obliterated his hearing on their way past his left ear.

The family room screen and doorframe ripped out of the wall as Señor Q bucked his way inside, bucked his way across the room, then bucked a horn through Larinda's back, goring her from her kidneys up into her rib cage. He raised her body up near the peak of the cathedral ceiling, shook her like he might shake every bull rider who had ever gone that eight-second distance with him if he got the chance again, bucked and spun and kicked and reveled in his pent-up fury, Judge and friends still hugging the wall, until he dropped down on all fours, snorting and staring at Owen. Larinda was still attached, the bull's horn protruding through her ribs. Q snorted again, remained frozen facing his tiny rodeo clown neighbor. Larinda's limp arm slowly raised the Tec-9, blood gushing from her mouth, her chest, her back. She peered down the barrel, Owen at the end of it. Judge's gun was twenty feet away, outside, useless.

"You will rot (unnhh)...in hell...for saving the judge, little man." Her finger curled.

Judge reached behind Geenie, grabbed the Glock from her holster, the gun this monster didn't know was there, stood and emptied its entire clip into her pained face and head. Smoke, blood, gray matter, her Tec-9, all of it settled around the family room, all of it neutralized. Señor Q bucked and spun and galloped out of the house, stopped to get his balance on the patio, and to face the hundreds of acres of rolling fields and hills and prairie in front of him. He spooked Bruce the cat, and the two were off in the direction of Q's never-ending pasture, Larinda Jordan's flopping carcass still attached to his head.

Owen lifted Mary Veronica up from the debris of the family room. She smiled sweetly at him, showing her dimples. "Thank you, Owen. Look, Owen honey..."

Jane's Baby

Owen had Judge's gun.

"You are dead to me, bitch." He raised the handgun, pointing it at her sideways like all good gangstas did. "Judge. Call nine-one-one and get Frannie Kitchens over here before I do something I'll regret. Or would regret. Eventually."

Judge wasn't particularly quick at punching in the numbers, his ears still ringing, plus he'd give Owen time to decide what was best for him. The police would have never known. Owen had been through enough, been hurt enough.

He deserved the satisfaction, Judge thought.

All us misfits do.

FORTY-SEVEN

Naomi's son and daughter were with her in D.C., mother and kids watching the Cowboys-Eagles playoff game on TV. Naomi took the call.

Larinda Jordon was confirmed dead, this time for sure, in Texas. A woman with her, an alleged accomplice, was being held for questioning.

She thanked the local Texas police chief for alerting her to the story before it went public. After she hung up the news outlets picked it up and fed the crawl at the bottom of the TV screen, the football game deep in the third quarter: "Breaking News. Missing domestic terrorist dead in bloody Texas encounter."

Naomi's son and daughter were on Christmas break, spending as much time with their convalescing mother as possible, Cowboys fans all. She'd remained in Georgetown, a three-bedroom condo rental across town from her destroyed condo. Too much still hurt...the trauma played out on the deck, in the common area, and at a nearby cross street...the loss of Edward Trenton...for her to ever return there. She'd sell it when it was livable again.

Another phone call, this one less of a surprise. She'd spent hours in conference with her Supreme Court peers on Thursday and Friday, discussing this topic in painstaking detail, but the weekend calls kept coming. The Court's decision was to be read two days from now, on Monday. On the phone was yet another one of The Nine who had voted differently than she had.

"Wishing your Cowboys luck, Madam Justice."

"Thanks so much. Today they need it. Philly's young quarterback is having the game of his life."

"He certainly is. Listen, Madam Justice, about Babineau v. Turbin..."

Of course it was about Babineau. All today's judicial calls were. Her vote had decided the case.

Jane's Baby

She concentrated, needed to block out the game so she could focus on the conversation. An internal avowal gathered steam. It steadied and emboldened her.

I am a Native American. I am a woman. I am a mother, a daughter, a feminist. I am a human being. I'm a U.S. Supreme Court associate justice, sworn to uphold the U.S. Constitution.
And, for a short time, I was Jane Roe's baby.
I am all these things, but only because I lived.

"Yes. My fourth call today about Babineau, Your Honor. What's on your mind?"

"Monday is a big day, Justice Coolsummer. Anything I can do to have you rethink your vote?"

Maybe in my heart I still am Jane's baby, with all the complexity, guilt, and appreciation this identity entails.
And this has changed me.

"No, not a thing, Your Honor."

About The Author – Chris Bauer

"The thing I write will be the thing I write." Chris wouldn't trade his northeast Philadelphia upbringing of street sports played on blacktop and concrete, fistfights, brick and stone row houses, and twelve years of well-intentioned Catholic school discipline for a Philadelphia minute (think New York minute but more fickle and less forgiving). He's had lengthy stops as an adult in Michigan and Connecticut, thinks Pittsburgh is a great city even though some of his fictional characters don't, and now lives in Doylestown, PA. He's married, the father of two, is a grandfather, still does all his own stunts, and he once passed for Chip Douglas of *My Three Sons* TV fame on a Wildwood, NJ boardwalk. As C.G. Bauer he's also the author of SCARS ON THE FACE OF GOD, an EPIC Awards runner-up for best in 2010 eBook horror, and the editor of the CRAPPY SHORTS short story collections.